Ger...
April 13, 1911,
~~Columbia Univ.~~
Cambridge, Mass.

ALSO BY FRANK O'CONNOR

Crab Apple Jelly

"It is impossible to read Mr. O'Connor's dialogue without delight; he uses a local Anglo-Irish patois with close fidelity indeed, but he so infuses each phrase with the character of its speaker, and rifts it so deep with the lyricism and wild humour of his own mind that it becomes a very rich, poetic medium, charged with greatness."

—KATE O'BRIEN, in The Spectator

THIS IS A Borzoi Book
PUBLISHED IN NEW YORK BY Alfred A. Knopf

The Common Chord

O Thou that from eleven to ninety reignest
In mortal bosoms, whose chase is this great world
And we in herds thy game . . .

The Common Chord

Stories and Tales

by FRANK O'CONNOR

New York · Alfred · A · Knopf

1948

THIS IS A BORZOI BOOK,
PUBLISHED BY ALFRED A. KNOPF, INC.

FIRST AMERICAN EDITION

CONTENTS

"News for the Church" and "The Babes in the Wood" originally appeared in *The New Yorker*.

The Common Chord

News for the Church

WHEN Father Cassidy drew back the shutter of the confessional he was a little surprised at the appearance of the girl at the other side of the grille. It was dark in the box, but he could see she was young, of medium height and build, with a face that was full of animation and charm. What struck him most were the long, pale, slightly freckled cheeks, pinned high up behind the grey-blue eyes, giving them a curiously Oriental slant.

She wasn't a girl from the town, for he knew all of these by sight, and most of them by something more, being notoriously an easy-going confessor. The other priests said that one of these days he'd give up hearing confessions altogether on the ground that there was no such thing as sin, and that even if there was, it didn't matter. That was part and parcel of his exceedingly angular character, for though he was kind enough to individual sinners, his mind was full of obscure abstract hatreds. He hated England; he hated the Irish government, and he particularly hated the middle classes, though, so far as anyone knew, none of them had ever done him the least bit of harm. He was a heavy-built man, slow-moving and slow-thinking, with no neck and a punchinello chin; a wine-coloured, sour-looking face, pouting crimson lips, and small, blue, hot-tempered eyes.

"Well, my child," he grunted in a slow and mournful voice that sounded for all the world as if he had pebbles in his mouth, "how long is it since your last confession?"

"A week, father," she replied in a clear, firm voice. That surprised him a little, for though she didn't look like one of the tough shots, neither did she look like the sort of girl who goes to confession every week. But with women you could never tell. They were all contrary, saints and sinners.

"And what sins did you commit since then?" he asked encouragingly.

"I told lies, father."

"Anything else?"

"I used bad language, father."

"I'm surprised at you," he said with mock seriousness. "An educated girl with the whole of the English language at your disposal! What sort of bad language?"

"I used the Holy Name, father."

"Ach," he said with a frown, "you ought to know better than that. There's no great harm in damning and blasting, but blasphemy is a different thing. To tell you the truth," he added, being a man of great natural honesty, "there isn't much harm in using the Holy Name either. Most of the time, there's no intentional blasphemy, but at the same time it coarsens the character. It's all the little things you don't indulge in that gives a body true refinement. Anything else?"

"I was tight, father."

"Hm," he grunted. This was rather more the sort of girl he had imagined her to be; plenty of devilment, but no real badness. He liked her bold and candid manner. There was no hedging or false modesty about her as about most of his women penitents. "When you say you were 'tight,' do you mean you were just merry or what?"

"Well, I mean I passed out," she replied candidly, with a shrug.

"I don't call that 'tight,' you know," he said with a reproachful note in his voice. "I call that beastly drunk. Are you often tight?"

"I'm a teacher in a convent school, so I don't get much chance," she replied ruefully.

"In a convent school?" he said with new interest. (He didn't like convent schools or nuns.) "Are you on holidays now?"

"Yes. On my way home."

"You don't live here, then?"

"No, down the the country."

"And is it the convent that drives you to drink?" he asked with an air of unshakable gravity.

"Well," she replied archly, "you know what nuns are."

"I do," he agreed in a mournful voice while he smiled

at her through the grille. "Do you drink with your parents' knowledge?" he added anxiously.

"Oh yes. Mummy is dead, but Daddy doesn't mind. He lets us take a drink with him."

"Does he do that on principle or because he's afraid of you?" the priest asked dryly.

"Ah, I suppose a little of both," she answered gaily, responding to his queer, dry humour. It wasn't often that women did, and he began to like this one a lot.

"Is your mother long dead?" he asked sympathetically.

"Seven years," she replied, and he realized that she couldn't have been much more than a child at the time and had grown up without a mother's advice or care. Having worshipped his own mother, he was always sorry for people like that.

"Mind you," he said paternally, with his hands joined on his fat belly, "I don't want you to think there's any harm in a drop of drink. I take it myself. But I wouldn't make a habit of it, if I were you. You see, it's all very well for old jossers like me that have the worst of their temptations behind them, but yours are all ahead, and drink is a thing that grows on you. You need never be afraid of going wrong if you remember that your mother may be watching you from heaven."

"Thanks, father," she said, and he saw at once that his gruff appeal had touched some deep and genuine spring of feeling in her, "I'll cut it out altogether."

"You know, I think I would," he said gravely, letting his eyes rest on her for a moment. "You're an intelligent girl. You can get all the excitement you want out of life without that. What else?"

"I had bad thoughts, father."

"Och," he said regretfully, "we all have them. Did you indulge them?"

"I did, father."

"Have you a boy?"

"Not a regular: just a couple of fellows hanging round."

"Och, that's worse than none," he said crossly. "You ought to have a boy of your own. I know there's old cranks that'll tell you different, but sure, that's plain foolishness. Those things are only fancies, and the best cure for them is something real. Anything else?"

There was a moment's hesitation before she replied, but it was enough to prepare him for what was coming.

"I had carnal intercourse with a man, father," she said quietly and deliberately.

"You what?" he cried, turning on her incredulously. "You had carnal intercourse with a man? At your age?"

"I know," she said with a look of distress. "It's awful!"

"It is awful," he replied slowly and solemnly. "And how often did it take place?"

"Once, father—I mean twice, but on the same occasion."

"Was it a married man?" he asked, frowning.

"No, father, single. At least, I think he was single," she added with sudden doubt.

"You had carnal intercourse with a man," he said

accusingly, "and you don't even know if he was married or single!"

"Ah, well, I assumed he was single," she said with real distress. "He was the last time I met him, but, of course, that was five years ago."

"Five years ago?" echoed Father Cassidy. "But you must have been only a child then!"

"That's all, of course," she replied. "He was courting my sister, Kate, but she wouldn't have him. She was running round with her present husband at the time. She only kept him on a string for amusement. I knew that, of course, and I hated her because he was always so nice to me. He was the only one that came to the house who treated me like a grown-up. But I was only fourteen at the time, and I suppose he thought I was too young for him."

"And were you?" asked the priest ironically. For some reason he had the idea that this young lady had no proper idea of the enormity of her sin, and he didn't like it.

"I suppose so," she replied modestly. "But I used to feel awful, being sent up to bed, and leaving him downstairs with Kate when I knew she didn't care for him. And then, when I met him again, the whole thing came back. I sort of went all soft inside. It's never the same with another fellow as it is with the first fellow you fall for. It's exactly as if he had some sort of hold over you."

"If you were fourteen at that time," said Father Cassidy, setting aside the obvious invitation to discuss the power of first love, "you're only nineteen now."

"That's all."

"And do you know," he went on broodingly, "that unless you can break yourself of this terrible vice once for all, it'll go on like that till you're fifty?"

"I suppose so," she said doubtfully, but he saw that she didn't suppose anything of the kind.

"You suppose so?" he snorted angrily. "I'm telling you so. And what's more," he added, speaking with all the earnestness at his command, "it won't be just one man, but dozens of men; and it won't be decent men, but whatever low-class sort of pups you can find that'll take advantage of you—the same horrible, mortal sin, week in, week out, till you're an old woman."

"Ah, still I don't know," she said eagerly, hunching up her shoulders in an ingratiating way. "I think people do it as much from curiosity as anything else."

"From curiosity?" he repeated in bewilderment.

"Well, you know what I mean," she said with a touch of impatience. "People make such a mystery of it!"

"And what do you think they should do?" he asked ironically. "Publish it in the papers?"

"Well, God knows 'twould be better than the way some of them go on," she said in a rush. "Take my sister, Kate, for instance. I admit she's a couple of years older than me, and she brought me up and all the rest of it, but in spite of that we're good friends. Ah, she's a decent sort of girl, you know, in her own way! We got on fine. She showed me her love-letters and I showed her mine. I mean we discussed things as equals, but ever since that girl got married she'd hardly throw a word to the cat. She talks to no one, only other married women, and they get in a huddle in a corner and whisper, whisper, whisper, and the moment you come into the room they begin to talk about the weather—exactly as if you were a blooming kid! I mean you can't help feeling that it's something extraordinary."

"Don't you try to tell me anything about immorality," said Father Cassidy angrily. "I know all about it already. It may begin as curiosity, but it ends as debauchery. There's no vice you could think of that gets a grip on you quicker and degrades you worse, and don't you make any mistake about it, young woman! Did this man say anything about marrying you?"

"I don't think so," she replied thoughtfully, "but of course that doesn't mean anything. He's an airy, light-hearted sort of fellow, and it mightn't occur to him."

"I never supposed it would," said the priest grimly. "Is he in a position to marry?"

"I suppose he must be since he wanted to marry Kate," she said with no great interest.

"And is your father the sort of man that can be trusted to talk to him?"

"Daddy?" she exclaimed aghast. "But I don't want Daddy brought into it!"

"What you want, young woman," said Father Cassidy with sudden exasperation, "is beside the point. Are you prepared to talk to this man yourself?"

"I suppose I am," she said with a smile, "but about what?"

"About what?" repeated the priest angrily. "About the little matter he so conveniently overlooked, of course."

"You mean—ask him to marry me?" she cried incredulously. "But I don't want to marry him."

Father Cassidy paused for a moment and looked at her anxiously through the grille. It was growing dark inside the church, and for one horrible moment he had the feeling that somebody was playing an elaborate and most tasteless joke on him.

"Do you mind telling me," he inquired politely, "am I mad or are you?"

"But I mean it, father," she said eagerly. "It's all over and done with now. It's something I'd always dreamed about, and it was grand, but you can't do a thing like that a second time."

"You can't what?" he asked sternly.

"I mean, I suppose you can, really," she said, waving her piously joined hands at him as if she were handcuffed, "but you can't recapture the magic of it. Terry's light-hearted and good-natured, but I couldn't live with him. He's completely irresponsible."

"And what do you think you are?" cried Father Cassidy, at the end of his patience. "Have you thought of all the dangers you're running, girl? If you have a child, who'll give you work? If you have to leave this country to earn a living, what's going to become of you?

I tell you, it's your bounden duty to marry this man, if he can be got to marry you—which, let me tell you," he added with a toss of his great head, "I very much doubt."

"To tell you the truth, I doubt it myself," she replied with a shrug that fully expressed her feelings about Terry and nearly drove Father Cassidy insane. He looked at her for a moment or two and then an incredible idea began to dawn on his bothered old brain. He sighed and covered his face with his hand.

"Tell me," he asked in a far-away voice, "when did this take place?"

"Last night, father," she said gently, almost as if she were glad to see him coming to his senses again.

("My God!" he thought despairingly, "I was right!")

"In town, was it?"

"Yes, father. We met on the train, coming down."

"And where is he now?"

"He went home this morning, father."

"Why didn't you do the same?"

"I don't know, father," she replied doubtfully, as if the same question had just struck herself.

"Why didn't you go home this morning?" he repeated angrily. "What were you doing round town all day?"

"Ah, I suppose I was walking," she replied uncertainly.

"And, of course, you didn't tell anyone?"

"There wasn't anyone I could tell," she said plaintively. "Anyway," she added with a shrug, "it's not the sort of thing you can tell people."

"No, of course," said Father Cassidy. "Except a priest," he added grimly to himself. He saw now how he had been taken in. This little trollop, wandering about town in a daze of bliss, had to tell someone her secret, and he, a good-natured old fool of sixty, had allowed her to use him as a confidant. A philosopher of sixty letting Eve, aged nineteen, tell him all about the apple! He could never live it down!

Then the fighting blood of the Cassidys began to warm in him. Oh, couldn't he though? He had never tasted the apple himself, but he knew a few things about apples in general and that apple in particular which little Miss Eve wouldn't learn in a whole lifetime of apple-eating. Theory might have its drawbacks, but there were times when it was better than practice. "All right, my lass," he thought grimly, "we'll see which of us knows the most!"

In a casual tone he began to ask her questions. They were rather intimate questions, such as a doctor or priest may ask, and, feeling broad-minded and worldly-wise in her new experience, she answered courageously and straightforwardly, trying to suppress all signs of her embarrassment. It emerged only once or twice in a brief pause before she replied. He stole a furtive look at her to see how she was taking it, and once more he couldn't withhold his admiration. But she couldn't keep it up. First she grew uncomfortable and then alarmed, frowning and shaking herself in her clothes as if something were biting her. He grew graver and more personal. She didn't see his purpose; she only saw that he was stripping off veil after veil of romance, leaving her with nothing but a cold, sordid, cynical adventure like a bit of greasy meat on a plate.

"And what did he do next?" he asked.

"Ah," she said in disgust, "I didn't notice."

"You didn't notice?" he repeated ironically.

"But does it make any difference?" she burst out despairingly, trying to pull the few shreds of illusion she had left tighter about her.

"I presume you thought so when you came to confess it," he replied sternly.

"But you're making it sound so beastly!" she wailed.

"And wasn't it?" he asked with lips pursed and brows raised.

"Ah, it wasn't, father," she said earnestly. "Honest to God, it wasn't. At least, at the time I didn't think it was."

"No," he said grimly, "you thought it was a nice little story to run home and tell your sister. You won't be in such a hurry to tell her now. Say an Act of Contrition."

She said it.

"And for your penance say three Our Fathers and three Hail Marys."

He knew that was hitting below the belt, but he couldn't resist the parting shot of a penance such as he might have given a child. He knew it would stick in that fanciful little head of hers when all his other warnings were forgotten. Then he drew the shutter and did not open the farther one. There was a noisy woman there, groaning in an excess of contrition. The mere volume of sound told him it was drink. He felt he needed a breath of fresh air.

He went down the aisle creakily on his heavy policeman's feet, and in the dusk walked up and down the path before the presbytery, head bowed, hands behind his back. He saw the girl come out and descend the steps under the massive fluted columns of the portico; a tiny, limp, dejected figure. As she reached the pavement she pulled herself together with a jaunty twitch of her shoulders and then collapsed again. The city lights went on and made globes of coloured light in the mist. As he returned to the church he suddenly began to chuckle, a fat good-natured chuckle, and as he passed the statue of St. Anne, patron of marriageable girls, he almost found himself giving her a wink.

The Custom of the Country

I.

ONE fine moonlight night Ernest Thompson, the English fellow, asked Anna Martin to come away for a week-end with him. Ernest was a fellow she had been doing a line with for close on a month; a tall chap with smooth oiled oak-coloured hair and a curiously raw, beefy face that went all off into points.

"That's a grand idea, Ernie," she said in her eager way. "I'll tell you what we'll do. We'll go to Glenamullen, and the Frawleys will put us up."

"Put us up?" said Ernest in surprise. "But I don't want anyone to put us up."

"What do you want so?" drawled Anna in the accent that her mother said was like a wind up a flue.

"I want to make love to you," said Ernest boldly.

"Go on!" cried Anna with a sinking heart. "And what do you think you're doing now?"

"Don't you want me to make love to you?" he asked earnestly, seizing her by the wrists and looking deep into her eyes.

"Ah, Ernie," she cried distractedly, trying to pull herself free, "if I did a thing like that I could never respect myself again."

"And why not?" asked Ernest indignantly. "I love you and you love me, or at least you say you do. What possible objection can there be? It would be different if you were going to have a baby."

"Ah, God, Ernie," she cried, losing the last shred of her wits at the very thought of such a possibility, "I couldn't, I couldn't, and that's all about it."

"But why not?" repeated Ernest fiercely.

"Because 'twould be a sin."

"Sssh!" hissed Ernest as two other lovers passed down the lane with the moonlight shining full on their idioty faces. The sight of them made Anna desperate. "How is it a sin?" he asked in a tense whisper.

" 'Tis always a sin unless people are married," she said.

"Always a sin?"

"Always, Ernie."

"Even suppose people are married already?"

"That's what we're taught anyway, Ernie."

"Well, I'm damned!" said Ernest.

She saw he had expected something different and was disappointed and hurt. She took out her cigarettes and offered him one, more by way of peace-offering than anything else. He refused it, and she saw he was mad with her. The match-flame showed her dark, plump, innocent face, all in smooth curves from the bumpy, boyish forehead to the broad, rounded chin, with the half-developed features nesting in the crinkles as if only waiting for a patch of sunlight to blossom out.

"I suppose you think I'm not fond of you now?" she drawled miserably, turning up her face to let out a column of smoke.

"What else can I think?" asked Ernest stiffly.

"Well, I am, if you want to know," she said, biting her lip to keep back the tears. "And God knows," she added with passion, "I wouldn't tell you a lie."

"Oh," said Ernest coldly in the voice of a judge summing up, "it's not your fault. It's just that you're inhibited."

"I suppose I am," agreed Anna, who didn't know from the sky over her what "inhibited" was. "I dare say it's the custom of the country. Maybe things are different with ye. Would an English girl do that if you asked her?"

"If she loved me, she would," said Ernest sulkily.

"And what would her family say?" asked Anna.

"They wouldn't be consulted," said Ernest shortly. "A woman's life is her own to do what she likes with, isn't it?"

2.

Anna's mother wouldn't have agreed with that at all. She was a widow woman of good family who had had the misfortune to marry one Willie Martin, a man of no class. She was a nice, well-preserved, well-spoken little roly-poly of a woman who sat for the greater part of the day in the kitchen behind the shop, very erect in her high-backed chair, her hands joined in her lap, while she thought of the past glories of her family.

She had a sallow face that looked very innocent down the middle and full of guile round the edges like a badly ironed pillow-case, and an air of great refinement and humility which suggested a soul of shot silk. Anna had good cause to know her mother's soul was made of tougher stuff. She was a woman of great principle, and if Anna bought a frock in the only fashionable shop in town, she had to pretend it was bought in some Catholic shop like Mulligan's where you couldn't get anything that wasn't two years out of date. Mrs. Martin didn't believe in helping those who dug with the wrong foot. She was full of family pride, and till the last maid left, having smashed the last bit of the family china off the kitchen wall and denounced "the Hungry Hayeses" as she called them to the seventh generation of horse-stealers, Mrs. Martin had never ceased in her humble, ingratiating way to persuade them to wear cap and apron, serve from the left, and call Anna "miss."

That she failed was entirely the doing of the Mahoneys, two mad sisters who kept a shop farther up the hill and corrupted Mrs. Martin's maids with tea and scandal. They were two tall women, one with the face of a cow and the other with the face of a greyhound; and the greyhound had a son who was going for the priesthood.

The madness of the Mahoneys took a peculiar form that made them think themselves as good as their neighbours. When Mrs. Martin had Anna taught to play the violin, they had Jerry taught to play the piano. When Anna and Jerry were both to have played at a convent concert, the Mahoneys, by a diabolical intrigue, succeeded in getting Anna's name left out of the program. Of course, Mrs. Martin refused to let Anna play at all, and her friend Sister Angela—a woman of great intellect —said she was perfectly right. Then Jeremiah Henebry Hayes, Mrs. Martin's brother, came home from America and stayed with her, driving off each day in a big car with the Stars and Stripes flying from the bonnet, and the madness of the Mahoneys reached such a pitch that they brought home a dissolute brother of their own from Liverpool and hired a car for him. They couldn't get rid of him after, and it was Mrs. Martin who used to give him the couple of Woodbines on tick.

Knowing nothing of Ernest's improper proposals to her daughter, she received him with great amiability, and waddled round after Anna, continually correcting her over her shoulder in a humorous, refined sort of way, not, as Anna well knew, in any hopes of improving her, but simply to show Ernest that she knew what was what.

"Well! well!" she said in mock alarm at one of Anna's outbursts of vulgarity, "where on earth do you pick up these horrible expressions, Anna? . . . I wonder do young ladies in England talk like that, Mr. Thompson?"

"I shouldn't say there are many young ladies anywhere who can talk like that, Mrs. Martin," replied Ernest with great gallantry.

"Oh, my!" exclaimed Mrs. Martin, deliberately misunderstanding him and throwing up her hands in affected horror. "You don't mean she's as bad as that, surely?"

"I mean, Mrs. Martin," said Ernest gravely, "that I think you have a wonderful daughter."

"Ah, I don't know," said Mrs. Martin, looking doubtfully at Anna as if she were some sort of beast she wouldn't like to pass off on a friend. "Of course, she should be all right," she added with great gravity, ironing out another crease or two in the middle of her face. "She comes of very good stock, on my side at least."

"I can well believe that, Mrs. Martin," said Ernest solemnly, his raw face shining like his well-oiled hair.

"I don't suppose you'd have heard of the Henebry Hayeses of Coolnaleama?" asked Mrs. Martin with quivering modesty. "You wouldn't, to be sure—how could you?"

"No," admitted Ernest reluctantly, feeling that this was a social gaffe of the first order like not knowing who the Habsburgs were. "I can't honestly say I have, but I knew at once that Anna was somebody out of the common."

"Of course," added Mrs. Martin, almost going into

convulsions of abnegation, "I believe people nowadays don't think as much of breeding as they used to, but I'm afraid I'm awfully old-fashioned."

"You're not old-fashioned at all, Ma," said Anna candidly. "You're antediluvian."

"Of course, her father's people weren't up to much," added Mrs. Martin, revenging herself in a ladylike way. "You can see it breaking out in her at times."

"He must have been a charming man," said Ernest, not following the domestic cut and thrust.

"Oh, charming," agreed Mrs. Martin ironically. "He might be alive yet only for that."

On the whole, though she wasn't of the enthusiastic sort, she was rather inclined to approve of Ernest. At any rate he was one cut above an Irishman of the same class.

"Of course," she said with great resignation, "he's not what you'd call a gentleman, but I suppose we can't expect everything."

"Well, anyway," retorted Anna, "I'm not what you'd call a lady either, so we suit one another fine."

"It's nice to hear it from your own lips anyway," said her mother, bridling up.

"Well, I'm not," declared Anna flatly, "and that's the holy bloody all of it. I'm not a lady, and I couldn't be a lady, and it's no use you trying to make me a lady."

"The language is delightful," chirped her mother with the affected lightness that always drove Anna mad. "I hope you talk like that to them when you go to England. They're sure to love it."

"Who said I was going to England?" bawled Anna, growing commoner than ever under such provocation. "He didn't ask me yet."

"Well, I hope when he does you won't forget you're a Catholic even if you do forget you're a lady," said her mother, waddling off to bed.

"A Catholic?" Anna cried in alarm. "What difference does that make?"

"Oh, none in the world," said her mother cheerfully over her shoulder. "Only you can't marry him unless he turns."

"Oh, Christ!" said Anna.

"I beg your pardon, Anna," said Mrs. Martin, turning in the doorway, a picture of martyred gentility. "Did I hear you say something?"

"I said I might as well stuff my head in the gas-oven as I'm about it," said Anna despairingly.

"Ah, well," said her mother complacently, "I dare say he'll turn. Most men do."

But Anna, lying awake, couldn't take it so lightly. Every morning now she was up at seven; gave her mother tea in bed before going to early Mass; did the shopping and minded the shop three nights a week; and a girl doesn't do things like that unless she has a man so much on her mind that everything she does seems to be done under his eye. "I have it bad all right," she thought in her common way. But even her commonness seemed different with Ernest. She had been brought up to look on it as a liability, but Ernest made it seem like a talent. It was bad enough being inhibited the first time, but being inhibited when it came to an offer of marriage seemed to her no better than treason or highway robbery.

When he did ask her a couple of weeks later, she looked in the glass, lit a cigarette, and threw herself into an arm-chair with her legs crossed; a boyish pose that her mother would certainly have denounced as vulgar and vile.

"You know I love you, Ernie, don't you?" she said tenderly, screwing herself up to use the queer English expressions she had picked up from him.

"I hoped so certainly," said Ernest cautiously. "Why?"

"If you don't you ought to," said Anna, breaking into the vernacular, "because the fact of the bloody matter is, I'm dotty about you."

"What's the difficulty?" asked Ernest with a frown.

"The difficulty is," said Anna, taking a puff of the cigarette and contriving to look as brassy as three film stars, "that by the time I'm finished you'll think I'm a proper little welsher."

Ernest grew pale. He rose and stood before the hearth, his hands behind his back.

"You mean you're married already?" he asked with great restraint.

"Married already?" echoed Anna. "What put that into your head?"

"Oh," he said, frowning, "or is it a kid? Mind," he added indifferently, "it doesn't matter to me. You needn't be afraid to tell me."

"Ah, for God's sake, Ernest," she cried, blushing madly, "what sort do you think I am?"

"Well," he said in genuine surprise, "I can't see any other difficulty."

"I'm a Catholic, Ernest," she said quietly.

"A Catholic?" said Ernest with great interest. "Are you really? I thought you were an R.C."

"Same thing."

"Are you sure?" asked Ernest doubtfully.

"Positive. But whatever you call it, the fact is, I can't marry a Protestant."

"Why not?" asked Ernest, growing red.

"Don't ask me," said Anna, blushing again at the thought of the reasons. "It's Ma—she's dotty about religion. It has something to do with the kids. She could tell you."

"I'll talk to your mother," said Ernest, and he meant it.

Mrs. Martin was sitting by the fire in the little back kitchen, and when he came in, she sprang to her feet and flustered about him in great concern, but for once Ernest was too angry for ceremony. Anna had never seen him so mad. He gripped the back of a chair and leaned on it like a man about to address a public meeting.

"Mrs. Martin," he said, "Anna tells me she can't marry me because of her religion. Is that true?"

"Oh," cried Mrs. Martin joyously, not forgetting her own manners in spite of his bad ones, "are you going to be married? Well, I think she's very lucky, Ernest, I do, indeed, and I hope you'll be very happy."

"So do I," said Ernest, not to be put off the scent, "but I'm blessed if I see how."

"Ah," said Mrs. Martin with a little shrug, "these things are nothing. We'll get over them. Of course," she added, just to show how easy it was, "if you were a Catholic ye could be married in the morning."

"No doubt," said Ernest curtly; "but you see I'm not a Catholic. I was brought up Church of England, and I see nothing wrong with that."

"Oh, indeed, I had some very dear friends that were Church of England," said Mrs. Martin, to show him that intolerance was something foreign to her nature; and she went on her knees before the fire with a poker. "You might even be able to get a dispensation," she added thoughtfully. "Mind you, I don't say you would, but 'twould be worth trying."

"A dispensation?" repeated Ernest hopefully. "What's that?"

"It's really permission from the Pope. You understand, of course, that if you got it the children would have to be brought up Catholics?" she asked with a shrewd glance over her shoulder.

"I don't give a rap how they're brought up," said Ernest. "That's Anna's look-out, not mine."

"Well, we could try it," said Mrs. Martin doubtfully, and Anna knew from her tone that, having got Ernest over the first fence, she wasn't going to be stopped by a little thing like a dispensation. A son-in-law that dug with the wrong foot indeed! She was out to make a convert of him. "Wouldn't that fire melt you?" she said with a sigh. "Of course," she added, lifting herself back into her chair and joining her hands in her lap, " 'twouldn't be much of a marriage."

"Why not?" asked Anna suspiciously.

"You'd have to be married out of the diocese," said Mrs. Martin cheerfully, not concealing the fact that she looked on a marriage where the Mahoneys couldn't see it as not much better than open scandal. "You can imagine what the neighbours would say," she added with grim amusement. "Haven't we lovely neighbours, Ernest?"

"God Almighty," said Anna with chagrin, "wouldn't you think mixed marriages were catching! Isn't it a wonder they wouldn't put us up in the Fever Hospital altogether?"

"Of course, Ernest," said Mrs. Martin with the meek air she put on whenever she was piqued, "if that's how Anna feels about it, I don't see why ye wouldn't get married in a registry office. I'm sure the Mahoneys would be delighted."

"Mrs. Martin," said Ernest oratorically, "I don't want Anna to do anything she doesn't think right, but I've got my principles too. My religion means as much to me as hers to her."

"I hope it means a great deal more, Ernest," said Mrs. Martin, getting in an extra poke at Anna, "but I suppose our church has to be more particular. You see," she said modestly, "we look on ourselves as the One True Church."

"And what do you think we look on ourselves as?" asked Ernest indignantly. "Mrs. Martin," he added in a tone of noble pathos, "why should you despise a man because he worships at a different altar?"

"Ah, well, 'tisn't alike, Ernest," replied Mrs. Martin with equal gravity. "After all, the Catholic Church was founded by Our Blessed Lord when he appointed St. Peter to be His vicar on earth. 'Tis hardly likely He'd choose someone like Henry VIII."

"Why not?" asked Ernest indignantly, feeling that some slight on the British people was intended.

"And all the wives, Ernest?" asked Mrs. Martin meekly.

"That would depend on the wives," said Ernest, the least bit pompously. ("My goodness," said Mrs. Martin afterwards, "I don't know did he even know what I was talking about.") "I don't think you should judge a man's actions without considering the circumstances. Anyhow, I'm marrying Anna, even if I have to become a Mohammedan. At the same time, I consider it unnecessary and unfair."

"Ah, well," said Mrs. Martin without rancour, spreading the tablecloth for supper, "maybe you'll think differently when you see the light yourself. And indeed," she added with a wounded laugh which showed that she thought Ernest rather lacking in good taste, "I hope we'll persuade you that we're a cut above Mohammedans."

Anna butted in before Ernest got the chance of defending Mohammedans, and over supper the talk fell on all the people who had married Catholics and been happy ever after. Mrs. Martin had it all from her friend, Sister Angela, in the convent.

"Who is this Sister Angela?" asked Ernest suspiciously.

"That's the nun that'll instruct you," said Mrs. Martin. "We were at school together—a simple sort of soul, but very clever. I'm told she's one of the three cleverest women in Europe. She instructed Anna for her First Communion."

"She did," said Anna, spoiling the performance as usual. "She lit a candle and offered us half a crown if we put our fingers in it."

"What on earth for?" asked Ernest.

"Hell," said Anna.

"I must say it doesn't seem to have had much effect," said her mother by way of no harm.

"You mean," said Ernest, putting down his cup, "that I've got to go back to Sunday school as if I was a kid?"

"Ah, well," said Mrs. Martin complacently, "you wouldn't even buy a car without finding out how it worked."

"A car?" said Ernest, stumped by this bit of feminine logic. "I don't see what cars have to do with it. And how long does this take?"

"Ah, not long," said Mrs. Martin comfortably. "Two or three months."

"Well, I'm damned!" said Ernest.

Anna nearly burst into tears. If he had asked her that night to come away for a week-end with him he mightn't have found her so inhibited.

3.

Next evening she brought him down to the convent, a horrible red-brick building on a hill overlooking the town, with a Sacred Heart on the lawn in front of it. After being shown down a long corridor that you could have skated on, with another life-sized statue at the end of it, into a parlour with open windows, a bookcase, and a picture of the Holy Family, Ernest was feeling very sorry for himself. Even Anna was a bit shaken.

"And you won't forget to call her 'sister,' Ernie?" she whispered coaxingly.

"I shall try," said Ernest, whose panic made him look coarse and bloated. "I can't promise anything, though."

Then the door opened, and in bounced Sister Angela, beaming at them with an array of buck teeth. She had a rather fine, emaciated face with a big-boned nose, and an intensely excitable manner exacerbated by deafness. Having been for years the bosom friend of a dotty old parish priest who had been favoured with visions of the Blessed Virgin, she was now collecting evidence to get him beatified. She had cut up and distributed his night-shirts among the poor, and they had worked some remarkable cures, but she still needed something really big in the way of a miracle.

She wrung both their hands simultaneously, beaming sharply from one to the other with a birdlike cock of her head.

"Anna, dear," she cooed, "I was so delighted when your mother told me. And this is your fiancé! What's his name? Speak a bit loud."

Anna did.

"Thompson?" said Sister Angela, beaming again as if this were a most delightful and unexpected coincidence. "He's not one of us, your mother says," she added, still clinging to Ernest's hand. "What persuasion is he?"

"Church of England," said Anna.

"No, no, not a bit," cried Sister Angela, shaking her head vigorously.

"I said he was Church of England," bawled Anna.

"Ooo! Church of England?" hooted Sister Angela, her whole face lighting up. Anna noticed that she had really lovely eyes. "The nearest thing to us," she added with a bob at Anna. "We never have any difficulty. Last month," she added, beaming at Ernest, "we had a sun-worshipper."

"Go on!" said Anna. "And did he turn?"

"I didn't like him," said Sister Angela, clamping her lips and shaking her head. "He was a mechanic. You'd think he'd know better. So silly! I wouldn't say he was sincere, would you?"

"I'll have to leave ye now," said Anna in panic, feeling that at any moment Ernest was going to burst out into an impassioned defence of sun-worshippers. She felt rather lonesome, leaving him there to be turned from an English lover into an Irish husband, and wasn't at all sure she would like the change. When she looked round to smile at him from the door, she saw that he liked it even less. It wrung her heart to see him with that queer trapped look.

She waited for him in a little paper-shop opposite the convent. When she saw him she ran out to meet him. His face was very red and he was so distraught that he even forgot to raise his hat to her.

"Well," she asked with a smile, "how did you get on?"

"Blessed if I know," said Ernest, with a wild glare in his blue eyes. "I've listened to some tall stories in my life, but she takes the biscuit."

"But what did she say?" wailed Anna with a sinking heart.

"She had nothing to say," said Ernest triumphantly. "I refuted her on every single point."

"She must have loved that," said Anna.

"I don't think she did, really," said Ernest, who some-times missed the point. "She began about Henry VIII and his wives. Nobody in this country seems to have heard of anything except Henry VIII. I said: *'De mortuis nil nisi bonum.'*"

"What does that mean?"

"'Let the dead rest,'" explained Ernest. "Whatever the man's weaknesses may have been, he can't come back to defend himself."

"And did you say 'sister'?" asked Anna.

"No," cried Ernest in anguish. "It sounds so damn silly! She said: 'I thought you were Church of England,' and I said: 'I was brought up Church of England, but for many years I have been an Abou Ben Adhemite.' And would you believe," added Ernest wonderingly, "that woman had never heard of Abou Ben Adhem!"

"Go on!" said Anna, biting her lip. "And who was he when he was at home?"

"Abou Ben Adhem?" exclaimed Ernest, stopping dead. "He was the bloke who said to the angel: 'Write me as one that loved his fellow men.' Abou Ben Adhem has been the great religious inspiration of my life," he added gravely.

"Well, I hope he inspires you now," said Anna, without any great confidence. Ernest simply had no idea of the seriousness of it. He said he'd make it all right next day and pretend he'd been thinking things over, but Anna felt it wouldn't meet the case at all. So did her mother. Mrs. Martin knew what the Mahoneys would say about atheists and unbelievers. She put on her best things and went down to the convent herself. When she returned she looked very grave and fluttered about the house, fussing about trifles, till she got on Anna's nerves.

"Well?" bawled Anna at last. "Can't you tell us did you see her?"

"Sister Angela?" said Mrs. Martin lightly. "She's not seeing visitors—poor soul!" she added with a sigh.

"Go on!" said Anna despairingly. "Why not?"

"She had a breakdown," said Mrs. Martin, with an

almost joyous air. "She won't be able to go on with the
instructions. He wasn't Church of England at all, but
some religion the nuns had never heard of."

"I know," said Anna. "An Abou Ben Something."

"Ah, well," said her mother resignedly, "if 'twas any
decent sort of religion they'd be bound to know about it.
They think it's probably something like the Dippers.
Of course, I knew he wasn't a gentleman. Reverend
Mother gave me the name of a Dominican theologian
you could go to, but she thinks you'd better not have
anything more to do with him."

"How soft she has it!" blazed Anna with tears of fury.
"Maybe if she could have got a man herself, she wouldn't
have been so smart about letting him go."

"Perhaps you'd sooner instruct him yourself?" said
her mother with ladylike viciousness.

"I will," said Anna desperately, "and make a better
job of it than they did."

She put on her hat and coat and strode blindly out
with no notion of where she was going. She passed the
little church on the hill, and the thought that she might
never walk down the steps of it in wreath and veil with
Ernest gave her a desperate courage. She knocked at the
presbytery door and asked for the curate.

"I'm Anna Martin," she said nervously, "and I'm en-
gaged to an English bloke that's over here on a job. He
wants to turn, but he can't make head or tail of what the
nuns tell him."

"Sit down and tell me about it," said the curate

amiably, turning off the wireless. "Will you have a fag?"

"I will," said Anna, crossing her legs and opening her coat. She liked the curate. "As true as God," she said with her lip quivering, "I'm nearly dotty."

"What religion is he?"

"An Abou Ben Something," said Anna. "You never heard of it?"

"I didn't," said the curate. "I thought you said he was English."

"He is," said Anna. "I don't know much about it. 'Tis something about loving your neighbour—the usual stuff. And damn little love there is knocking round when you start looking for it," she added bitterly.

"Ah," said the curate, "we'll soon put him right for you."

"You won't have any trouble with him," said Anna, "so long as you don't mind what he says. He's the best fellow in the world only that he likes to hear himself talk."

At the presbytery gate the following evening she gave Ernest final instructions. Desperation had changed Anna. She was masterful and precise, and Ernest by this time had begun to realize that there were a lot of things he didn't know.

"And mind," said Anna, "you're to call him 'father.'"

"I shan't forget," said Ernest.

"And whatever the hell you do, don't contradict him," said Anna. "There's nothing they hate like being contradicted."

After that she felt she had done all she could, so she went to the chapel and said a prayer. When she met Ernest later on she had every reason to be satisfied. The curate and Ernest had got on like a house afire, and even though it was only his first lesson, Ernest said he was converted already.

One Saturday afternoon six weeks later he made his profession of faith and renounced all his previous heresies, including Abou Ben Adhemism, made his first confession, was baptized, and received absolution for all the sins of his past life. Unfortunately the Mahoneys had got hold of the convent version of it and were putting it round that he was a Turk. Mrs. Martin countered this by exaggerating his wealth, rank, and education. He cut a grand figure next morning, coming from the altar with Anna, beautifully dressed, his hands joined and his oiled head bowed. It was a sunny morning in autumn, and as they came out of the church, an old market woman threw her arms round him and kissed him on both cheeks. "Wisha, God bless you, my lovely boy!" she bawled, and at the sight of Ernest's blush, Anna realized how far he had travelled to win her and was moved to tears of joy.

"All right, Ernie boy," she said. "I'll make it up to you."

4.

On the Holyhead boat Ernest began to behave in a very queer way. He disappeared into the saloon and when Anna saw him again he was tight. It wasn't in the least like him and it worried her.

"Hallo, boy," she said, taking him by the arm. "Anything wrong?"

"Why?" asked Ernest, in a maudlin tone. "Do I look as if there was something wrong?"

"You look like a man that was going back to jail," replied Anna candidly.

"Jail?" exclaimed Ernest, breaking free of her and looking at her with dumbfounded eyes. "Why should you say that?"

"I don't know," said Anna in alarm. "You're not, are you?"

"As a matter of fact," replied Ernest, "I probably am."

"Go on!" she said with fictitious lightness. "What did you do? Pinch something?"

He was really outraged at that and drew himself up with an air of injured dignity.

"Do I look like a thief?" he asked in a pained voice.

"You could be a damn sight worse from my point of view," replied Anna, and at that moment it struck her that in some ways he wasn't at all unlike the pictures of Henry VIII. "You're not going to tell me you're married already?"

Ernest leaned over the edge of the boat as if he were going to be sick and nodded, too full for words.

"That's grand," said Anna with bitter restraint. "And kids, I suppose?"

"Two," said Ernest in a choking voice.

"Sweet of you to tell me," said Anna, going white.

"Well, can you blame me?" Ernest asked, drawing himself up with something like real dignity. "I loved you. I worshipped you. I knew from the first moment that you were the only woman for me. I simply had to have you."

"Oh, you had me all right, Ernie," said Anna, unable even at this most tragic moment of her life to be anything but common.

But in spite of Ernest's appeals and even his tears, she left him at Holyhead and returned home. She might be common but she wouldn't deliberately do something she thought was wrong. She felt sure she was going to have a baby; that was the only thing that was lacking to her degradation.

Her mother on the whole was very good about it. Even the baby she accepted with resignation as being the will of God—anything that couldn't be concealed from the Mahoneys seemed to be her definition of the will of God. But Anna couldn't accept it with such resignation. The whole road was humming with spite. When she went into town she ran the gauntlet of scores of malicious eyes. "She knew, she knew! Sure, of course she knew! Didn't Sister Angela warn her? It was all grandeur and false pride. She wanted to say she could get a husband— a pasty-faced thing like that!" But the pitying ones were worse. "Ah, wisha, poor Anna! Sure, she was very simple. Wouldn't you think she'd know that a foreigner like that was too sweet to be good?"

One night she was sitting in the back kitchen listening to her mother and a neighbour whispering in the shop, and when the neighbour had gone Anna strode out and leaned against the jamb of the door with arms folded, blowsy and resentful.

"What 'poor Anna' were ye talking about?" she asked.

"Ah, indeed, Anna, you may well ask," said her mother.

"But why the 'poor Anna'?" her daughter went on reasonably. "After all, I didn't marry a boozer or a fellow that beat me, like that one. I'm going to have a kid, which is more than a lot of them can say. I got some fun out of life anyway."

"I hope you'll tell everyone that," said her mother encouragingly. "They'll be all delighted to know you're not down-hearted about it. I'm sure you won't be long getting a husband."

"Why?" asked Anna. "Must I be 'poor Anna' before I can get a husband too?"

"I'm afraid you'll have to be a great deal more," said her mother.

"That sounds as if 'twas going to be great fun," said Anna.

"Fun is hardly what a girl in your position ought to be looking for," said her mother tartly.

"Do you know I was thinking that?" said Anna in a heart-breaking drawl. "It just crossed my mind that I wasn't suited to my situation at all." ("Oh, Cripes!" she thought, as she suddenly realized what she was saying, just like the last maid when she was giving notice, "there goes the blooming china!" At that moment she realized that there wasn't a drop of Henebry Hayes blood left in her veins; from head to foot she was pure Martin, a woman of no class.) "I'm not grand enough for this neighbourhood at all, Ma," she went on recklessly. "I think I'll have to go somewhere I'm better suited."

She crossed the shop under her mother's eyes and began to mount the stairs. She was suddenly filled with a great sense of liberation and joy. The strain of being a real Henebry Hayes is something you don't appreciate till it is removed. "I'm common," she thought delightedly. "Poor Ernest doesn't know what he's going to get in me. Poor lamb, he has no notion!"

And then, filled with tender longing, she sat down and began to scrawl a long, loving, rambling, illiterate letter to the man who had made her commonness worth while.

Judas

I'LL FORGET a lot of things before I forget that night. As I was going out the mother said: "Sure, you won't be late, Jerry?" and I only laughed at her and said: "Am I ever late?" As I went down the road I was thinking it was months since I had taken her to the pictures. You might think that funny, Michael John, but after the father's death we were thrown together a lot. And I knew she hated being alone in the house after dark.

At the same time I had troubles of my own. You see, Michael John, being an only child, I never knocked round with girls the way others did. All the chaps in the office went with girls, or at any rate they let on they did. They said: "Who was the old doll I saw you with last night, Jerry? Aha, Jerry, you'd better mind yourself, boy, or you'll be getting into trouble!" Paddy Kinnane, for instance, talked like that, and he never saw how it upset me. I think he thought it was a great compliment. It wasn't until years after that I began to suspect that Paddy's acquaintance with dolls was about of one kind with my own.

Then I met Kitty Doherty. Kitty was a hospital nurse, and all the chaps in the office said a fellow should never go with hospital nurses—they knew too much. I knew when I met Kitty that that was a lie. She was a well-educated, superior girl; she lived up the river in a posh locality, and her mother was on all sorts of councils and committees. She was small and wiry; a good-looking girl, always in good humor, and when she talked, she hopped from one thing to another like a robin on a frosty morning.

Anyway, she had me dazzled. I used to meet her in the evenings up the river road, as if I was walking there by accident and very surprised to see her. "Fancy meeting you!" I'd say, or "Well, well, isn't this a great surprise?" Then we'd stand talking for half an hour and I'd see her home. Several times she asked me in, but I was too nervous. I knew I'd lose my head, break the china, use some dirty word, and then go home and cut my throat. Of course, I never asked her to come to the pictures or anything like that. I knew she was above that. My only hope was that if I waited long enough I might be able to save her from drowning, the White Slave Traffic, or something of the sort. That would show in a modest, dignified way how I felt about her. Of course, I knew at the same time I ought to stay at home more with the mother, but the very thought that I might be missing an opportunity like that would be enough to spoil a whole evening on me.

This night in particular I was nearly distracted. It was three weeks since I'd seen Kitty. You know what three weeks are at that age. I was sure that at the very least the girl was dying and asking for me and that no one knew my address. A week before, I'd felt I simply couldn't bear it any longer, so I made an excuse and went down to the post-office. I rang up the hospital and asked for her. I fully expected them to say that she was dead, and I got a shock when the girl at the other end asked my name. "I'm afraid," I said, "I'm a stranger to Miss Doherty, but I have an important message for her." Then I got completely panic-stricken. What could a girl like Kitty make of a damned deliberate lie like that? What else was it but a trap laid by an old and cunning hand. I held the receiver out and looked at it. "Moynihan," I said to it, "you're mad. An asylum, Moynihan, is the only place for a fellow like you." Then I heard her voice, not in my ear at all, but in the telephone booth as if she were standing before me, and I nearly dropped the receiver with terror. I put it to my ear and asked in a disguised voice: "Who is that speaking, please?" "This is Kitty Doherty," she said rather impatiently. "Who are you?" "I am Monsieur Bertrand," said I, speaking in what I hoped was a French accent. "I am afraid I have de wrong number." Then I put down the receiver carefully and thought how nice it would be if only I had a penknife handy to cut my throat with. It's funny, but from the moment I met Kitty

I was always coveting sharp things like razors and pen-knives.

After that an awful idea dawned on my mind. Of course, I should have thought of it before, but, as you've probably guessed, I wasn't exactly knowledgeable. I began to see that I wasn't meeting Kitty for the very good reason that Kitty didn't want to meet me. That filled me with terror. I examined my conscience to find out what I might have said to her. You know what conscience is at that age. I remembered every remark I'd made and they were all brutal, indecent or disgusting. I had talked of Paddy Kinnane as a fellow who "went with dolls." What could a pure-minded girl think of a chap who naturally used such a phrase except—what, unfortunately, was true—that he had a mind like a cess-pit.

It was a lovely summer evening, with views of hillsides and fields between the gaps in the houses, and that raised my spirits a bit. Maybe I was wrong, maybe she hadn't found out the sort I was and wasn't avoiding me, maybe we might meet and walk home together. I walked the full length of the river road and back, and then started off to walk it again. The crowds were thinning out as fellows and girls slipped off up the lanes or down to the river. As the streets went out like lamps about me I grew desperate. I saw clearly that she was avoiding me; that she knew I wasn't the quiet, good-natured chap I let on to be but a volcano of brutality and lust. "Lust, lust, lust!" I hissed to myself, clenching my fists.

Then I glanced up and saw her on a tram. I forgot instantly about the lust and smiled and waved my cap at her, but she was looking ahead and didn't see me. I ran after the car, intending to jump on it, to sit on one of the back seats on top and then say as she was getting off: "Fancy meeting you here!" (Trams were always a bit of a problem. If you sat beside a girl and paid for her, it might be considered forward; if you didn't, it looked mean. I never quite knew.) But as if the driver knew what was in my mind, he put on speed and away went the tram, tossing and screeching down the straight, and I stood panting in the middle of the road, smiling as if missing a tram was the best joke in the world and wishing all the time I had the penknife and the courage to use it. My position was hopeless. Then I must have gone a bit mad, for I started to race the tram. There were still lots of people out walking, and they stared after me, so I lifted my fists to my chest in the attitude of a professional runner and dropped into a comfortable stride which I hoped vaguely would delude them into the belief that I was in training for a big race.

Between the running and the halts I just managed to keep the tram in view all the way through town and out at the other side. When I saw Kitty get off and go up a hilly street I collapsed and was just able to drag myself after her. When she went into a house on a terrace I sat on the curb with my head between my knees till the panting stopped. At any rate I felt safe. I could now walk up and down before the house till she came out, and accost her with an innocent smile and say: "Fancy meeting you!"

But my luck was dead out that night. As I was walking up and down out of range of the house I saw a tall chap come strolling up at the opposite side and my heart sank. It was Paddy Kinnane.

"Hullo, Jerry," he chuckled with that knowing grin he put on whenever he wanted to compliment you on being discovered in a compromising situation, "what are you doing here?"

"Ah, just waiting for a chap I had a date with, Paddy," I said, trying to sound casual.

"Begor," said Paddy, "you look to me more like a man that was waiting for an old doll. Still waters run deep. . . . What time are you supposed to be meeting him?"

"Half eight," I said at random.

"Half eight?" said Paddy in surprise. " 'Tis nearly nine now."

"I know," said I, "but as I waited so long I may as well give him another few minutes."

"Ah, I'll wait along with you," said Paddy, leaning against the wall and taking out a packet of fags. "You might find yourself stuck by the end of the evening. There's people in this town and they have no consideration for anyone."

That was Paddy all out; no trouble too much for him if he could do you a good turn.

"As he kept me so long," I said hastily, "I don't think I'll bother with him. It only struck me this very minute that there's a chap up the Asragh road that I have to see on urgent business. You'll excuse me, Paddy. I'll tell you about it another time."

And away I went hell for leather to the tram. When I reached the tram-stop below Kitty's house I sat on the river wall in the dusk. The moon was rising, and every quarter of an hour the trams came grunting and squeaking over the old bridge and then went black out while the conductors switched the trolleys. I stood on the curb in the moonlight searching for Kitty. Then a bobby came along, and as he seemed to be watching me, I slunk slowly off up the hill and stood against a wall in the shadow. There was a high wall at the other side too, and behind it the roofs of a house shining in the moon. Every now and then a tram would come in and people would pass in the moonlight, and the snatches of conversation I caught were like the warmth from an open door to the heart of a homeless man. It was quite clear now that my position was hopeless. The last tram came and went, and still there was no Kitty and still I hung on.

Then I heard a woman's step. I couldn't even pretend to myself that it might be Kitty till she shuffled past me with that hasty little walk of hers. I started and called out her name; she glanced over her shoulder and, seeing a man emerging from the shadow, took fright and ran. I ran too, but she put on speed and began to outdistance me. At that I despaired. I stood on the pavement and shouted after her at the top of my voice.

"Kitty!" I cried. "Kitty, for God's sake, wait for me!"

She ran a few steps further and then halted, turned, and came back slowly down the path.

"Jerry Moynihan!" she whispered, lifting her two arms to her breasts as if I had found her with nothing on. "What in God's name are you doing here?"

I was summoning up strength to tell her that I just happened to be taking a stroll in that direction and was astonished to see her when I realized the improbability of it and began to cry instead. Then I laughed. I suppose it was nerves. But Kitty had had a bad fright and now that she was getting over it she was as cross as two sticks.

"What's wrong with you, I say," she snapped. "Are you out of your senses or what?"

"Well, you see," I stammered awkwardly, half in dread I was going to cry again, "I didn't see you in town."

"No," she replied with a shrug, "I know you didn't. I wasn't out. What about it?"

"I thought it might be something I said to you," I said desperately.

"No," said Kitty candidly, "it wasn't anything to do with you. It's Mother."

"Why?" I asked almost joyously. "Is there something wrong with her?"

"I don't mean that," said Kitty impatiently. "It's just that she made such a fuss, I felt it wasn't worth it."

"But what did she make a fuss about?" I asked.

"About you, of course," said Kitty in exasperation. "What did you think?"

"But what did I do?" I asked, clutching my head. This

was worse than anything I'd ever imagined. This was terrible.

"You didn't do anything," said Kitty, "but people were talking about us. And you wouldn't come in and be introduced to her like anyone else. I know she's a bit of a fool, and her head is stuffed with old nonsense about her family. I could never see that they were different to anyone else, and anyway, she married a commercial herself, so she has nothing much to boast about. Still, you needn't be so superior. There's no obligation to buy, you know."

I didn't. There were cold shivers running through me. I had thought of Kitty as a secret between God, herself, and me and that she only knew the half of it. Now it seemed I didn't even know the half. People were talking about us! I was superior! What next?

"But what has she against me?" I asked despairingly.

"She thinks we're doing a tangle, of course," snapped Kitty as if she was astonished at my stupidity, "and I suppose she imagines you're not grand enough for a great-great-grandniece of Daniel O'Connell. I told her you were a different sort of fellow entirely and above all that sort of thing, but she wouldn't believe me. She said I was a deep, callous, crafty little intriguer and that I hadn't a drop of Daniel O'Connell's blood in my veins." Kitty began to giggle at the thought of herself as an intriguer.

"That's all she knows," I said bitterly.

"I know," said Kitty with a shrug. "The woman has no

sense. And anyway she has no reason to think I'm telling lies. Cissy and I always had fellows, and we spooned with them all over the shop under her very nose, so why should she think I'm lying to her now?"

At that I began to laugh like an idiot. This was worse than appalling. This was a nightmare. Kitty, whom I had thought so angelic, talking in cold blood about "spooning" with fellows all over the house. Even the bad women in the books I'd read didn't talk about love in that cold-blooded way. Madame Bovary herself had at least the decency to pretend that she didn't like it. It was like another door opening on the outside world, but Kitty thought I was laughing at her and started to apologize.

"Of course I had no sense," she said. "You're the first fellow I ever met that treated me properly. The others only wanted to fool around with me, and now because I don't like it, Mother thinks I'm getting stuck-up. I told her I liked you better than any fellow I knew, but that I'd grown out of all that sort of thing."

"And what did she say to that?" I asked fiercely. It was—how can I describe it?—like a man who'd lived all his life in a dungeon getting into the sunlight for the first time and afraid of every shadow.

"Ah, I told you the woman was silly," said Kitty, getting embarrassed.

"Go on!" I shouted. "I want to know everything. I insist on knowing everything."

"Well," said Kitty with a demure little grin, "she said

you were a deep, designing guttersnipe who knew exactly how to get round feather-pated little idiots like
me. . . . You see," she added with another shrug, "it's
quite hopeless. The woman is common. She doesn't understand."

"But I tell you she does understand," I shouted frantically. "She understands better than you do. I only wish
to God I was deep and designing so that I'd have some
chance with you."

"Do you really?" asked Kitty, opening her eyes wide.
"To tell you the truth," she added after a moment, "I
thought you were a bit keen the first time, but then I
didn't know. When you didn't kiss me or anything, I
mean."

"God," I said bitterly, "when I think of what I've been
through in the past couple of weeks!"

"I know," said Kitty, biting her lip. "I was the same."
And then we said nothing for a few moments.

"You're sure you're serious?" she asked suspiciously.

"I tell you, girl," I shouted, "I was on the point of committing suicide."

"What good would that be?" she asked with another
shrug, and then she looked at me and laughed outright—
the little jade!

It is all as clear in my mind as if it had happened last
night. I told Kitty about my prospects. She didn't care,
but I insisted on telling her. It was as if a stone had been
lifted off my heart, and I went home in the moonlight
singing. Then I heard the clock strike, and the singing

stopped. I remembered the mother at home, waiting, and began to run again. This was desperation too, but a different sort.

The door was ajar and the kitchen in darkness. I saw her sitting before the fire by herself, and just as I was going to throw my arms about her, I smelt Kitty's perfume round me and was afraid to go near her. God help us, as if it would have told her anything!

"Hallo, Mum," I said with a laugh, rubbing my hands, "you're all in darkness."

"You'll have a cup of tea?" she said.

"I might as well," said I.

"What time is it?" she said, lighting the gas. "You're very late."

"Ah, I met a fellow from the office," I said, but at the same time I was stung by the complaint in her tone.

"You frightened me," she said with a little whimper. "I didn't know what happened you. What kept you at all?"

"Oh, what do you think?" I said, goaded into retorting. "Drinking and blackguarding as usual."

I could have bitten my tongue off when I'd said it; it sounded so cruel, as if some stranger had said it instead of me. She turned to me for a moment with a frightened stare as if she was seeing the stranger too, and somehow I couldn't bear it.

"God Almighty," I said, "a fellow can have no life in his own house," and away with me upstairs.

I lit the candle, undressed and got into bed. I was wild.

A chap could be a drunkard and blackguard and not be made to suffer more reproach than I was for being late one single night. That, I felt, was what you got for being a good son.

"Jerry," she called from the foot of the stairs, "will I bring you up your cup?"

"I don't want it now, thanks," I said.

I heard her give a heavy sigh and turn away. Then she locked the two doors front and back. She didn't wash up, and I knew my cup of tea was standing there on the table with a saucer on top in case I changed my mind. She came slowly up the stairs, and she walked like an old woman. I blew out the candle before she reached the landing in case she came in to ask me if I wanted anything else, and the moonlight came in the attic window and brought me memories of Kitty. But every time I tried to imagine her face while she grinned up at me, waiting for me to kiss her, it was the mother's face that came up with that look like a child's when you strike him the first time—as if he suddenly saw the stranger in you. I remembered all our life together from the night the father—God rest him!—died; our early Mass on Sunday; our visits to the pictures; our plans for the future, and Christ, Michael John, it was as if I was inside her mind and she sitting by the fire, waiting for the blow to fall! And now it had fallen, and I was a stranger to her, and nothing I ever did could make us the same to each other again. There was something like a cannon-ball stuck in my chest, and I lay awake till the cocks started crowing.

Then I couldn't bear it any longer. I went out on to the landing and listened.

"Are you awake, Mother?" I asked in a whisper.

"What is it, Jerry?" she said in alarm, and I knew she hadn't slept any more than I had.

"I only came to say I was sorry," I said, opening the room door, and then as I saw her sitting up in bed under the Sacred Heart lamp, the cannon-ball burst inside me and I began to bawl like a kid.

"Oh, child, child," she cried out, "what are you crying for at all, my little boy?" and she spread out her arms to me. I went to her and she hugged me and rocked me just as she did when I was only a nipper. "Oh, oh, oh," she was saying to herself in a whisper, "my storeen bawn, my little man!"—all the names she hadn't called me since I was a kid. That was all we said. I couldn't bring myself to tell her what I'd done, and she wouldn't confess to me that she was jealous; all she could do was to try and comfort me for the way I'd hurt her, to make up to me for the nature she'd given me. "My storeen bawn," she said. "My little man!"

The Holy Door

I.

POLLY DONEGAN and Nora Lalor met every morning outside the chapel after eight o'clock Mass. Both were very pious, but apart from that they had little in common. Nora was the prettier, with a soft round face and great round wondering eyes. She was exceedingly shy and a bit of a dreamer as well as being crazily inquisitive. Her father was Jerry Lalor, the builder, a man who had been vice-commandant of the Volunteers during the Troubles.

Polly was a tall girl with coal-black hair, a long, proud, striking face, and an air of great calm and determination. As they went down the hill from the church she saluted everybody with a pleasant, open smile, accepting invitations from anyone who asked her out. Nora went through the torments of the damned whenever anyone asked her—torments equally compounded of curiosity and timidity.

Nora had a knack that Polly found rather upsetting of bringing the talk round to the facts of life. Whenever she did, Polly put on a blank and polite air and without the least effort retreated into her own thoughts about what they should have for dinner, not to be shaken out of them till Nora said with an injured air: "You're not listening to a word I say."

"Oh, I was, Nora," Polly would cry in great indignation. "But I must be rushing now or I'll be late for breakfast."

Nora could see quite plainly that Polly wasn't even interested in the facts of life. Nora could never hear enough about them. She had the same feeling about them as about ghosts and could as little resist talking herself into a state of hysteria about them. Love and marriage were the ghosts that most terrified the maiden soul of Nora, because she had thought so long about God's inscrutable purpose in creating mankind in two sexes that she could hardly bring herself to look the statue of a saint in the eyes without wondering what he'd look like without his clothes.

It's not easy in our church to look very far without facing the problem, because there are statues inside the door and in each of the side chapels and along the columns of the arcade. It makes the church very gay, but poor Nora found it hard not to see them all like Greek statues with nothing on, and whatever it was about their faces and gestures they seemed more improper that way than any Greek divinities. To a truly pious mind there is something appalling in the thought of St. Aloysius Gonzaga without his clothes.

"Oh, Nora," said Polly when she mentioned it, "what funny things you think of!"

"But after all," said Nora with a touch of fire, "they must have had bodies like you and me."

"Indeed, Nora," said Polly, "they'd be very queer without them," and it was quite clear to Nora that Polly simply hadn't considered the implications. "At any rate, it has nothing to do with us."

"Oh, I wouldn't be too sure of that, Polly," said Nora with some spirit. "We may find it has quite a lot to do with us when we get married."

"Oh, do you think so, Nora?" asked Polly politely. "Anyway, I don't expect it'll ever worry me."

"Why not?" asked Nora eagerly, imagining that for once Polly's fastidiousness would be revolted by something.

"Ah," said Polly thoughtfully, "I could never imagine myself married. I always hated having Susie in the room with me. She was never done talking."

"If talking was all there was in marriage!" said Nora darkly.

"Oh, I think talking is the worst of all, Nora," said Polly patiently. "I can't imagine anything worse when you want to be alone."

"Oh, there's a shock in store for you so," said Nora.

"What sort of a shock, Nora?" asked Polly.

"Oh, of course you can't describe it, because people

will never discuss it with you. People you've known since you were a child go on as if you couldn't even be told about it."

"Do they really?" asked Polly with a giggle. "I wonder what it can be."

"Polly," asked Nora, "if you get married before me, will you tell me all about it?"

"Oh, I will to be sure, girl," said Polly offhandedly, but her tone showed Nora that she didn't really understand the implications.

"But I mean everything, Polly," she said broodingly, fixing Polly with her big brown earnest eyes.

"Oh, why wouldn't I, Nora?" cried Polly impatiently, showing that Nora's preoccupation with the facts of life struck her as being a bit uncalled for. "Anyway, you'll be married long before I will. I never had any inclinations for it somehow."

But whatever about the inclinations—and Polly was telling the truth about that—she was the first to get an actual offer. Charlie Cashman was a great friend of Nora's father and a regular visitor to her house. He had even shown a certain weakness for her, but she had always treated him with great coolness. He was an airy, excitable man with a plump, sallow face, which always looked as if it badly needed a shave; a pair of keen, grey eyes in slits under bushy brows; hair on his cheekbones, hair in his ears and hair in his nose as well. He wore a dirty old grey cardigan, a tweed suit, and a cap. Nora didn't like him—even with his clothes on. She told herself it was the cleft in his chin, which always betokened a sensual nature, but it was really the thought of all the hair. It made him look so animal.

In many ways he was a good catch. He had been her father's commandant during the Troubles. He owned the big hardware store in town, which his father had left him against his mother's wishes. Mrs. Cashman and Charlie had never got on, and she had wanted the shop for her other son, John Joe; but after letting Charlie work as a shop assistant in Asragh all his life, the old man had suddenly turned round and left him everything. Even Mrs. Cashman herself was in the house only on sufferance.

He was even well read as the townspeople went. Once he found Nora reading St. Francis de Sales and asked her if she had ever read *Romeo and Juliet,* but he asked it with such a sly and double-meaning air that he only repelled her worse than ever. She gave him a cold and penetrating glance that should have frozen the blood in him.

"As a matter of fact I have," she said steadily, just to show him that true piety didn't exclude a study of the grosser aspects of existence.

"What did you think of it?" asked Charlie.

"I thought it contained a striking moral lesson," said Nora.

"Go on," said Charlie with a flicker of a grin. "What was that?"

"It showed what unrestrained passion can lead people

to," said Nora with the air of a Christian martyr announcing the Gospel truths to a Roman centurion.

Her father, a big man with an astonished face, looked at them and said nothing, but that night after Charlie had gone he glanced at Nora with a terrible air.

"What's that book Charlie Cashman was talking about?" he asked.

"*Romeo and Juliet,*" she said with a start. "It's there on the shelf behind you. In the big Shakespeare."

He took down the book and looked even more astonished.

"That's a funny sort of way it's written," he said. "What is it about?"

She told him the story as well as she could, while he smoothed his chin.

"But they were properly married?" he asked.

"They were," said Nora. "Why?"

"Ah," said her father cantankerously, "that was a funny way to take him up. 'Tisn't as if there was anything wrong in it." He strode to the foot of the stairs with his hands in his trousers pockets while Nora watched him with a hypnotized air. "Mind you," he said, "I don't want to force the man on you, but there's many a girl in this town would be very glad to have him."

That was all that was said, but Nora resolved to die like a Christian martyr sooner than marry a man with as much hair as Charlie. At the same time, of course, she didn't altogether like to see him switch his attention to Polly. To her mind, it only showed the flighty, sensual sort of man he was, and she was far too fond of Polly to wish her married to him. Her interest in the whole thing was quite unselfish.

The Donegans too wanted to catch Charlie, and Polly, being a good-natured girl, felt if she was going to get married at all she ought to do it in a way that would oblige somebody. She didn't mind the hair, and she seemed to take a genuine liking to Charlie. Polly had no brains; she never even knew which of the two factions was the government of the moment, but Charlie could explain it all to her in the most interesting way. He seemed to her a man of really gigantic intellect, and listening to him was as good as a sermon from a great preacher. It caused a certain coldness between the two girls, but Polly was self-centred and hard-hearted, and Nora got the worst of that bargain.

2.

Charlie asked Polly where she'd like to go for her honeymoon, and Polly looked rather troubled.

"Ah, 'twould cost too much," she said in her tangential way. "We'll go somewhere else."

"Not at all, girl, not at all," said Charlie recklessly. "We'll go wherever you like."

"Lourdes?" asked Polly doubtfully. "Is that far, Charlie?"

"Lourdes?" repeated Charlie with a baffled air. "What do you want to go there for?"

"Oh, it's only for the sake of the pilgrimage," said Polly. "Did you ever read the life of Bernadette, Charlie?"

"No," said Charlie, "but we'll go to Lourdes."

Everything was arranged, the tickets bought and the hotel room reserved, when one day Polly met Nora in the street. Nora blushed; she was thinking about all she had said of Charlie to Polly, which by now had probably got back (it hadn't, but in that Nora was judging by herself), and she smiled timidly and held out her hand.

"Well," she said, "I wish you the best of luck," but her tone was regretful as if she felt that Polly would probably need it.

"Oh, Nora," cried Polly with a delighted laugh, "you'd never guess where we're going on the honeymoon. Oh, Nora, would you ever come? I'd love to have you with us."

Now, it was like Polly to want to bring Nora with them, and at the time it didn't really strike Nora as queer, because she began to wonder whether she couldn't get the money out of her father.

"Oh, where is it?" she asked eagerly.

"Lourdes," said Polly. "Isn't it marvellous?"

"Lourdes?" cried Nora, aghast. "But surely you knew about Lourdes?"

"No," said Polly in great surprise. "Oh, don't tell me it's not allowed, Nora?"

" 'Tisn't that at all," said Nora in alarm, "but it's supposed to be very unlucky for honeymoons. I only heard of one girl that chanced it, and she died inside a year."

"Oh, Law, Nora," cried Polly with bitter disappointment, "how is it that nobody told me that, or what sort of people do they have in those travel agencies?"

"Well, I suppose they took it for granted you knew."

"And even Charlie!" cried Polly in anguish. "He's supposed to be an educated man. You'd think he'd know about it."

She rushed away at once to tell Charlie, whom she already looked on as a walking encyclopædia, and they had their first fight. Charlie was now all set for Lourdes and a night or two in Paris on the way, and he fumed and stamped at Nora Lalor and her blasted pisherogues, but you didn't catch a prudent girl like Polly endangering her safety and happiness because of the bit of inconvenience it might cause. And two days before the wedding everything had to be cancelled, and they went to Connemara instead.

They arrived there in a car one very wet evening, and Polly said rather dismally that it wasn't in the least like what she had expected. It wasn't the only thing that was unlike what she expected, nor was she the only one who was disappointed. She had brought a little statue of the Blessed Virgin, which she put on the table by her bed before she said her night prayers and undressed. She was a little surprised at the way Charlie looked at her, but not really upset. She patted the bed and said it was just the sort of bed she liked and that she needed it after the journey. Then she turned and saw the queer

grin on Charlie's face. It wasn't like anything she had
ever seen before and it filled her with vague alarm. Then
Charlie got into the bed beside her and she gave a loud
gasp that could be heard through the whole hotel.

For the rest of the night there was one thought and
one thought only in Polly's brain, which was not usually
retentive of ideas. "Can it be? Is it possible? Why didn't
somebody tell me?" She kept herself from flying from
the room with shrieks by repeating aspirations to herself.
"Jesus, mercy, Mary, help!" was her favourite. She
thought of all the married women she had ever known
from her mother on, fat, pious, good-natured women
whom you saw every morning at Mass, and wondered
if they had lived all their lives through with this secret in
their hearts. She knew exactly now what it was that Nora
had been trying to find out and why no one had ever
told her. There was only one faint hope: that after years
she might get used to it as they seemed to have done. But
then it all began again, and she muttered aspirations loud
enough for Charlie to hear, and knew she could never,
never get used to it; and when it was over, a bitter anger
smouldered in her heart against all the nonsense that
was written about it by people like Shakespeare. "Oh,
what liars they are!" she thought, wishing that she could
lay hands on one of them just for five minutes. "What
liars!"

She didn't get a proper wink of sleep until morning,
and when Charlie tried to rouse her for breakfast she
snarled at him and then rolled herself up to sleep until

lunch. During the meal she scarcely once opened her mouth, but looked gloomily out through the windows at a landscape that was as dark as her soul. After coffee she said she was going for a walk.

"A walk?" cried Charlie. "But will you look at the rain, woman!"

"Oh," she said quickly, "you needn't come if you don't want to. I'd just as soon be by myself."

"I'll do nothing of the sort, woman," snapped Charlie, surprised and rather frightened at this queer sequel to a marriage night, and they plunged out in the torrents of mountain rain. It was a typical Connemara day, with deceptive intervals during which a blue patch appeared in the sky or a ray of light brought out a rich mournful colour from the bogs and lakes. Polly, head down and hands in the pockets of her mackintosh, strode on, trying to shake off the nightmare of the previous night and the still worse nightmare that was to come.

"Now will you come back?" snarled Charlie when he was wet to the skin.

"Ah, what nonsense!" cried Polly. "We have heaps of time still before dark."

"Oh, all right," said Charlie. "You can walk until dark if you like. I'm going back to the hotel. I'm lucky if I haven't double pneumonia already. Are you coming?"

"No."

"Go to hell!" snapped Charlie. Nice words to use on the first day of a honeymoon! Polly went on till she came to a mountain cottage. A nice old woman came out and asked her in out of the rain. Then nothing would do her but that Polly should change, and in a Connemara petticoat of bright crimson Polly sat in front of the fire and drank the tea that the old woman made for her. As the evening wore on, her heart grew lighter. The old man came in, and Polly asked him quite flightily what he thought of his new daughter-in-law, and when she heard that the old couple had six children, all in America, she realized that you could get used to hell. Before she left with the old man, who was escorting her across the bog in the darkness, she threw her arms round the old woman and kissed her.

"Oh," she cried, almost delirious with relief, "you have no idea what you've done for me. When I came here I thought my heart was going to break, but now I feel life is worth living again."

The day after they returned from the honeymoon, Nora called. Charlie was in the shop as she passed through and she smiled shyly at him. Herself and Polly had tea in the kitchen and then went upstairs to the best room, overlooking the main street. Nora noticed with satisfaction that Polly looked a bit tired, but Polly put it down to the fatigue of the journey. Then Nora lit a cigarette and sat back, prepared to hear the truth at last.

"Well," she asked with a knowing smile, "and what does it feel like to be married?"

"Oh, all right, Nora," replied Polly perfunctorily, though Nora noticed that for a moment her face looked even more ravaged than before.

"And how do you find Charlie?" asked Nora, her smile growing broader.

"Oh, I suppose he's much the same as anyone else," replied Polly with a far-away look, glancing out through the lace curtains at the red-brick houses on the other side of the street.

"And is that all you're going to tell us?" asked Nora with a laugh.

"Oh, what ever do you mean, Nora?" Polly asked indignantly.

"I thought you were going to advise me whether I should get married or not," added Nora lightly, but with the growing conviction that she would have to fight for any little bit of information she managed to extract.

"Oh, Law, Nora," cried Polly with a distraught air, "I don't think it can ever be right to discuss things like that."

"Oh," said Nora with chagrin, feeling that, like the country from whose bourne no traveller returns, marriage never seemed to allow anyone back to tell you what it was like, "was it as bad as that?"

"I think I'd sooner not talk about it at all, Nora," said Polly firmly, and she bowed her head, and her smooth forehead became fenced with wrinkles, and a second chin began to peep from below the first. Nora knew that when Polly set her face like that, wild horses wouldn't drag another word out of her.

3.

So that was how married life began for Charlie and Polly. Charlie had this shop in the main street; a shop like a cave, buckets hanging and spades stacked at either side of the front door, and when you went in, the hardware department was on your right and the general store on your left. Charlie looked after the first, and Polly, with a little girl, the other. Charlie's end of it was really well looked after; there wasn't a bit of agricultural machinery for miles around that he didn't know the inside of and for which he couldn't at a pinch produce at least the substitute for a spare part.

Polly wasn't so brilliant, but she was careful and polite. In every way she was all a wife ought to be; obliging, sweet-tempered, with no flightiness about her, and so modest that she wouldn't even allow Charlie to put on the light while she dressed for Mass of a winter's morning. Mrs. Cashman had had a good selection of holy pictures before, but Polly brought a whole gallery of them, and the bedroom was covered in them. There was also a Lourdes clock which played the Lourdes hymn at the appropriate hours—very soothing and devotional—but at the same time Charlie was just the least bit disappointed. He couldn't help admitting that to himself. "Romeo, Romeo, wherefore art thou Romeo?" he would suddenly find himself declaiming. Italian

women were probably different. It was probably the
sun. He was a restless man, and he had hoped marriage
would settle him. It hadn't. When he had closed the shop
for the night and should have been sitting upstairs before the fire with his pipe and his book, the longing
would suddenly seize him to go out to Johnny Desmond's instead. It was very disconcerting. To counter
it, he began enumerating his blessings. He had expected
nothing under the will, and now he had everything.
Sometimes in the dark he poked his way down to the
shop, switched on the lamp over the cash desk, and took
out the will. He always liked the style of the will; the
way it carefully excluded all possibility of misunderstanding. In its own way it was as powerful as Shakespeare.

One murky afternoon when there was no business doing in the shop, his mother came in and found him por-
ing over it. He gave her a quizzical grin. She was a
cranky old woman, doubled up with rheumatics.

"I see what you're at," she said resignedly. "I see it
all."

"Aha," said Charlie with a chuckle, slapping his hairy
paw on the will, "that's fine, devotional reading."

"You were always too smart for your poor slob of a
brother," she said philosophically. "But take care you
wouldn't be keeping the bed warm for him yet."

"What's that you say?" shouted Charlie, startled in
spite of himself.

"God spoke first," said his mother, taking a packet

of rice from behind the other counter. "Many a better cake didn't rise."

She went out, banging the house door behind her, and left Charlie gaping. The will, lying on the desk before him, had lost its magical power. Because there was a clause in it, a clause to which Charlie had never given a thought—why would he?—entailing the property on his children, or failing them on John Joe's. Failing them—that was the snag. And John Joe already had four and another one coming. With head down and hands in his trousers pockets, Charlie paced moodily to the shop door and stood there, leaning against the jamb, his legs crossed and his cap pulled low over his eyes. His mother could read him like a book.

The least thing was enough to set him off. At the first stroke of the Angelus he put up the shutters and had his supper. Then he lit his pipe and strolled to the hall door for a look up and down the main street, on the off chance of seeing somebody or something. He never did, but it was as well to make sure. Then he went back to the kitchen, dragging his feet as he usually did before setting out to Johnny's. It was a way they had of announcing that they weren't moving in the right direction. His mother had gone out to the chapel, and Polly was sitting at the table under the window. Charlie took a deep breath, removed his hands from his trousers pockets, raised his head, and squared his shoulders.

"Well," he said briskly, "I might as well take a little turn."

"Wisha, you might as well, Charlie," said Polly without resentment.

It was only what she always said, but in Charlie's state of depression it sounded to him like a dead key on the piano. He felt it was a hard thing that a married man of a year's standing had no inclination to stop at home, and that Polly had no inclination to make him. Not that she could have, even if she had tried, but he felt that a little persuasion wouldn't have been out of place.

"The mother wasn't talking to you?" he asked keenly.

"No, Charlie," replied Polly in surprise. "What would she talk to me about?"

"Oh, nothing in particular," said Charlie with a toss of his head. "She was just remarking that you were a long time about having a family," he added with a touch of reproach.

"Oh, Law, Charlie," cried Polly aghast. "Wasn't that a very queer thing for her to say?"

"Was it, I wonder," said Charlie, as if to himself, giving her a sideway glance from the corner of his eye.

"But, Charlie," she exclaimed, drawing herself up, "you don't think I won't have children, do you?"

"Oh, no, no, no," replied Charlie hastily, fearing lest he might have gone too far. "But 'twould suit her fine if you hadn't. Then the place would go to John Joe's kids."

"Oh, how could it go to John Joe's children?" cried

Polly in alarm. "I thought your father left it all to you."

"To me, and my children," corrected Charlie. "As long as I have no children I have no say over who it goes to."

"Oh, Law, Charlie," she cried, "isn't that a terrible worry to you?"

"Well, as a matter of fact it is," said Charlie, scratching his poll reflectively. "You see, I put a lot of work into the place, and no one likes to be working for someone else. . . . You wouldn't see a doctor?" he added.

"I'd have to ask Father Ring first," said Polly thoughtfully.

That upset Charlie again. He nearly told her it was Father Ring she should have married, but remembered in time that she'd be bound to confess it. There is nothing a good-living woman likes better than confessing her husband's sins.

4.

But Charlie's remarks brought Polly for the first time up against the serious things of life. It made her very thoughtful, but it was a week or so before she could bring herself to talk to Nora about it. It was a thing you could only discuss with a woman, and Nora was the only intellectual woman she knew.

Nora, it seemed, wasn't inclined to take it as seriously as Charlie. According to her, there was a lot of chance in it. Some people went on for years without having a child, while others didn't even wait for their time to be up. It was quite shocking when you came to think of it, but Polly somehow never did get round to thinking of it. If you were really in trouble, there was always the Holy Door. Johnny Fleming, the barrister, and his wife had been married for ten years without having a child, and they had made the pilgrimage. Then they started, and now people were beginning to say that it was about time they made another pilgrimage to shut off the power.

"I suppose I could go next year if nothing happens," said Polly doubtfully.

"You must go this year if you're going at all," said Nora. "It's only opened once in seven years."

"Oh, I could never wait as long as that," cried Polly, overcome.

"Well, it's rather dangerous to be too long about having the first," said Nora sagaciously. "There was a woman up our road waited till she was thirty-eight, and she died."

"Oh, Law" said Polly, a little peeved. "I suppose 'tis wrong to be criticizing, but really, the Lord's ways are very peculiar."

So back she went to Charlie with the story. Charlie screwed up his face as though he were hard of hearing, a favourite trick of his whenever he wanted to gain time.

"Where did you say?" he asked.

"Rome," said Polly.

"Rome?" repeated Charlie with a mystified air. "What the blazes do you want to go to Rome for?"

"It's the pilgrimage of the Holy Door," said Polly. "You wouldn't know about that?" she asked, in the trustful tone she used to indicate the respect she had for his learning.

"No," replied Charlie, playing up to the part of the intellectual husband. "What sort of door?"

"A holy door," said Polly.

"A *holy* door," repeated Charlie, stroking his plump, stubby chin.

" 'Tis only opened once in seven years, and 'tis good for people without families," prompted Polly hopefully.

"Is that so?" asked Charlie gravely. "Who told you about that, Polly?"

"Nora Lalor," said Polly.

"Tut, tut, tut," clucked Charlie impatiently. "Ah, I wouldn't say there'd be much truth in that, Polly."

"Oh, Law, Charlie," she cried in ringing tones, outraged at his incredulity, "you surely don't think people like the Flemings would go all that way unless there was something in it?"

"Oh, no, no, no, I dare say not," said Charlie hastily, seeing that anything further he said was likely to be reported back to Father Ring. "But I'm afraid I couldn't get away just now."

"Well, I'll have to get away, Charlie," said Polly with quiet decision. "It might be too late if I left it for another seven years. Nora says 'tis very dangerous."

"And a hell of a long time it'll be before that one is in any danger," snapped Charlie fierily.

His bad temper didn't last long, though. It was an excuse for an outing, and Charlie loved an outing. He had never been farther than London before; Paris staggered him; and while the train was passing through the Alps in the late evening he wedged himself in the corridor with his elbows on the rail while tears of excitement poured down his hairy cheeks. After all, he couldn't forget he was going to the homeland of Romeo and Juliet.

He quickly made friends with the other two occupants of the carriage, a fat Dutchman in shirt-sleeves who ate sausages and spooned shamelessly with the woman with him, who he said was his wife. The sight was too gross for Polly, and she went and stood in the corridor, but not to look at the scenery.

"Isn't she beautiful?" said the Dutchman, stroking his wife affectionately under the chin.

"Oh, grand, grand!" agreed Charlie enthusiastically, nodding and smiling encouragement to the woman, who couldn't speak English and to all appearances didn't know much of any other language either.

"That's a nice-looking girl with you," said the Dutchman. "Who is she?"

"Polly?" said Charlie, looking at the figure in the corridor. "Oh, that's the wife."

"Whose wife?" asked the Dutchman.

"Mine," said Charlie.

"And don't you love her?"

"Love her?" echoed Charlie, giving another peep out at the sombre figure of Polly. "I'm dotty about her, of course."

"Then why do you not kiss her?" asked the Dutchman. "Women love it. Look at this!"

"Ah, mine wouldn't," said Charlie in alarm. "In Ireland we don't go in much for that sort of thing."

"And what do you go in for?"

"Well," replied Charlie a little doubtfully, seeing that he didn't quite know himself—apart from politics, which didn't sound quite right—"we're more in the sporting line—horses and dogs and so on."

"Ah," said the Dutchman, shaking his head, "you can't beat women."

Charlie went out to Polly, who was leaning with her back to the compartment with a brooding look on her face.

"Oh, Charlie," she said in a troubled voice, "how do they do it? A wonder the woman doesn't drop dead with shame! I suppose they're Protestants, are they, Charlie?"

"I dare say, I dare say," said Charlie, thinking it was better not to try and explain.

5.

It was a great outing, and it lasted Charlie in small talk for a month. The grapes like gooseberries, and night coming on and every little café with sopranos and tenors and baritones all bawling away about love—*amore, mio cuore, traditore*—you could see where Juliet got it from. But Juliet's homeland didn't seem to have done much for Polly, and the fellows in Johnny Desmond's began to drop sly remarks about doors of one sort and another, while old Mrs. Cashman, getting over her alarm at the prospect of a miracle, declared loudly that it would be a poor look-out for a woman like her to be relying on a son that had to take his wife to Rome. And, indeed, it didn't take a miracle to start John Joe's wife off, for the poor wretch had only to look at her.

But Polly, to give her her due, was every bit as upset as Charlie was. Sixty pounds odd the pilgrimage had cost them and they had absolutely nothing to show for it. If the Holy Door couldn't do a thing like that it couldn't be so holy after all. She blamed Nora Lalor a lot for the bad advice she had given her.

"But after all, Polly," said Nora reasonably, "you mustn't expect too much. It might be something mental."

"Oh, how could it, Nora?" cried Polly in a fury. "I'm surprised at you saying a thing like that."

"But why not?" asked Nora with a touch of asperity. "If you didn't feel attracted towards Charlie—"

"Oh," said Polly vaguely and guardedly, but with a dim comprehension dawning in her eyes, "would that make a difference?"

"It might make all the difference in the world, Polly,"

said Nora severely. "After all, there was Kitty Daly. She was married eight years and hadn't a family, and then one night she imagined her husband was Rudolph Valentino, and everything went smack smooth after that."

"Rudolph Valentino," said Polly. "Who was he?"

"He was a film star," said Nora.

"But why would she do that?" asked Polly incredulously.

"Well, I suppose he was a nice-looking man, and you know what Jerome Daly is like."

"Would there be a picture of him that I could see?" asked Polly.

"I wouldn't say so," said Nora. "Anyway, he's dead now, so I don't suppose 'twould be right. But, of course, there are plenty of others just as good."

"Oh, I don't think it could ever be right," cried Polly with a petulant toss of her head. She was feeling very sorry for herself. She knew quite clearly that that sly thing, Nora, was trying to worm out of her what Charlie really did to her, and she was torn asunder between the necessity for revealing something and the desire not to reveal anything at all. "I'm sure Father Ring would say it was wrong."

"I don't see why he would," said Nora coolly. "After all, it was done for a good purpose."

Polly had no reply to that one. But at the same time the temptation lingered. The following Saturday evening she went to confession to Father Ring. Her sins didn't take long to tell. They were never what you'd call serious.

"Father," she said as she finished, "I want to ask your advice."

"What about, my child?" asked Father Ring.

"It's my husband, father," said Polly. "You see, we haven't any children, and I know it's a terrible worry to him, so I went on the pilgrimage to the Holy Door in Rome, but it didn't do me any good."

"Go on," said Father Ring.

"So then a friend of mine was telling me about another woman that was in the same position. It seems she imagined that her husband was Rudolph Valentino."

"Who was he?"

"Some sort of fellow on the pictures," said Polly.

"But what put it into her head that he was her husband?" asked Father Ring with a puzzled frown.

"Oh, she only imagined it," said Polly in distress. "It seems he was a very nice-looking fellow, and her husband is an insignificant little man. . . . Of course, I could understand that," she added candidly. "Charlie is a very good fellow, but he doesn't look right somehow."

"Charlie?" exclaimed the priest in astonishment. "But he's a fine-looking man."

"Oh, would you think so?" asked Polly with interest. "Of course, I might be wrong. But anyway, this woman had a child after."

"What did she call him?" asked the priest suspiciously.

"I don't know, father," replied Polly. "Why? Does it make any difference?"

"It doesn't," said the priest. "I was just wondering."

"But tell me, father," said Polly, "I wonder would it ever be right?"

"Ah, I don't say that there would be anything wrong about it," said Father Ring, pulling aside the curtain before the confessional and peeping out the darkened church. "Of course, she did it with a good object."

"That's what Nora—that's what my friend said," added Polly, amazed at the intellect of that little gligeen of a girl.

"Provided, of course, that she didn't get any pleasure out of it," added Father Ring hastily. "If she got carnal pleasure out of it, that would be a different thing."

"Oh," said Polly with a shocked air, "you don't think she'd do that?"

"What I mean," said the priest, "is, more than the natural pleasure."

"The natural pleasure?" repeated Polly with a stunned air.

"However," said Father Ring hastily, "I don't think you're in any danger of that."

It was shortly after this occasion that Charlie began to notice a change in the atmosphere in Johnny Desmond's. Charlie was very sensitive to atmosphere. First, a drunken, sarcastic little scut from the County Council passed a remark about Polly and the new teacher,

Carmody. Now, Carmody was a relative of Father Ring's, a good-looking, plausible Kerry man who put on great airs with the women. Charlie greeted the remark with a sniff and a laugh and was almost on the point of telling them how Polly wouldn't let him switch on the light while she dressed for Mass. Then he began to wonder. Somehow or other, the remark stuck. When next Polly's name was mentioned in connection with Carmody he scowled. It was clear that something was going on and that he was the victim and the laughing-stock. He couldn't bear that. It might be that in her innocence Polly was being indiscreet. On the other hand it might well be that, like many another woman before her, she was only letting on to be innocent to get the chance of being indiscreet. A man could never tell. He went home feeling very upset.

He strode into the hall and snapped a command to Polly, who was sitting in the darkness over the range. She rose in surprise and followed him obediently up the stairs. In the sitting-room he lit the gas and stooped to look up under the mantel as though to see if the burner was broken.

"Sit down," he said curtly over his shoulder.

"Oh, Law, what is it at all, Charlie?" asked Polly nervously.

Charlie turned and stood on the hearth-rug, his legs apart, his cap drawn down over his eyes, and seemed as if he were studying her through his two hairy cheekbones.

"Tell me, Polly," he said in a reasonable tone such as he felt became a man whose wife had just been unfaithful to him, "did I do anything to you?"

"Oh, what ever do you mean, Charlie?" she asked in bewilderment. "What could you do to me?"

"That's just what I'd like to know," said Charlie, nodding sagaciously. "What I did out-of-the-way."

"Oh, Charlie," she exclaimed in alarm, "what a thing to say to me! I never said you did anything out-of-the-way."

"I'm glad to hear it," said Charlie, nodding again and looking across the room at the picture of a sailing-ship in distress. "I suppose you don't know the new teacher in the school?" he added by way of no harm.

"Is it Mr. Carmody?" she asked with a suspicion of a blush.

"That's the very man," said Charlie. "I see you do know him."

"I met him a couple of times with Mrs. MacCann," said Polly patiently. "What about him?"

"Now, is that all?" asked Charlie accusingly. "You might as well tell me the truth, now, and not have me drag it out of you."

"Oh, what do you mean?" cried Polly, sitting bolt upright with indignation. "What would you drag out of me? I don't know what's after coming over you at all, Charlie."

"Hold on, now, hold on," said Charlie commandingly, raising one hand for silence. "Just sit where you are for a minute." He put his hands behind his back, tilted forward on his toes, and studied his feet for a moment. "Do you know," he added gravely, fixing his eyes on her again. "that 'tis all over the town that you and Carmody are carrying on behind my back? . . . Isn't that a nice thing to have said about your wife?" he asked, raising his voice.

Up to that moment he had only partly believed in her guilt, but he no longer had any doubt when he saw the way she changed colour. It was partly anger, partly shame.

"Oh," she cried in a fury, tossing her handsome black head, "the badness of people! This is all Nora Lalor's doing. Father Ring would never repeat a thing like that."

"Father Ring?" exclaimed Charlie with a start, seeing that others were in the secret from which he was excluded. "What has he to do with it?"

"I see it all now," cried Polly dramatically. "I should never have trusted her. I might have known she'd bell it all over the town."

"What would she bell?" snapped Charlie impatiently. At the very best of times Polly wasn't what you'd call exactly lucid, but when anything happened to upset her, every joint in her mind flew asunder.

"She said," explained Polly earnestly, wagging a long arm at him, "that she knew a woman called Kitty Daly that had a child after imagining her husband was Rudolph Valentino."

"Rudolph who?" asked Charlie with a strained air.

"You wouldn't know him," replied Polly impatiently. "He's an old fellow on the pictures. He's dead now."

"And what has he to do with Carmody?" asked Charlie anxiously.

"He has nothing whatever to do with Carmody," shouted Polly, enraged at his stupidity.

"Well, go on, woman, go on," said Charlie, with his face screwed up into a black knot in the endeavour to disentangle the confusion in which she had plunged him.

"Oh, I know it couldn't be wrong, Charlie," said Polly positively, flying off at another tangent. "I asked Father Ring myself was it wrong for her."

"Wrong for who?" snarled Charlie, almost beside himself.

"The woman that thought her husband was Rudolph Valentino, of course," said Polly warmly.

"Christ Almighty," groaned Charlie, "do you want to drive me mad?"

"But when you won't listen to me!" cried Polly passionately. "And Father Ring said there was no harm in it so long as she was doing it for a good purpose and didn't get any pleasure out of it. . . . Though indeed," she added with great candour, "I'm sure I have no idea what pleasure she could get out of it."

"Ah, botheration!" shouted Charlie, shaking his fists at her. "What goings-on you have about Rudolph Valentino! Don't you see I'm demented with all this hugger-mugger? What did you do then, woman?"

"I went to the pictures," said Polly with an aggrieved air.

"You went to the pictures with Carmody?" asked Charlie encouragingly, only too willing to compound for an infidelity with an indiscretion.

"Oh, what a thing I'd do!" cried Polly in a perfect tempest of indignation. "Who told you that I went to the pictures with Mr. Carmody? This town is full of liars. I went with Nora, of course."

"Well?" asked Charlie.

"Well," said Polly in a more reasonable tone, "I thought all the old men on the pictures were terrible. How people can bear the sight of them night after night I do not know. And then, as we were coming out, Nora asked me wasn't there any man at all that I thought was good-looking, and I said: 'Nora,' I said, 'I always liked Mr. Carmody's appearance.' 'Oh, did you?' said Nora. 'I did, Nora,' said I. Now, that," said Polly flatly, bringing her palm down on her knee, "was all that either of us said; and of course I might be wrong about his appearance, though I always thought he kept himself very nicely; but anyone that says that I went to the pictures with him, Charlie, all I can say is that they have no conscience. Absolutely no conscience."

Charlie stared at her for a moment in stupefaction. For that one moment he wondered at himself for ever thinking that Polly could have it in her to carry on with a man, and more that any man in the world would be fool enough to try and seduce her. *Amore, mio cuore, traditore,* he thought despairingly. Quite clearly Italian women must be different. And then the whole thing began to dawn on him and nearly suffocated him with rage.

"And do you mean to tell me," he asked incredulously, "that you went to Father Ring and asked him could you think I was Charlie Carmody?"

"Rudolph Valentino, Charlie," corrected Polly. "It was Nora Lalor put Mr. Carmody into my head. . . . You don't think it makes any difference?" she added hastily, terrified that she might unwittingly have drifted into mortal sin.

"You asked Father Ring could you think I was Rudolph Valentino?" repeated Charlie frantically.

"Oh, surely, Charlie," said Polly, brushing this aside as mere trifling, "you don't think I'd do it without finding out whether 'twas a sin or not?"

"God Almighty!" cried Charlie, turning to the door, "I'm the laughing-stock of the town!"

"Oh, you think too much about what people say of you," said Polly impatiently. "What need you care what they say so long as 'tis for a good object?"

"Good object," cried Charlie bitterly. "I know the object I'd like to lay my hands on at this minute. It's that Nora Lalor with her cesspool of a mind. By God, I'd wring her bloody neck!"

6.

That was nothing to what Nora did later. Somebody, Charlie discovered, had put it about that it was really his fault and not Polly's that they had no family. Of course, that might quite well have been a misconception of Polly's, for he learned from a few words she dropped that she thought his mother was a witch and that it was she who was putting the spells on her. A girl who would believe that was quite capable of blaming it on the butcher's boy. But somehow Charlie suspected that the malice behind it was Nora's and not Polly's. The Carmody business was only a flea-bite to it, for it lowered him in the estimation of everybody. And it was clever, because he wasn't in a position to prove the contrary. Worst of all, he doubted himself. He was a nervous man; the least thing was enough to set him off, and for weeks and weeks he brooded over it till he had almost convinced himself that the woman was right; he wasn't like any other man; God had heaped so many heavy burdens on him that this was all he could expect.

Now, the Cashmans had a maid called Molly—Molly O'Regan—a country girl with a rosy, laughing, good-natured face and a shrill, penetrating voice. She was one of the few people he knew who wasn't afraid of his mother, and in his bachelor days when she brought him his shaving water of a morning she always leaned in the door and showed him just enough of herself to interest a half-wakened man. "Come in, girl," he would whisper, nodding and beckoning, "come in and shut the door." "What would I come in for?" Molly would ask with an air of surprise. " 'Pon my soul," he would say admiringly, "you're most captivating!" "Captivating?" Molly would shriek. "Listen to him! There's capers for you!" "You're like a rose," he would say, and then give one wild bound out of the bed, which landed him within a few feet of her, while she gave another shriek and banged the door behind her.

It was astonishing how like a rose she seemed with all those religious women around him. Sometimes when his mother and Polly were out he followed her up to the bedroom and had a bit of a skirmish with her. "Sweet Jesus," she cried, "what would I do if one of them walked in? And all the holy pictures!" And she flashed a wondering look at all the coloured pictures, the statues, and the Lourdes clock. "Isn't it true for me?" she cried. "A wonder you wouldn't have a bit of shame in you!"

"I declare to my God," said Charlie with a grin, "they set off your beauty. When you get married I'll give you the lot as a wedding present."

"As a wedding present?" yelped Molly. "How do you know I'd have them? God forgive me for saying it, but 'tis more like a chapel than anything else."

"As a matter of fact," said Charlie, "that's the idea. You knew I was starting a religious order of my own, didn't you?"

"A religious order?" echoed Molly. "I did not."

"Oh, that's quite true," said Charlie gravely. "I'm only waiting for authority from Rome."

"What sort of a religious order?" asked Molly suspiciously—she wasn't too bright in the head, and as she said herself, with the blackguard Charlie Cashman you'd never know where you were.

"An order of Christian married couples," replied Charlie. "The old sort of marriage is a wash-out. Purity is what we're going in for."

"Purity?" shrieked Molly in a gale of laughter. "And you in it!"

And then one autumn evening Molly whispered to him that she was going to have a baby. She wept and said her old fellow would have her sacred life. Charlie shed a few tears as well and told her not to mind her old fellow; while he had a pound in the bank he'd never see her short for anything. He meant it too, for he was a warm-hearted man and always had a soft spot in his heart for Molly. But, best of all, it had killed for ever whatever doubts he might have had about himself. In the dusk he went up to Johnny Desmond's overflowing with delight and good nature. From this out they could make what jokes they liked about him, but these would be nothing to his own secret joke over them. It didn't matter if it took twenty years before they knew it. A load had been lifted from his mind. He was in the wildest spirits, drinking and joking and making up rhymes.

Next morning, coming on to dawn, he woke with a

very bad taste in his mouth. He glanced round, and there, in the light of the colza-oil lamp burning before the statue of the Sacred Heart, was Polly beside him in the bed. She looked determined even in sleep. The Lourdes clock, which was suffering from hallucinations and imagining it was an alarm clock, was kicking up merry hell on the mantelpiece. He knew it was really playing "The bell of the Angelus calleth to pray," which is a nice, soothing, poetic thought, but what it said in his mind was "You're caught, Charlie Cashman, you can't get away." He realized that if the truth about Molly ever got known, the fat would be in the fire. Polly would leave him; the Donegans would hound him down; Father Ring would denounce him from the altar, and his little business would go to pot. And in spite of it all, he wouldn't be able to leave the business to his son. "You're caught, Charlie Cashman, you can't get away," the clock sang with a sort of childish malice.

The skill with which he manœuvred Molly out of the house would have done credit to an international statesman. He got her into lodgings in Asragh with a bit of money in her name at the bank, and no one was a ha'porth the wiser. But it never is the difficulties you can calculate on that upset you in an hour of crisis. How was Charlie to know that Molly, without a job to do, would find time hanging heavy on her and start spending hours in the Redemptorist church? After a couple of months he started to get the most alarming letters. She talked of telling Polly, of telling her father, of spending the rest of her life in a home, doing penance. When he saw her one night in a back street in Asragh— the only place they could meet in comparative safety —he was shocked at the change in her. She was plumper and better-looking but her eyes were shadowy, and her voice had dropped to a sort of whine.

"Oh, Charlie," she sighed with a lingering, come-to-Christ air, "what luck or grace could we have, and we leading a life of sin and deception?"

"A lot of deception, but damned little sin," said Charlie bitterly. "What do you want me to do?"

"Oh, Charlie," she said, "I want you to get finished with the deception as well as the sin. Be said by me and confess it to your wife."

"Ah, what a thing I'd do!" snapped Charlie, scowling and stamping. "Do you know what she'd do?"

"What would any woman do when she'd find you truly repentant?" asked Molly ecstatically.

"She'd take bloody good care I had cause," said Charlie.

He persuaded her against it, but at the same time it was a nerve-racking business. In the evenings after his supper he lit his pipe and took his usual prowl to the door, but he couldn't bring himself to leave the house. Anything might happen while he was away. Nora Lalor, for instance, might drop in and tell the whole thing to Polly, and what would become of him then? He had a trick of making up little rhymes to amuse himself, and one that he made at this time ran:

Brass, boys, brass, and not only buttons,
The older we gets, the more we toughens.

The older Charlie got, the less he toughened; that was
his trouble.

"Wisha, wouldn't you go for a little stroll?" Polly
would ask considerately.

"Ah, I don't feel like it," Charlie would say with a
sigh.

"Oh, Law," she would cry in gentle surprise, "isn't that
a great change for you, Charlie?"

Once or twice he nearly snapped at her and asked
whose fault it was. Sometimes he went to the house
door and stood there for a full half-hour drinking in the
misery of the view in the winter dusk: the one mean
main street where everyone knew him and no one wished
him well. It was all damn well for Romeo, but Romeo
hadn't to live in an Irish country town. One night it got
so bad with him that he actually packed his bag, intending to slip away and never return. Each morning he
prowled about in wait for Christy Flynn, the postman, to
intercept any anonymous letter there might be for Polly.
As he didn't know which of them were anonymous, he
intercepted them all.

Then one morning the blow fell. It was a solicitor's
letter. He left the shop in charge of Polly and went down
to Curwen Street to see his own solicitor, little Timsy
Harrington. Curwen Street is a nice quiet street, rosy
and warm even on a winter's day, and signs on it; the

cheapest call you could pay there would cost a pound. Charlie knew his call would cost him more than that, but he smoked his pipe and tried to pass it off in a light-hearted, man-of-the-world way, as if collecting affiliation orders was the one job to which he had dedicated his life. That didn't go down with Timsy Harrington, though.

"Wisha, God Almighty, Mr. Cashman," he said in his shrill, scolding old woman's voice, "I'm astonished at you! An educated man like you! If you wanted it, couldn't you do it to anyone else but the Regans? Didn't father and son stop in bed for eight months, letting on they were paralysed, in hopes of getting a couple of pounds out of the insurance company?"

When Charlie went back along the main street, he felt as if he were bleeding from twenty gashes. He swore if he got out of this scrape that he'd live a celibate the rest of his days. Outside the shop he was accosted by an old countryman with a long, innocent face.

"Good morrow, Charlie," he said confidentially, giving Charlie a glimpse of a bolt in the palm of his hand. "I wonder would you have e'er an old nut that'd fit it?"

"I'll try, Tom," said Charlie with a sigh, taking it from him and turning it over in his hand. "Did you ask Polly?"

"There's no one in the shop, Charlie," said the old man.

"Christ Almighty!" muttered Charlie. "Leave me this and I'll see what I can do for you," he added hastily. "You'll excuse me, but I'm very busy at the moment."

He opened the shop door, tiptoed in, and stood with

his head cocked. He could hear Polly moving with stallion strides about the bedroom, and his heart misgave him. He went softly up the stairs and opened the bedroom door a few inches. She was throwing clothes, shoes, and statues all together in a couple of suitcases with positive frenzy. Charlie pushed the door in a little farther; looked at the suitcases, then at her, and at last managed to work up an insinuating smile.

"What's up, little girl?" he asked with a decent show of innocent gaiety.

He saw from her look that this particular line was a complete wash-out, so he entered cautiously, closing the door behind him for fear of being overheard from the shop.

"Aren't I in trouble enough?" he asked bitterly. "Do you know what the O'Regans want out of me?"

"Oh," cried Polly with the air of a tragedy queen, "if there was a man among them he'd shoot you!"

"Two hundred pounds!" hissed Charlie, his high, hairy cheekbones twitching. "Isn't that a nice how-d'ye-do?"

"Oh," she cried distractedly, "you're worse than the wild beasts. The wild beasts have some modesty, but you have none. It was my own fault. Nora Lalor warned me."

"Nora Lalor," said Charlie severely, "will be the ruination of you. She was in here again this morning—you needn't tell me. I can see the signs of her."

"Don't attempt to criticize her to me," stormed Polly.

"Get out of my sight or I won't be responsible."

"Whisht, woman, whisht, whisht, whisht!" hissed Charlie, dancing in a fury of apprehension. "You'll be heard from the shop."

"Oh, I'll take care to be heard," said Polly, giving her rich voice full play. "I'll let them know the sort of man they're dealing with. I'll soho you well."

"So this is married life!" muttered Charlie in a wounded voice, turning away. Then he paused and looked at her over his shoulder as if he couldn't believe what he saw. "Merciful God," he said, "what sort of woman are you at all? How well I didn't go on like this about the schoolmaster!"

"What schoolmaster?" asked Polly in bewilderment, her whole face taking on a ravaged air.

"Carmody," said Charlie reproachfully. "You thought it was my fault and I thought it was yours—what more is in it? We both acted with a good purpose. Surely to God," he added anxiously, "you don't think I did it for pleasure?"

"Oh," she cried, beside herself, "wait till I tell Father Ring this! Wait till he knows the sort of comparisons you're making. With a good purpose! Oh, you blasphemer! How the earth doesn't open and swallow you!"

She pushed him out and slammed the door behind him. Charlie stood on the landing and gave a broken-hearted sigh. "So this is married life!" he repeated despairingly. He returned to the shop and stood far back at the rear, leaning against the stove-pipe. It was a sunny morning, and the sunlight streamed in the windows and glinted on the bright buckets hanging outside the door. Then he started as he saw Nora Lalor, wearing a scarlet coat, come out of the butcher's shop and give a furtive glance across the street. If he had had a gun at that moment, he would have shot her dead.

He heard Polly come downstairs and open the door of the hall. Slowly and on tiptoe he went to the shop door, leaning his shoulder against the jamb and looking up the main street after Nora. He saw her red coat disappear round the corner by the chapel. The old farmer, who was standing outside the post-office, thought that Charlie was hailing him, but Charlie shook his head and frowned. The old farmer leaned resignedly back against the wall of the post-office while Charlie cocked his ear. He heard Polly addressing a small boy in that clear voice of hers, which he knew could be heard at the opposite side of the street.

"Dinny," she said, "I want you to run down to Hennessey's and ask them to send up a car."

Charlie was so overcome that he retreated to the back of the shop again. Polly was going home. It would be all round the town in five minutes. Yet he knew he wasn't a bad man; there were plenty worse, and their wives didn't leave them. For one wild moment he thought of making a last appeal to her, for the sake of the love between them, but one glance into the hall at Polly sitting bolt upright in her blue serge costume, her cases beside her and her gloves and prayer-book on the hall stand,

and Charlie knew that love wasn't even in the running. He went to the shop door and beckoned another small boy.

"I want you to find Father Ring and bring him here quick," he whispered fiercely, pressing a sixpenny bit into the little boy's palm. "Mr. Cashman sent you, say. And tell him to hurry."

"Is it someone sick, Mr. Cashman?" asked the little boy eagerly.

"Yes," hissed Charlie. "Dying. Hurry, now!"

After that he paced up and down the shop like a caged tiger till he saw Father Ring rounding the corner from the chapel. He walked up to meet him.

"What is it at all, Charlie?" the priest asked anxiously. "Is it the mother?"

"No, father," said Charlie desperately, seeing the twitching of curtains in top rooms. "I only wish to God it was," he ground out in a frenzy.

"What is it at all, tell me?" asked Father Ring as they entered the shop.

"Ah, I'm in great trouble, father," said Charlie, tossing his head like a wounded animal. Then he fixed his eyes on a spot of light at the back of the shop and addressed himself to it. "I don't know did you hear any stories about me?" he inquired guardedly.

"Stories, Charlie?" exclaimed Father Ring, who, being a Kerryman, was able to fight a better delaying action than Charlie himself. "What sort of stories?"

"Well, now, father, not the sort I'd like you to hear,"

replied Charlie with what, for him, was almost candour.

"Well, now you mention it, Charlie," said Father Ring with equal frankness, "I fancy I did hear something. . . . Not, of course, that I believed it," he added hastily, for fear he might be committing himself to too much.

"I'm sorry to say you can, father," said Charlie, bowing his head and joining his hairy hands before him as he did at Mass on a Sunday.

"Oh, my, my, Charlie," said Father Ring, giving him a look out of the corner of his eye, "I'm sorry to hear that."

Charlie looked at the floor and nodded his head glumly a couple of times to show that he shared the priest's regrets.

"And tell me, Charlie," whispered Father Ring, pivoting himself on his umbrella as he leaned closer to Charlie, "what way did herself take it?"

"Badly, father," replied Charlie severely. "Very badly. I must say I'm disappointed in Polly."

This time it was he who looked at Father Ring out of the corner of his eye, and somehow it struck him that the priest wasn't as shocked-looking as he might be.

"I'd expect that, mind you," said Father Ring thoughtfully, nodding.

"By God," thought Charlie, "he's not shocked!" There was something that almost resembled fellow-feeling in his air.

"But heavens above, father," Charlie said explosively, hitting his palm with his fist, "the woman is out of her mind. And as for that Lalor girl, I don't know what to say of her." Father Ring nodded again, as much as to say that he didn't know what to say of her either. "I know she's a good-living girl, and all the rest of it," Charlie went on cantankerously, "but girls with no experience of life have no business interfering between married couples. It was bad enough without that—I needn't tell you that. And there she is now," he said, cocking his thumb in the direction of the hall, "with her bags packed and after ordering a car up from Hennessey's! She's prepared to make a show of me before the whole town! Sure, that's never right."

"Well, now, Charlie," whispered the priest, "women are contrairy; they are contrairy; there's no denying it. I'll have a word with her myself."

He opened the house door gently, peeped in and then went into the hall on tiptoe as if he were entering a room where there was someone asleep. Charlie held the door slightly open behind him to hear what went on. Unfortunately, the sight of the priest going in had given the farmer the notion of business as usual. Charlie looked round and saw his long, mournful face in the doorway.

"Charlie," he began, "I hope I'm not disturbing you—"

Charlie, raising his clenched fists in the air, did a silent war-dance. The old farmer staggered back, cut to the heart, and then sat on the sill of the window with his stick between his legs. Another farmer came along, and the old man began to tell him his troubles, with long, accusing glances back at Charlie, who was glued to the door with an agonized look on his face.

"My poor child," he heard Father Ring say in a shocked whisper, "you were in the wars? I can see you were."

"Well, I'm going home now, father," replied Polly listlessly.

"And where better could you go?" exclaimed Father Ring as if he was trying to disabuse her of any idea she might have of remaining. " 'Tis that husband of yours, I suppose? 'Tis, to be sure. I need hardly ask."

"I'd rather not talk about it, father," said Polly politely but firmly. "I dare say you'll hear all about it soon enough."

"I dare say I will," said Father Ring. "People in this town seem to have little better to do. 'Pon my word, I believe I saw a few curtains stirring on my way down. You'll have an audience."

"Well, indeed, father," said Polly in the same weary, indifferent tone, "I never minded much what they saw."

"Sure, you never had anything to conceal," said Father Ring, overwhelming her with agreement as his way was. "I suppose you remember the case of that little girl from Parnell Street a few weeks ago?"

"No, father, I'm afraid I don't," replied Polly without interest.

"Sure, you couldn't be bothered," said Father Ring. "Ah, 'twas a sad business though. She was only nineteen. She was married at ten and the baby was born at one."

"Oh, my, father," said Polly politely, "wasn't that very quick!"

"Well, now you mention it, Polly, it was," said the priest smoothly. "But that wasn't what I was going to tell you. To avoid being noticed, the poor child came home at four in the morning. And would you believe it, Polly, not a soul in that street went to bed that night! Sure, that's never natural! I say that's not natural. Where's that blackguard of a husband of yours till I give him a bit of my mind?" he cried indignantly, turning on his heel. "Charlie Cashman! Charlie Cashman! Where are you, you scoundrel?"

"Here I am, father," said Charlie meekly, taking two paces forward till he stood between the crimson curtains with a blaze of silver from the fanlight falling on his bowed head.

"Aren't you ashamed of yourself?" shouted the priest, hitting the air with his umbrella.

"I am, father, I am, I am," replied Charlie in a broken voice, without looking up.

"Oh, that's only all old connaisseuring, father," cried Polly distractedly, jumping to her feet and grabbing gloves and prayer-book. "Nobody knows what I went through with that man." She opened the hall door; the hall was flooded with silver light, and she turned on them with bowed head, drawing a deep breath through her nose, as beautiful and menacing as a sibyl. "I'm going home to my father now," she continued in a firm voice. "I left the keys on my dressing-table, and you can give Hennessey's boy the bags."

"Polly," said Father Ring sternly, leaning on the

handle of his umbrella, "what way is this for a Child of Mary to behave?"

"Ah, 'tis all very fine for you to talk, father," cried Polly scoldingly, "but I had to live with him and you hadn't. I'd sooner live with a wild beast than with that man," she added dramatically.

"Polly," said Father Ring mildly, "what you do in your own house is your business; what you do in the public view is mine. Polly, you're in the public view."

For the first time in Charlie's life he found himself admiring Father Ring. There was a clash and a grating of wills like the bending of steel girders, and then Polly's collapsed. She came in and closed the door. "Now, Polly," said Father Ring affectionately, "inside that door I don't want to interfere between ye, good or bad. Make what arrangements you like. Live with him or don't live with him; sleep in the loft or sleep in the stable, but don't let us have any more scandal like this morning."

"I wouldn't be safe from him in the stable," said Polly rebelliously. She felt that for the first time in her life she had been met and mastered by a man, and it rankled. At any moment now she was ready to turn nasty, and Father Ring saw it. But Charlie only noticed the falsehood about himself.

"You wouldn't be what?" he cried indignantly. "When did I ever raise a finger or say a cross word to you?"

"Now, Charlie, now!" said Father Ring, raising his hand. "And, woman alive," he added good-humouredly, "can't you bolt your door?"

"How can I," stormed Polly, as sulky as a spoiled child, "when there's no bolt on it?"

"That's easily remedied," said Father Ring.

"Then tell him to send out for a carpenter and have it done now," she said vindictively.

"Send out for a what?" shouted Charlie, cocking his head as if he couldn't believe his ears. "Is it mad you are? My God Almighty, what a thing I'd do; send out for a carpenter to put a bolt on my wife's door!"

"Very well," she said, opening the hall door again, "I'll go home to my father."

"Hold on, now, hold on!" cried Charlie frantically, dragging her back and closing the door behind her. "I'll do it myself."

"Then do it now," she cried. "Because out of this I will not stir till 'tis done."

"Do what Polly tells you, Charlie," said the priest quietly. He saw the danger wasn't over yet. Charlie gave her a murderous glare and went out to the shop. There was a crowd gathered outside on the pavement discussing the wrongs of the poor old farmer, who was the object of the most intense sympathy. Charlie came back after a moment with a brass bolt, a screwdriver, and a couple of screws.

"Show me that bolt," said Polly menacingly. The devil was up in her now. The priest might have bested her, but she still saw a way of getting her own back. Charlie knew that next day herself and Nora Lalor would be splitting their sides over it, and in that moment he vowed a holy war against all women to the day of his death. "I'm going home to my father's," she said, clamping her long lips. "That bolt is too light."

"Get a heavier one, Charlie," said Father Ring quietly. "Now, don't argue, there's a good man."

Argument was about the last thing in Charlie's mind at that moment. Murder would have been nearer the mark. He flung the bolt at Polly's feet, but she didn't even glance at him. When he went back to the shop this time, the crowd was surging round the door.

"Bad luck and end to ye!" he shouted, taking out his spleen on them. "Have ye no business of yeer own to mind without nosing round here?"

"Mr. Cashman," said a young man whom Charlie recognized as the old farmer's son, "you have a bolt belonging to my father."

"Then take it, and to hell with ye," snarled Charlie, taking the bolt from his coat pocket and throwing it at them.

"Oh, begor, we won't trouble you much from this day out," said the young man fierily. "Nor more along with us."

"Go on to hell to ye!" snapped Charlie, beside himself, and he went back to the hall with an iron bolt in his hand. "That's a stable bolt," he said, addressing himself to no one in particular.

"Put it on," said Polly.

Charlie turned on his heel and went upstairs. Father Ring followed him. He stood in awe, looking at all the holy pictures. Then he held the bolt while Charlie used the screwdriver. He was so mad with rage that he used it anyhow.

"You're putting that screw in crooked, Charlie," said the priest. "Wait now till I put on my specs and I'll do it for you."

"Let her go, let her go," said Charlie on the point of breaking down. "It doesn't matter to me now whether she goes or stays. I'm nothing but a laughing-stock."

"Now, Charlie, Charlie," said the priest good-naturedly, "you have your little business to mind."

"For my nephews to walk into," said Charlie bitterly.

"Ah, now, God is very good," said Father Ring. "You're a young man yet. Begor," he added, giving Charlie a quizzical look over the specs, "I did a few queer jobs in my time, but this is the queerest one yet." He saw that Charlie was in no state to appreciate the humour of it, and gave him a professional look through the spectacles. "Ah, well, Charlie," he said, "we all have our burdens. You have only one, but I have a dozen, not to mention the nuns, and they reckon two on a count."

As they came down the stairs Charlie's mother appeared out of the kitchen as if from nowhere, drying her hands on her apron; a little bundle of rags, bones, and malice with a few wisps of white hair blowing about her.

"Aha," she cackled, as if she were speaking to herself, "I hear the Holy Door is shut for the next seven years."

7.

But as she was so fond of saying herself, "God spoke first." It seemed as though after it Polly never had another day's luck. She fell into a slow decline and made herself worse instead of better by drinking the stuff Mrs. Cashman brought her from the Wise Woman, and by changing about from the Nine Fridays to the Nine Tuesdays, and from the Nine Tuesdays to the Nine Mondays —a far more efficacious devotion, according to Nora, who had tried them all.

Charlie wasn't much better off. A scandal like that is never good for a man's business. The Donegans and their friends cut him. The shop began to go down, and Charlie went down with it. He paid less attention to his appearance, served the counter unshaven and without collar and tie; grew steadily shabbier and more irritable and neglected-looking. He spent most of his evenings in the pub, but even there people fought shy of him. Only Old Crone and a few more of the congenitals welcomed his company. The professional men and the civil servants treated him as a sort of town character, a humorous, unreliable fellow without much balance. That, to Charlie, who felt he had put them there, was the bitterest blow, and in his anxiety to reinstate himself with them he boasted and quarrelled and did the boolim generally.

But the funny thing was that from the time she fell ill,

Polly herself softened towards him. Her family were the first to notice it. Like everything else in Polly, it went to extremes, and, indeed, it occurred to her mother that if the Almighty God in His infinite mercy didn't release her soon, she wouldn't have any religion left.

"Ah, wisha, I don't know," she would say with a vacant look. "I don't know is he much worse than anyone else."

"Oh, Polly, how can you say that?" her mother would cry.

"Ah," said Polly broodingly, "I had some very queer temptations myself that no one knew about. Father Ring said once that I was very unforgiving. I think now he was right. All our family were always vindictive."

After that she began to complain about being nervous in the room alone and Mrs. Cashman offered to sleep with her.

"Oh," said Polly impatiently, "I could never bear another woman in the room with me."

"And what do you want so?" asked Mrs. Cashman with her hands on her hips, at her wits' end.

"What I want," said Polly with more truth than she knew, "is a man. I think I'd like Charlie to come back."

"Is it that fellow?" cried Charlie's mother aghast. "That scut—that—I have no words for him. Oh, my! Is it a man that would shame his poor wife the way that ruffian did?"

"Oh," said Polly fractiously, "the way ye talk one'd think he was at it night, noon, and morning. Ye have as much old goings-on about one five-minutes!"

Mrs. Cashman decided that she was going a bit soft
in the head. When a married woman begins to reckon
her husband's morals in terms of hours and minutes, she
is in a bad state. Polly asked Charlie meekly enough if
he'd mind coming back to keep her company. Charlie
would have been just as well pleased to stay as he was,
where he could come in and go out as he liked, but he
saw it was some sort of change before death and did as
she asked him.

It was cold comfort for Polly. Too much mischief had
been made between them for Charlie to feel about her
as a man ought to feel about his wife. The pair of them
would like awake in the grey, flickering light of the colza-
oil lamp with all the holy pictures round them and the
Lourdes clock on the mantelpiece, ticking away whenever it remembered it, and making wild dashes to catch
up on whatever time it had missed, and Charlie's
thoughts would wander, and he'd think if it was God's
holy will to take Polly, it would mean another chance for
him; another chance of an old doll that would fling
herself into his arms without asking Father Ring's permission like the Yeoman Captain's daughter in the old
song:

> *A thousand pounds I'll give thee*
> *And fly from home with thee;*
> *I'll dress myself in man's attire*
> *And fight for Liberty.*

And while Charlie was making violent love to the Captain's daughter, Polly, lying beside him, thought of how her poor bare bones would soon be lying in the stony little patch above Kilmurray, while another woman would be lying where she was lying now, with Charlie's arms round her.

"I suppose," she said in a low voice one night when he was just fancying that she must have dropped off to sleep, "you're only waiting till the sod is over me?"

"What's that?" asked Charlie in astonishment and exasperation, looking round at her as she lay with one arm under her head, staring out into the shadows.

"You're only waiting till I'm well rotten to get another woman in my place," Polly went on accusingly.

"Ah, what a thing I'd think of!" snapped Charlie, as cross as a man jolted suddenly out of his sleep, for her words were like a torch that caught the skirts of the Captain's daughter slipping out by the side door, and he felt it was shameful for him in his health and strength to be plotting like that against a sick woman.

"Nothing matters to you now only to best John Joe and have a son that'll come in for the shop," said Polly with the terrible insight of the last loneliness. "Only for the shop you might have some nature for me."

"And when the hell had I anything but nature for you?" shouted Charlie indignantly, sitting up in bed. "What do you think I married you for? Do you think 'twas for money?"

"If you had any nature for me you wouldn't have disrespected me," Polly went on stubbornly, holding tight to her grievance.

"And what about you?" said Charlie. "You had to think I was some ould divil on the pictures! There's nature for you!"

"I did it with a good object," said Polly.

"Good object!" snorted Charlie. He was on the point of telling her that Juliet and the Captain's daughter didn't do the things they did with a good object, or any object at all except getting the man they wanted most in the world. But he knew she wouldn't understand. Polly lay for a long time drawing deep breaths through her nose.

"Don't think or imagine that I'll rest quiet and see you married to another woman though," she added in a very determined voice. "You may think you'll be rid of me, but I'll make full sure you won't. All our family would go to hell's gates to be revenged."

"Ah, Christ Almighty," shouted Charlie, giving one wild leap out of bed that landed him into the middle of the floor. "Leave me out of this! This is my thanks for coming back here! Leave me out!"

"Mind what I say, now," cried Polly, pointing a bony arm at him from the shadows. She knew well she had him on a tender spot. Herself or Mrs. Cashman would have made no more of meeting a ghost than of putting out the milk for the cat, but Charlie had enough of the rationalist in him to be terrified. His mother had brought him up on them. "Our family was ever full of ghosts," she added solemnly. "You won't have much comfort with her."

"My trousers!" cried Charlie, beside himself with rage and terror. "Where the hell is my bloody trousers?"

"I'm giving you fair warning," Polly cried in a blood-curdling voice as he poked his way out of the room in his nightshirt. "I'll soho ye well, the pair of ye!"

8.

She died very peacefully one evening when nobody was in the room but old Mrs. Cashman. Even in death she made trouble for Charlie. Her last wish was that she wouldn't be buried in Kilmurray at all but in Closty, the burial-ground of the Donegans. It wasn't, as she patiently explained, out of any malice towards Charlie. She wouldn't mind being buried with him; it was the thought of having ultimately to lie with him and the other wife and to rouse herself at the last day to put in an appearance side by side with her that determined her to die a Donegan. Of course, when it became known, it made things many times worse for Charlie and suggested that, at the very least, he had some hand in putting her into the grave. Nora thought it was a very fitting decision.

However, as she was coming down from the bedroom where Polly was laid out in her Child of Mary shroud, she thought she heard a sound from the direction of the shop. The door was closed, all but an inch or two, but

Nora was of a very inquisitive disposition. She pushed
it in quietly. The shop was quite dark, several of the
outside shutters being up, but in the little bit of light that
came from the street she saw the figure of a man and
realized that the noise she had heard was weeping. It
gave Nora quite a shock, for it had never once occurred
to her that Charlie was the sort of man who would hide
himself away and weep. She was a warm-hearted girl.
She went in and touched him lightly on the arm.

"I'm sorry for your trouble, Charlie," she said timidly.

"I know that, Nora," he muttered without looking
round. "I know you are."

"She'll be a terrible loss to you," she added, not very
sincerely.

"Ah, she was unfortunate, Nora," said Charlie broodingly. "She was a fine woman, a lovely woman. I don't
know what bad luck was over us."

"Wha⁺ better luck could ye have and the poor orphan
cheated?" cried a harsh inexpressive voice from the hall,
and Nora started with terror. There was Mrs. Cashman
standing in the doorway with her hands on her hips.
Her voice and appearance were like those of an appari-
tion, and for the first time Nora remembered that Polly
had come to the conclusion that Mrs. Cashman was a
witch and putting spells on her. "She's better off, Nora,
girl," added the old woman.

"I suppose so," agreed Nora doubtfully, resenting her
appearance just at a moment when Charlie was ready to
talk to her.

"She was a good girl and a just girl and she loved her God," hissed Mrs. Cashman, aiming every word at Charlie under Nora's guard. "It would be a bad man that would go against her dying wishes."

"Ah, who talked of going against them?" snarled Charlie with the savagery of a goaded beast, and lunging past them he went out the hall and banged the door behind them.

"Did you see that, Nora?" asked Mrs. Cashman, grabbing her by the arm.

"He's very upset," said Nora in alarm.

"Upset?" cackled Mrs. Cashman. "How upset he is! She's not in her grave yet, and already he's planning who he'll get in her place. That's how upset he is. But he's not done with me yet, the blackguard!"

It was a real shock to Nora, and for the first time it occurred to her that perhaps after all Charlie might have been misjudged—if men could ever be misjudged. From all accounts of what they did to poor women when they had them stripped, they couldn't, but on the other hand, if there had been some foul play by Mrs. Cashman, wouldn't it be dreadful?

She went to the funeral in the carriage with Mrs. Cashman. The moment she got out of the carriage outside the Closty graveyard, she knew there was something very wrong. The Donegans were there, a half-dozen different families, and on their own ground they had taken complete control of the funeral. Charlie was only an outsider. He was standing beside the hearse with his hands crossed before him, holding his hat, and a look of desperation on his dark monkey face. There was a little knot of Donegans behind the open hearse and another little knot by the graveyard gate. Others beside herself had seen what was happening, and men who had known Charlie were standing in a semicircle a hundred yards down the road. Her father was standing a little ahead of them but sufficiently far away not to become involved if any crossness broke out. There was a scowl on his battered old face; his lips pouted out and his eyes almost shut while he noted everything that went on out of the corners.

The procession into the graveyard was to be the signal for the demonstration. Polly, poor soul, had come back to her own at the last and her own would know how to protect her. Charlie would never be allowed past the cemetery gate and he knew it, and knew he would be alone against half a dozen men younger than himself. The coffin was eased out and four Donegans got under it. And just at that moment Nora left Mrs. Cashman's side and went up and stood by Charlie.

It was exactly as though she had blown a whistle. Her father raised his head and looked back at the semicircle of men behind him and then, pulling the lapels of his coat together, came and placed himself at the other side of Nora. Old Jerry Lalor was a peace-loving man, but he couldn't stand by and see his own daughter molested by a Donegan. And one by one a half-dozen middle-aged men came up and joined the party. They too hadn't particularly wanted to get involved in a row between Charlie and the Donegans, but they were old Volunteers and couldn't very well stand aside and let their commandant and vice-commandant be hustled about by the seed of land-grabbers and policemen. Charlie, with Nora by his side, followed the coffin through the gate while her father and the others stood aside waiting their turn. The Donegans glowered but did nothing else. As they emerged at the grave Father Ring looked up at Charlie and Nora from under his bushy brows.

"Thanks, Nora, thanks," said Charlie in a low voice as the service concluded. "You were always a good friend."

Even Nora at her most complacent wouldn't have described herself as a good friend of Charlie's, but the fact that he had understood all the implications of what she had done showed her that he had better feelings than he was generally given credit for.

After Polly's death everyone noticed the change in him. His clothes were brushed; his boots were polished; his face was shaved; and no matter what hour of the morning you visited the shop, he had a collar and tie on. He spent more time in the shop and less in Johnny Desmond's. After a couple of days he stopped going to Johnny's altogether. It was put down at once to the fact that he was looking for someone to take Polly's place. But who'd have him? That wasn't quite so clear. Any respectable woman would be lowering herself by marrying him. The general impression seemed to be that he'd marry Molly, and Nora supposed this would only be proper, but somehow she couldn't help feeling it would be a pity. Mrs. Cashman, who saw all her beautiful plans for the future of John Joe's children going up in smoke, felt the same, so she put it round that Molly had since got into trouble with another man. She hadn't, poor soul, but this was the best Mrs. Cashman could do to decrease her market value. Nora for the first time included him in her prayers and asked the Holy Ghost to help him in making the right choice.

One night a couple of weeks after, when she was on her way back from the chapel, she looked in. She was astonished at Mrs. Cashman's sourness.

"You'll have a cup of tea?" said Charlie.

"No, I won't, Charlie, honest," she said hastily, alarmed at the puss the old woman had on her. "I'm rushing home."

"I'll go up with you," he said at once, giving a look at himself in the mirror.

"If you're back before me, the key will be in the window," said his mother sourly.

"Why?" he snapped. "You're not going out again?"

"You don't think I'm going to stop in the house alone?" she bawled.

"Really, Charlie," said Nora in distress, "there's no reason for you to come with me at all."

"Nonsense!" he said crossly, and led the way to the hall door. It was a moonlit night, and the street was split with silver light. The abbey tower was silhouetted against it, and the light broke through the deeply splayed lancets of the chancel, making deep shadows among the foundered tombstones.

"I really only came in to know how you were getting on," she said.

"Ah, I'm all right," said Charlie. "Only a bit lonely, of course."

"Ah," she said with a half-smile, "I suppose you won't always be that way."

No sooner had she said it than she could have dropped dead with shame. It wasn't in line at all with the noble spirit that had animated her in the graveyard. Charlie gave her a long queer look with his eyes screwed up in slits and then crossed the road and sat against the bridge.

"Tell me, Nora," he asked, folding his arms and looking at her keenly from under the peak of his cap, "what would you do if you were in my position?"

"Oh, I don't know, Charlie," she replied in alarm, wondering how on earth she could extricate herself from this embarrassing fix. "What's to prevent you?"

He sighed.

"You know the sort of things Polly said," he added moodily.

"Ah, I don't think I'd mind that at all," she replied vaguely. "After all, Polly was a sick woman."

"She was, she was," agreed Charlie, nodding once or twice. "Would it ever be right, do you think, to go against a dying woman's wishes?"

"Well, of course, that would depend, Charlie," said

Nora with sudden gravity, for like many of her race she combined a strong grasp of the truths of religion with a hazy notion of the facts of life.

"You mean on whether 'twas done with a good object or not?" asked Charlie keenly. The only thing he had learned from years with Polly was the importance of doing things with a good object.

"Exactly," she said, a little surprised to find him so well versed in religious matters. "And whether the wishes were reasonable or not."

"And you don't think they were?" asked Charlie hopefully.

"I wouldn't say so, Charlie," she replied doubtfully. "But of course Father Ring could tell you that better than I could."

"I dare say, I dare say," said Charlie, without any great interest, as it seemed to Nora. "Tell me, Nora," he added sharply, "do you believe in things like that?"

"Like what, Charlie?" she asked in surprise.

"I mean ghosts and things of that sort," he said, with a nervous glance that took in the ruined abbey, its slender tapering tower soaring up from the cluster of ragged gables with tall irregular battlements that looked like cockades in the moonlight.

"Well, we're taught to believe in them," she replied with a little shudder.

"We are," sighed Charlie. "But you never saw one yourself?"

"No," said Nora doubtfully.

"Nor I," said Charlie.

They resumed their walk home. Nora saw now what he was driving at. Polly had said she'd haunt him and she was a woman of her word. Anything she had ever said she would do she had done, and there was no saying that as a pure spirit she would have changed much. Charlie himself had lost a great deal of the rational cocksureness of his rebel youth. He had lived so long with credulous women that he was becoming almost as credulous as they. He was reckoning up his chances of backing in case Polly's ghost got out of hand. Nora couldn't give him much comfort, for her own belief in ghosts was largely determined by the hour of day, and at ten o'clock of a moonlight night it was always particularly strong.

When they parted, Nora blamed herself a lot. It was very unmaidenly of her first to call at all, and secondly to ask Charlie point-blank what his intentions were; and for one terrible couple of minutes after she had asked she had dreaded that he might think that it mattered to her. Of course it didn't, except for his own sake, because though she had got to appreciate certain good points in him, there was no possible question of a Child of Mary like herself marrying a man who, whatever his good points might be, had done such terrible things with Molly O'Regan—even if Polly had been an unobtrusive ghost.

There were others who weren't quite so certain. When Charlie got home he stood in the hall in surprise. There was something queer about the house. The hall was in darkness; there was light in the kitchen, but it wasn't

the gaslight. With all the talk about ghosts, it upset
Charlie. "Are you there, Mother?" he called nervously.
There was no reply; only the echo of his own voice.
Three steps took him to the kitchen door, and his heart
almost stopped beating. The fire was out; the greater
part of the kitchen was in shadow, but two candles in
two brass candlesticks were burning on the mantelpiece,
and between them, smiling down at him, a large, silver-
framed photograph of Polly.

The next moment he was blind with rage, seeing how
he was being baited. He snatched the photograph down
and dashed upstairs to his mother's bedroom. She—the
picture of aged innocence—was kneeling by the bedside
with her hands joined, and she looked round at him in
surprise.

"Was it you left that in the kitchen?" he shouted
angrily.

"What is it?" she asked in mock ignorance, rising to
her feet and screwing up her eyes as she reached out for
the picture. "Oh," she asked, "isn't it pretty? I found it
today in one of her drawers."

"Put it back where you found it," he stormed. "And
don't attempt to do anything of the kind again. Don't
attempt it, I say!"

"Oye, why not?" she asked with a pretence of concern,
picking up the photograph and studying it. "Wouldn't
anyone like it—a picture of his poor wife? Unless he'd
have something on his conscience!"

"Never mind about my conscience," shouted Charlie.

"Fitter for you to look after your own."

"Aha," she bawled triumphantly, throwing off the mask, "my conscience have nothing to trouble it."

"No," said Charlie bitterly. "You have it too well seasoned."

"And don't think but she sees it all, wherever she is," cried the old woman, raising her skinny paw to indicate the direction in which Polly might be supposed to exist. "Take care that she wouldn't rise from the grave and haunt you; you and that little whipster you were out gallivanting with!"

"What gallivanting?" snarled Charlie. "You don't know what you're talking about."

"Maybe I'm blind?" bawled his mother. "Walking into the graveyard alongside you as if she had you caught already! Aha, the slyboots, the pussy-cat with her Novenas and her Nine Fridays! She thinks we don't know what she's up to, but God sees ye, and the dead woman sees ye; and what's more, I see ye. And mark my words, Charlie Cashman, that's the hand that'll never rock a cradle for you!"

9.

Two days later Charlie happened to be serving behind the counter when something attracted his attention. He looked round and saw Father Ring busily admiring the goods in the shop window. As he did so, the priest looked up and smiled, but when Charlie put down the parcel he was wrapping to come out to him, Father Ring frowned and shook his head. He raised one finger and pointed it significantly in the direction of the house door. Charlie nodded glumly. Then with his thumb the priest made another sign to indicate the direction he was walking in, and Charlie nodded again. He could translate a bit of business like that as well as anyone, and he knew that Father Ring wanted to talk to him somewhere his mother wouldn't know about it. So he left the little girl in charge of the shop and strolled nonchalantly through the town, past the abbey, where he had halted a couple of nights previously with Nora, and found Father Ring, leaning over the selfsame bridge, letting on to be studying the plant life in the river. When Charlie appeared he did a pleasant little act to indicate his surprise and pleasure at this unexpected meeting. It was, as he said, a really delightful day; a spring day. The mist had dimmed the blue of the sky to green, and the green of the young leaves to blue.

"Whisper, Charlie," said the priest, putting his left hand on Charlie's shoulder and bending his head discreetly across the other one, "I had a visit from your mother."

"My mother!" echoed Charlie in surprise.

"Your mother," said the priest gravely, studying his face before he made another little excursion over his shoulder. "She's afraid you're going to get married again," he whispered in amusement.

"She's easily frightened," said Charlie grimly.

"That's what I told her," said Father Ring. "Of course, I know you'll keep this to yourself. She seems to think there ought to be a special commandment to stop you. Of course," he added with a shocked air, "I told her I wouldn't dream of interfering with you."

"You did, to be sure," said Charlie watchfully, knowing that this was precisely what Father Ring was doing.

"You know the girl I mean?" asked Father Ring, studying him hard.

"I believe so, father," said Charlie, giving nothing away.

"A nice girl," said Father Ring, more by way of a question than anything else.

"A very nice girl," said Charlie.

"And a courageous girl, mind you," said Father Ring. "It took a bit of spirit to do what she did the day Polly was being buried. Of course," he added, admitting her little weakness, "she should have been married years ago." Then he pounced. "Tell me, Charlie," he asked anxiously, "you wouldn't be thinking about her, would you? I hope I'm not being inquisitive?"

"You're not, to be sure," exclaimed Charlie.

"Because it just struck me if you were, I might be able to put in a good word for you," said Father Ring. "Of course, she hasn't much experience of life. You know what I mean?"

"I do," said Charlie, who realized as well as the priest that there might be some little difficulties to be removed if a modest girl like Nora was to be persuaded to marry a public sinner like himself. But at the same time he wasn't going to be bounced into anything. He had made a fool of himself once before. "Well now, father," he said with a great air of candour, turning towards the river as if for recollection, "I'll tell you exactly the way I'm placed. You know the old saying: 'Once bitten, twice shy.'"

"I do, I do," said Father Ring, turning in the same direction, as if his thought and Charlie's thought might meet out there on the river. Then he started suddenly and gave Charlie a look of astonishment. "Ah, I wouldn't say so, Charlie," he said. "I wouldn't say that at all."

"Well, maybe I'm putting it too strongly, father," said Charlie.

"I think so, Charlie. I think you are," said Father Ring eagerly. "Mind you, I'd say she was a different class of woman entirely. More feminine, more clinging—that's under the surface, of course."

"You're probably right, father," said Charlie, nodding but sticking fast to his own point. "But there's one thing you might notice about me," he went on, looking at the priest out of the corner of his eye. "You mightn't think it, but I'm a very highly strung man."

"You are, you are," said Father Ring with great anxiety. "I noticed that myself. I wonder would it be blood pressure, Charlie."

"I was never the same since the Troubles," said Charlie. "But whatever it is, I want something that'll steady me up."

"You do, you do," said the priest, trying to follow Charlie's drift.

"If I had a family," said Charlie, "I'd be a different sort of man entirely."

"You would," said Father Ring with a crucified expression. "I can see you're a domesticated sort of man by nature."

"And," added Charlie with a wealth of meaning in his tone, "if the same thing was to happen me as happened me before, I might as well throw myself in there." He pointed at the river, scowling, and then drew a deep breath and took a step back from the priest. "This very minute," he added dramatically.

"Ah, but you don't think it would, Charlie?" asked Father Ring in alarm.

"But you see, father," said Charlie, punching the air with his fist, "I don't know whether it would or not."

"You don't, you don't, to be sure you don't," muttered the priest, his whole face smoothing out in the glow of perfect understanding. "I can see it quite plainly now. And of course," he added conspiratorially, "if you were to marry the other girl—what's that her name is?—Peggy or Kitty or Joan—that boy of hers would come in for the business."

"That's the very thing, father," said Charlie savagely. "That's what has me demented."

"It has, it has of course," said Father Ring, smiling at the sheer simplicity of it. "Of course, Nora is a nicer girl every way, but a bird in the hand is worth two in the bush. I know how you feel. I'd be just the same myself."

So Charlie returned to the shop with his problem not only unsolved but made twice as clear by the parish priest's understanding of it. Nora, as he said, was a nice girl, but a bird in the hand was worth two in the bush. And Charlie felt he had never really had a bird of any breed; nothing but a few tail feathers out of Molly before she too flew into the bush. And there was more in it even than Molly. What he hadn't told the priest at all was the lonesomeness that came over him at times, whenever he thought of his son, his little boy. He was a warm-hearted man; how else could he feel? Once he had got out the car and driven off to the little village where the kid was being nursed, watched him coming home from school, and then followed him and slipped a halfcrown into his hand. Whatever the inconveniences of Molly might be, they slipped out of sight when he thought of bringing home the little fellow and seeing him go to a decent school like any Christian.

But then all of a sudden his mind would slip a cog and he would think of the scene outside the graveyard, and Nora, with her face grave and pale, stepping up to his side. "In comes the Captain's daughter, the Captain of the Yeos"; "Romeo, Romeo, wherefore art thou, Romeo?" and he would be seventeen again and ready to risk his life for poor old Ireland or anything else that happened to come handy. "Out of the love I bear thee, yield I my life for thee." Whatever misfortune was on

Charlie, he knew he could never be like any other sensible man, but would keep on to the day he died, pining for something a bit larger than life.

That night the temptation to go to the pub was almost overwhelming. He put on his coat and went out, but when he reached the door he turned away again. That was where people went only when their problems had grown too much for them. He went off for a stroll in the country, and on his way back, as if by magic, his feet led him round a lot of back lanes till he found himself passing Nora's door. He passed it and then turned back.

"Can I come in?" he asked, pushing in the door. She was sitting there in the dusk and rose to meet him, flushed and eager.

"Oh, come in, Charlie," she said, and there was no doubting the real pleasure in her voice. "You'll have a cup of tea?"

"I'll have a bucket," said Charlie. "Since I gave up the drink I have a throat like a lime-kiln."

"And did you give it up entirely?" she asked incredulously.

"Oh, entirely," said Charlie. " 'Tis bad stuff."

"Oh, aren't you great?" she exclaimed, but Charlie didn't know whether he was or not. He felt suspended in a sort of mind-world with the prospect either of a further ascent or a shocking bad fall. When he had drunk his tea he strolled up and down the kitchen and leaned against the doorpost, looking out at the people passing by in the dusk. When she rose to light the gas, he stopped her, resting his big hands on her shoulders.

"Sit down," he said shortly. "I want to have a word with you."

Her face grew pale and her big brown eyes took on a wide, unwinking stare, but she did what he told her.

"I'm in great trouble," said Charlie.

"Oh, Law!" she exclaimed. "What trouble?"

"I had a talk with Father Ring today," said Charlie.

"I heard that," said Nora. (There was very little she didn't hear.) "What did he want?"

"He wanted me to get married," replied Charlie with a grim smile.

" 'Tisn't much when you say it quick," said Nora with a rising colour. From Charlie's announcement that he was in great trouble she had drawn the obvious conclusion that Father Ring wanted him to marry someone he didn't want to marry, and who else could that be but Molly O'Regan? "I suppose he didn't tell you who?" she added.

"As a matter of fact, he did," said Charlie with the same grim smile.

"Well," said Nora with a touch of heat, "I wonder how people can have the audacity to interfere in other people's business like that."

"Ah, well," said Charlie, a little surprised to hear her talk like that of the priest, " 'twas intended as a kindness. I'll give the man his due. He meant it well—for both parties."

"Well, I hope you told him you'd do whatever he

wanted," said Nora with the same note of severity in her voice.

"Well, to tell you the truth, Nora," said Charlie, "I didn't. That's what I wanted to explain to you. You know the way I feel about it. I'm lonely down there in the house with no one but the mother. I'd like to get married. I know 'twould be the makings of me, but the fact of the matter is, I couldn't bring myself to it. 'Tis the shop. I admit it. I can't help it. Whatever sort I am, I'm made like that. 'Twould be different if I could be certain, absolutely certain, that I'd have a child that'd come in for the business when I'm gone."

"You mean the same thing that happened with Polly might happen again?" asked Nora with a start. Somehow she couldn't associate Molly O'Regan with child-lessness, but she saw nothing strange in the assumption that Charlie and Molly would have to start again from scratch. She was better up in the subtleties of the moral law than in those of common law.

"I mean I broke my heart once before," snapped Charlie, "and I don't want to do it a second time."

"But you don't think the same thing would ever happen twice?" she asked with a hypnotized stare.

"But how do I know, girl?" cried Charlie desperately. "You might think I'm being unreasonable, but if you were through it with a man, you'd feel just the same. Did Polly ever say to you that she thought the mother was putting a spell on her?" he added sharply.

"She did," admitted Nora.

"And what do you think of it?" asked Charlie.

"I don't know what to think," said Nora, the dusk producing its periodical change in her views about the invisible world.

"When I married Polly first," said Charlie reflectively, "she said: 'Many a better cake didn't rise.' The other night when we were discussing it again, she said: 'That's the hand that'll never rock a cradle for you.'" He looked at Nora to see if she was impressed, but, seeing that Nora in her innocent way applied his mother's prophecy to Molly O'Regan, she wasn't as impressed as she might have been. Charlie was disappointed in her. The scene wasn't going as it ought to have gone. "What sort of knowledge would a woman like that have?" he asked.

"I couldn't imagine, Charlie," replied Nora, with nothing like the awe one might have expected.

"And then there's Polly," said Charlie, adding another threatening spectre to the group. "So you see the way I'm placed," he went on after a moment. "If I don't marry the girl—always assuming, of course, that she'd have me," he interjected tactfully with a glance at her—"I'm destroying my own happiness. If I do marry her and anything goes wrong, I might as well cut my throat and hers while I'm about it. What the hell am I to do?"

"I'm sure I couldn't advise you, Charlie," replied Nora steadily, almost as though she was enjoying his troubles, which in a manner of speaking, seeing that they were deferring a decision that wasn't altogether agreeable to her, she was. "What do you think yourself?"

At that moment Charlie didn't quite know what to think. He had come there expecting at least as much sympathy and understanding as he had got from Father Ring. Even a few tears and kisses wouldn't have been out of place from his point of view.

"*If* I could be sure she cared for me," he said with an infinity of caution, drawing closer to her, "I'd tell her the same thing I told Father Ring and ask her to come away to Dublin with me for a couple of days."

"But for what, Charlie?" asked Nora with real interest.

"For what?" repeated Charlie in surprise. Charlie was under the illusion most common among his countrymen that he always made himself very clear. "Nora," he went on with a touch of pathos, "I'll be absolutely frank with you. You're the only one I can be frank with. At this moment you're the only real friend I have in the world. My position is hopeless! Hopeless! There's only one thing that will break the spell of bad luck. That's to have the honeymoon first and the marriage after."

It was dark, but he watched her closely from under the peak of his cap and saw that he had knocked her flat. No one had ever spoken to her like that before.

"But wouldn't that be a terrible sin, Charlie?" she asked with a quaver in her voice.

"Not if 'twas done with a good object," said Charlie severely, answering her out of her own book.

"Oh, I'm sure she'd do it even without that," said Nora bitterly.

"If she loved me she'd do it," said Charlie, with hope springing up in his heart.

"Love?" cried Nora scornfully, springing from her chair, and suddenly all her maiden airs dropped from her and she was a mature, raging, jealous woman. "Ah, don't be deceiving yourself like that, my dear man. That one doesn't love you."

"Who? Who doesn't love me?" asked Charlie, taking a step towards her.

Then it was her turn to be staggered.

"Weren't you talking about Molly O'Regan?" she asked.

"Molly O'Regan?" cried Charlie, raising his head as though to bay. "What the hell put that into your head, woman? Sure, God Almighty, I have only to marry Molly O'Regan in the morning, and her son will come in for the property. Isn't that the very thing I was telling you?"

"Oh," said Nora distractedly, drawing back from him with a look of horror, "don't say any more to me."

"But, my God, girl," groaned Charlie, thinking of his beautiful scene entirely wasted on her and the impossibility of beginning it all over again, like a detective story once you've found out who the murderer is, "sure, you must know I don't give a snap of my fingers for Molly O'Regan! You were the first woman I ever cared a damn about, only you wouldn't have me when I was there for the asking. Even Father Ring knew that."

"Oh," she cried, as if she was just ready to go into hysterics, "I couldn't do it, I couldn't do it."

"No, no, no, no," said Charlie in alarm, shaking her arm and speaking as though such an idea had never crossed his mind. "I know that quite well. Whisht, now, whisht, or you'll be heard."

"You must never, never say a thing like that to me again," she said, looking at him with terrified eyes as if he was a devil in human shape.

"But, my God, woman," he cried indignantly, "you're missing the whole point. I never asked you. I'd never have mentioned it only you asked me yourself what I told Father Ring. Surely you understand that?"

It seemed she didn't, not altogether anyhow, and Charlie strode to the door with his hands clasped behind his back and a gloomy look on his face.

"I'm sorry if I upset you," he said over his shoulder. "You're the only woman I ever loved, and I wanted to explain."

She was staring at him incredulously, brushing back the loose black hair from the front of her forehead with an uncertain hand. If he had only known it, she was thinking what a very queer way the Holy Ghost had chosen to answer her prayer. He waited for some sign of relenting in her, but there was none, and he heaved a deep sigh and left. Crossing the bridge when the abbey tower was all black and spiky against the sky and the lights in the back of the little shops were reflected in the shallow river, he was like a man demented. He knew he had made a fool of himself again, and this time for good. Soon it would be in everyone's mouth that the madman, Charlie Cashman, had tried to destroy a second girl. He knew how it would be interpreted. The girl who had stood by him when no one else would do it—this was her thanks. And it all came of Romeo and Juliet, the Captain's daughter, and the rest of the bloody old nonsense. There was some curse on him. Nora would tell her father and Father Ring; between them they would raise up a host of new enemies against him; nobody would do business with him—a foolish, idle, dreamy, impractical man!

10.

When Charlie woke next morning to the full horror of the new scrape he had got himself into, he realized that there was only one thing left for him to do. He must cut his losses and rescue whatever little was left him from the wreck. At the same time he didn't want to do anything too overt. He let a week pass by, waiting for the chance of an interview with Tim O'Regan. One morning he saw him coming down the street and went to the door.

Tim was an ex-soldier; small, gaunt, and asthmatic, dressed in a blue serge suit that was no bluer than his face, and a muffler wrapped about his throat. Tim let on not to see Charlie, and Charlie waited till he was almost past before he spoke.

"Hallo, Tim," he said jocosely. "I didn't recognize you."

Tim paused and turned, giving nothing away.

"Oh, hallo," he said huskily, as if he hadn't recognized Charlie either.

"Tell me, Tim," said Charlie confidentially, one shoulder hunched and one eye screwed up in a playful grin, "how much of that couple of hundred have you left?"

"Begor, to tell you the truth," replied Tim with a throaty chuckle, "there's damn little of it left."

"I was thinking that, mind you," said Charlie with a roguish smile. "I thought you had a thirsty sort of look on you. Is Johnny's too far for you?"

"Begor, I think I could just make it," said Tim.

Johnny Desmond gave them a queer look when they came in, but Charlie, seemingly in the best of spirits, rattled away about everything under the sun, till at last it began to dawn on them that he had opened negotiations for Molly and the kid. When they separated, nothing had yet been said, but it was all understood. That was not by any means Charlie's intention, but every time he tried to bring himself to inquire for Molly, he would give one glance at Tim's mean poker face and at once find himself thinking of the scene outside the graveyard, and then it was as if Holy Ireland, Romeo and Juliet, and all the romantic dreams of his youth started with a wild cry from their slumber. He knew he was letting his chance go by and cursed himself for his own indecision. It was terrible, but he couldn't help it; he was an unfortunate, dreamy man.

Later that morning he had to go to the bank. For a full week he had been haunting the shop, in dread to move the length of the street without someone with him. He gave one quick glance first to see that the coast was clear and then strode briskly off. He hadn't gone a hundred yards when the heart almost died within him. Jerry Lalor was coming down the same pavement. Charlie looked round frantically for some shop he could dive into, but there was none. "Brass, boys, brass!" he groaned to himself, wondering at the same time whether Jerry would cut him or hit him. But to his great surprise Jerry showed no sign of anger; only a slight surprise at Charlie's furtive air.

"Good morrow, Charlie," he said, sticking his thumbs in the armholes of his vest. "As you won't say it yourself," he added.

"Oh, good morrow, good morrow, Paddy," cried Charlie with false heartiness, trying to read the signs on the other man's battered face. "I'm just rushing up to the bank," he said.

"The bank?" asked Jerry slyly. "Are you sure 'tisn't the presbytery?"

"What the hell would I be doing at the presbytery?" Charlie exclaimed with a watchful smile.

"Don't ask me," replied Jerry with grave humour. "Who was it was telling me you were thinking of taking the field again? I believe your patrols were seen."

"Patrols, Jerry?" said Charlie in mystification. "Ah, I'm too old for that sort of thing now."

"Ah, I hope not, Charlie," said Jerry. "Begor," he said, squaring his shoulders, "I don't know that I'd mind shouldering the old shotgun again in a good cause. Well," he added, moving on, "mind what you're doing, old man."

He left Charlie open-mouthed on the pavement, looking after him. What the blazes did Jerry Lalor mean? he thought, scratching his poll. "Mind what you're doing" —was that the sort of advice you'd expect from a man whose daughter you had just been trying to seduce? "Mind what you—" Was the man mad or something? Charlie took a few steps after him, intending to ask him in for a drink and sound him to see what he meant, but then stopped again. What he could not understand was why old Jerry, who had the devil's own temper, was taking his advances to Nora in that spirit. Had Nora given him a censored version of the story? Then it flashed across his mind that Jerry hadn't been referring to Nora good, bad, or indifferent. "The patrols" he was referring to were Charlie's few words with Tim O'Regan. In that town news never took long to travel. A flash of lightning; a wild hope—had Nora been afraid to tell him? But then Charlie's face fell again. No woman could keep a thing like that to herself. If she hadn't told her father, she had told someone else, and sooner or later the story was bound to reach him. Charlie heaved a bitter sigh. More

fool he not to have come to terms with the O'Regans before the storm broke over his head.

He went on towards the bank, but his luck seemed
to be dead out that morning. Just as he was turning in
the door, Father Ring came out. Charlie gave him a tortured glance, but before he even had time to think of an
escape Father Ring was shaking him by the hand.

"You're looking well, Charlie," he said earnestly.

"Ah, I'm not feeling too good, father," said Charlie,
thinking bitterly how far the priest was from the truth.

"Tell me, Charlie," the priest said confidentially, "you
didn't do any more about that little business we were
discussing?"

"To tell you the truth, father," said Charlie candidly,
"I did not."

"Take your time," said Father Ring, nodding. "But let
me know if you change your mind. To tell you the
truth," he added, "I wouldn't be surprised if there was a
soft corner there for you, and the father wouldn't let her
go empty-handed. You know what I mean?"

"I do, father," groaned Charlie, and as Father Ring
went round the corner to the chapel he stood on the steps
of the bank with his head in a whirl. It was a spring day,
a sunshiny day that made even the main street look
cheerful, but Charlie was too confused for cheerfulness.
The whole thing was becoming too much for him. For
a week he had skulked like an assassin in the shop in
dread of Jerry Lalor and Father Ring, and here they were
both like lovers. And yet Nora went to confession to

Father Ring! Admitting that he wouldn't let on what she did tell him, he couldn't conceal what she didn't. It was quite plain that she hadn't told either him or her father about Charlie. Now, what purpose would a girl have for concealing it? Modesty? Modesty in Charlie's mind was associated with nothing but hullabaloo. There was another flash of light like fireworks in his head, and then darkness again as sudden and profound. "Christ!" he thought despairingly. "I'm going dotty! 'Tis giving up the drink in such a hurry!"

"Morra, Charlie," said a farmer, going in, but Charlie didn't even answer him. His face was screwed up like a man's who'd forgotten what he'd come for. Then all of a sudden he took a deep breath, drew himself erect, and was off like a hare to Nora's house.

She came out the hall when she heard him banging on the door and gaped at him with horror-stricken eyes, but he rudely pushed her back into the kitchen before him.

"Sit down, sit down," he said shortly.

"What would I sit down for?" she asked in a low voice, and then her knees seemed to give way and she flopped into a chair by the door, her hands joined in her lap and her big brown eyes looking up in holy terror.

"When can you marry me?" asked Charlie, standing over her like a boxer, ready to knock her flat if she rose again.

"Why?" she asked in a dead voice. "Wouldn't Molly O'Regan have you?"

"Ha, ha," said Charlie with a bitter laugh, "I see the tomtoms were working this morning."

"I suppose you think we don't know that 'tis all arranged?" she asked, throwing back her head to toss aside the stray curl that fell across her brows.

"The trouble with you," said Charlie vindictively, "is that you always knew everyone else's business and never knew your own. You knew all about managing other people's lives, but when you met the one man that ever loved you, you let him slip. That's how much you knew. Now you're trying to do the same thing again."

"If you loved me, you wouldn't ask me to disrespect myself," she said with mournful accusation.

"And if I didn't love you," snapped Charlie, "I wouldn't ask you at all. Now, I'm asking you properly, and mind you," he added threateningly, "this time you're not going to get a second chance! Once and for all, will you marry me?"

"But why should you?" she asked in a vague hysterical tone, rising with her hands thrown out and her head well back. "You know now the sort of woman I am. You need never respect me any more."

"What the hell is up with you?" shouted Charlie, almost dancing with fury. Whatever he said to this girl seemed to be all wrong.

"There's nothing up with me," she answered in a reasonable tone, which was as close to lunacy as anything Charlie had ever heard. "I know what I am now—that's all."

"And what are you?" asked Charlie in alarm.

"You ought to know," she said triumphantly. "I didn't slap your face, did I?"

"You didn't what?" cried Charlie with an agonized air.

"Oh," she cried in a rapture of self-abasement, "I deceived myself nicely all these years. I thought I was a good woman, but you knew better. You knew exactly what I was: a cheap, vulgar, sensual woman that you could say what you liked to. Or do what you liked to. I suppose it's the just punishment for my pride. Why would you marry me when you know you can have me for nothing?"

Charlie had another flash of inspiration. This time it was inspiration mixed with pity and shame that flooded his whole being. He suddenly saw the girl was fond of him and had thought about him till she was ready for anything. Jessica, Juliet, the Captain's daughter; the whole blooming issue in one! This was the real thing, the thing he had always been searching for and never found. He caught her in his arms and kissed her.

"God forgive me," he said thickly. "The finest woman in Ireland, and I tormenting you like that. I'll make it up to you though. Put on your things and we'll see your old fellow and the priest."

"No, no, no," she cried hysterically, like a Christian martyr offering herself to the lions, "I don't want you to do anything you don't want to do. I'm not afraid— of ghosts or anything. Really, I'm not."

"Whisht, whisht, whisht," said Charlie.

"But what'll you do if your mother puts spells on me?" she asked in a dazed tone, putting her hand to her forehead.

"Roast her over a slow fire," snapped Charlie. He was his own man again; aged seventeen, a roaring revolutionary and rationalist, ready if necessary to take on the whole blooming British Empire and the Catholic Church. "Now, listen to me, girl," he said, taking her by the shoulders and looking into her eyes. "No one is going to put spells on you. Make up your mind for that! And no one is going to haunt you either. That's only all old women's blather, and Christ knows we had enough of that to last us for the rest of our lives. The pair of us are a match for anyone and anything. Now, tell me what you're doing."

"I'm making the dinner," said Nora, blinking and smiling at being called back to anything so prosaic as a dinner.

"We're having dinner at the hotel," said Charlie firmly. "Now, Mrs. Cashman, take off that apron and come on down town with me. And hurry!"

He stood behind her grinning as she put on her hat. She put it on sideways and her face was blotched beyond anything a powder-puff could repair, but Charlie didn't give a damn. He felt grand. At last he had got what he'd always wanted, and he knew that the rest would come. (It did too, and all Mrs. Cashman's spells didn't delay it by an hour.) As for Nora, at that moment she had no notion what she had got, but she had an alarming suspicion that it was the very opposite of what she had always desired.

(Which, for a woman, is usually more or less the same thing.)

Don Juan (Retired)

ONE fine summer evening Joe French went into Casserly's pub. Joe was a tall, well-built young man, an insurance agent by trade, with a broad, smooth, pleasant face; very pious and going just a shade bald in front. He dressed well, spoke well, and had never drifted into any of the sloppy ways of young men in Irish country towns. Barring one disappointment with a girl called Celia Goodwin, who had walked out on him and run off with a commercial traveller, his life had been uneventful enough.

There were two people in the pub before him: the barman, Jimmy Matthews, and Spike Ward, the motor-driver. They weren't talking. Jimmy had his two elbows on the counter and was studying the daily paper; when Joe came in he looked up in a scared sort of way. Jimmy was the leader of the local Republicans, and it may have been that which gave him the air of something peeping out of a burrow. He was tall, with a haggard face like a coffin, a rather modish mop of black hair going white at the temples, and a pair of pince-nez that gave him a cast-iron intellectual expression. Spike was sitting with his back to the window, wearing a shabby old bowler hat and a pair of riding-breeches. It was nearly ten years since he'd given up the horse and car, but he still continued to dress the part.

" 'Tis hot, Mr. French," said Jimmy, rubbing his hands briskly as if he meant that it was cold, and cocking his ears for the order. "A pint, I suppose?"

"Oh, a pint, Jimmy," chuckled French, taking out his pipe. "Have one with me?"

"I never touch it, Mr. French," said Jimmy, leaning his two palms on the counter and bending nearly half-way across it. Jimmy was a man of the most ungainly attitudes.

"I suppose you see enough of it," said French without rancour.

"I see too much of it at times," said Jimmy candidly, readjusting the pince-nez.

"I suppose you could never manage to finish that, Spike?" asked French, giving a look at the motor-driver, who was sitting in front of an all but empty glass. Spike looked at it thoughtfully.

"Hardly, Mr. French," he drawled, without a trace of a smile on his lean and melancholy visage. "That was one of the two things my poor mother warned me against."

"And I suppose the other was women?" said French

with a grin, giving Jimmy the wink to fill them up.

"Ah, how did you know?" drawled Spike wonder-ingly.

"Oh, my Lord!" said Jimmy in disgust. "Is that bloom-ing man talking about women again?"

"Mr. French," asked Spike reproachfully, "did I bring up the subject of women?"

"You thundering rogue," shouted Jimmy, busy with the beer-engine, "do you ever do anything else? Sitting there all day on your behind, bragging and boasting!"

"Bragging and boasting?" gasped Spike on an ascend-ing scale, as he raised his head feebly like a man coming up for air. "I said one couple of words to this gentleman here, and I'm accused of bragging and boasting!"

"Ah, what else is it?" asked Jimmy impatiently. "And I wouldn't mind," he added, in the candid tone of a factory hooter, "only that 'tis all blooming lies!"

"Go on!" said Spike wonderingly, with a great air of interest as if only now was he discovering the full extent of Jimmy's malice. "So I'm a liar as well? Is there any-thing else now while you're at it?"

"My sweet Lord!" cried Jimmy, pointing to one cor-ner of the bar. "Didn't I hear you there last night, spin-ning yarns about the English lady up the glen that you said wanted to bring you back to London with her?"

"And wasn't I the fool," Spike asked plaintively, "not to do it instead of wasting the best years of my life in this misfortunate hole? Sure, there's nothing in this country for anyone."

"What a fool you were!" cried Jimmy bitterly. "Getting them to pay for drinks for you! I only wish I could knock it down as easy. . . . Thanks, Mr. French. . . . And I wouldn't mind," he added vigorously, "if you were a decent-looking man itself, but a little jackeen like you that's only two hands higher than a duck." He flashed a joyous look at French and threw back his head with a loud guffaw. "Only two hands higher than a duck," he repeated, making an adroit half-turn to the till, turning his half-closed eyes reflectively to heaven while he did the sum, and holding his fingers poised above the cash register as if he was going to perform a piano solo.

"Now, don't be personal," said Spike, rising slowly and with great dignity.

"Thanks, Mr. French," said Jimmy. Then he twiddled at his pince-nez, folded his arms, and looked Spike up and down. "You ought to be thoroughly ashamed of yourself," he said severely, "talking like that about a woman of birth and education."

"Now," said Spike gravely, coming towards the counter, "there's the mistake you're always making. Birth have nothing to do with it."

"What's the secret so, Spike?" asked French.

"Oh, education," said Jimmy, with another guffaw, toppling back against the shelves with his arms still folded.

"Nor education either," said Spike severely. "A man might be able to talk Greek and Latin and still not be able to entertain a society woman."

"Ah, for God's sake," shouted Jimmy in exasperation, shooing him off as if he were a straying hen, "what do you know about society women?"

"What do I know about society women?" asked Spike, lifting his pint and studying it with a detached air. "I'll tell you. There's as much difference between a society woman and any other sort of woman as there is between one pint and another." Then he lifted his glass politely and almost drained it.

"Of course, there's something in what you say," said French. "Some of these society women are rotten."

"Oh, shocking, shocking," agreed Jimmy gravely.

"They're what?" asked Spike incredulously, putting down his glass and approaching French as if he hadn't heard him properly. "What's that you said?"

"Ah, you have only to look at the Sunday papers," said French.

"Mr. French," said Spike imploringly, "I beg and beseech you, don't mind what you read in the papers! You'll soon be as bad as this man here for the papers. . . . He's getting softening of the brain from them," he added, with a reflective look at Jimmy. "Sure, my God above, women are the same the whole world over, society women and every other sort of women."

"Ah, but you're taking it to the fair, Spike," said French. "You know yourself that English society women have no moral standards."

"Moral standards?" said Spike, gaping at him.

"He never heard of them," cried Jimmy with a crow

of glee, throwing himself across the counter.

"Didn't I?" asked Spike.

"Are you going to stand the man a drink?" shouted Jimmy.

"Maybe you think I can't?" said Spike.

"I think you're too blooming close," said Jimmy.

"Go on!" said Spike with quiet irony. "That's a charming character you're giving me. I'm a bragger and a boaster; I'm a liar; and now I'm close as well! See what it is to have friends!" He took a halfcrown from his breeches pocket and laid it solemnly on the counter. "Bite that now and see is it all right," he said with an expressionless countenance. "Mr. French," he added in a pitying tone, "I'm surprised at you. 'Pon my word, I'm surprised!"

"But I know I haven't the experience, man," said French with a good-humoured chuckle, pulling at the knee of his trousers. "Sure, that's why I'm trying to get a few tips from you."

"I hope they're better than the tips he gives for the horses," said Jimmy.

"Seeing that you know as much about women as you do about horses," drawled Spike, "I can't see 'twould be much use to you."

"Mr. French," said Jimmy eagerly, "isn't it amazing, isn't it positively amazing, that we have a respectable woman left in the town?"

"But I have to live in the town, man," retorted Spike gravely.

"And you won't tell us the secret?" said French with a grin.

"What secret?" asked Spike.

"How you have them all tumbling over themselves for you," said French. "How well they don't do it for Jimmy or me!"

"Two good-looking men, begor!" said Jimmy with another guffaw.

"Now, there ye are again," said Spike sadly, looking from one to the other as if he didn't know which was the worse. "A thing is only human nature, ordinary flesh and blood, the same in the highest and the lowest; and ye go on as if 'twas something a man ought to go and get patented."

"Oh insured," said French, but Spike ignored this facetiousness.

"Now, I'll give ye a simple example," he said thoughtfully. "Twenty odd years ago I was going up to town in the train; that was before I got the old car. As we were waiting in Doulough a certain young lady got in. I won't tell ye her name. I got to know it after. She was the daughter of a respectable shopkeeper in the town; a fine, well-educated, good-looking girl. Well, we got into conversation—I was a better-looking man in those days than I am now—and when I found she was stopping in Crane's Hotel I thought I might as well stop there too.

"Well, to make a long story short, I went along to her bedroom that night. That was twenty-one years ago," added Spike, half-closing his eyes as he made it up, "twenty-one years ago the first of next May. I suppose if I met that girl in the street tomorrow she'd hardly know me, but would you believe me when I say that hardly a day passes but I think of her?"

He gave them both a look, took a few paces to the door and spat out, glanced up and down the street, and then came back to the counter. French and Jimmy were looking at him in fascination.

"Next morning," he added gravely, "I was getting up, and as I did I noticed something. 'This and that,' says I. 'Were you—?' 'What did you think?' says she, and first she blushed and then she smiled and drew the clothes up about her. 'But why didn't you tell me?' says I. 'What business is it of yours?' says she, laughing into my face. 'Twas the courage of the girl that struck me. I went home, but, begor, I couldn't stop thinking about her. Now," he added, cocking his head at French, "you might think that I'm a bad man, but I'm not. God knows, I hadn't much at the time, but I took my pen in my hand and sat down and wrote asking her to marry me."

"You didn't?" said French with a grin.

"I did," said Spike. "And do you know what she said? 'Dear Mr. Ward, please don't worry yourself about me. I have no claim on you. On the contrary, I owe it to you that at last I know what Life is.' I never forgot that," said Spike with a sigh. " 'I know now what Life is.' And she hardly more than a child!"

"What a child she was!" said Jimmy. "She had sense

enough not to marry you." Then as it gradually began
to dawn on him that Spike had diddled them again and
that he had been hanging on his words like any of the
poor caubogues of the town, he affected an air of great
contempt. "Anyway," he added, "what is it, only more
of your lies?"

"Lies?" echoed Spike with real indignation.

"What else is it?" shouted Jimmy.

"After all," said French, waking out of his own pri-
vate day-dream, "we have only your own word for it."

"And what the hell do you expect?" asked Spike
scornfully. "A signed receipt?"

"We want you to prove it, man," said Jimmy boister-
ously, pouring them out fresh pints. "What's the good
of you coming in here, day after day, telling us about all
the women you say fell in love with you when we don't
know whether they did or not? Can't you go out and
prove it?"

"There was a time I could prove it," said Spike, a bit
taken aback.

"But what's the use when you can't prove it now?"
cried Jimmy, delighted at the way they had managed
to corner the evasive Spike.

"I'm not the man I was twenty years ago," said Spike
with noble pathos.

"Nor never were, Spike," said Jimmy with finality.
"You might as well admit it, boy. You never were."

"I'd lay a quid on it now you couldn't get off with a

decent woman in this whole town," said French with a grin.

"That I couldn't get off with a woman," echoed Spike with a trapped look. "Maybe ye'd come down to something within my means?"

"All right so," said Jimmy joyously. "We will. We'll make it ten bob, and I'll put up five of it. But you'll blooming well have to prove it," he added sternly. "We're not going to pay out our good-looking ten bob just for another of your tall yarns." And he went off into another guffaw, thinking of the grand story he'd have for the fellows in the bar that night. Spike grew very red. He was thinking the same. A lot of Spike's little comforts depended on the impression he could make on the poor caubogues of the town, who were never likely to see anything of high life. He drained his pint slowly and turned to go.

"Take care but I would," he said menacingly.

"You'd better," bellowed Jimmy good-humouredly, "or you need never show your face in this bar again. . . . I have you now, you blooming chancer!" he shouted after Spike.

"Just to show you," Spike added over his shoulder, "what a man can do. . . . Freeing Ireland," he said with a look at French. "A pack of old women that can't free themselves." He returned from the pavement to hurl a final shaft at Jimmy. "Who am I calling a woman to?" he asked. "Sure, you're neither fish, flesh, nor good red

herring. I don't know what sort of misfortunate article
are you."

"One minute now and I'll be with you, Spike," said
French, finishing his own drink in a hurry.

"And don't forget to bring us back the proofs, Spike!"
shouted Jimmy after them. All the way down the main
street they could hear him laughing to himself.

"Jimmy is a terrible card," chuckled French good-
naturedly. It was an unusual sight to see himself and
Spike strolling down town together, but French found
himself curiously attracted to the man. He had never
met anyone like him before. He tried to get him to talk
about the English lady up the glen that had wanted to
bring him back to London with her, but Spike wouldn't.
He was too mad. His pride had been deeply hurt. He
went along with a very red face, answering only in
monosyllables.

French accompanied him in the direction of his home.
He lived a little outside the town, on the Asragh road.
As they reached the top of the hill there was a lane off to
the left with a number of thatched and whitewashed
cottages in it. A good-looking, red-headed girl was coming down towards the main street, and when he saw her
Spike suddenly halted.

"Hold on a minute," he said, his face clearing suddenly. "I want to have a word with this girl."

"Oh, there's no hurry," said French.

"I met this girl before somewhere," muttered Spike
to himself. "What the hell is that her name is? Mary—

Mary—'twill come to me in a minute."

"Would you sooner I went on?" asked French, suddenly remembering about the bet and feeling rather awkward.

"Oh, hang round, hang round," said Spike, scarcely moving his lips. "It mightn't be any good. . . . Hallo, Mary," he added in a queer, unctuous drawl, a broad smile flickering across his melancholy beery face as he raised his battered old bowler with antique courtesy. " 'Tis a cure for sore eyes to see you. Where were you all this time?"

"See you later, Spike," said French in confusion, and went on. He didn't look round till he reached the bend of the road, and then he saw Spike and the girl coming slowly towards him with bowed heads, deep in conversation. The light was turning, and the little plantation beside the road was filling with a tangle of shadows. The two of them stood for a while talking, with the smoke of the town rising behind them; then the girl gave a hasty glance around, and they quickly crossed the wall. They did it so quickly that French nearly missed them. He waited for a while and then strolled idly back, glancing into the plantation. After that he retraced his steps and sat on the side of the road, smoking his pipe. He had plenty to think about. Of course, if what Spike said was true and all women were alike, he could understand why it was that Celia had run off with the commercial traveller. His bitterness against her, he realized, should now be transferred to the whole sex. They were all a terrible lot, the best of them unworthy of a member of his confraternity.

It was nearly an hour before Spike and the doll came out again, but the time did not seem long in passing. They got over the wall hastily, and this time they separated without as much as a word or a glance. The girl squared her shoulders and went down the road with her head in the air, just as though she were admiring the scenery. Spike didn't give her as much as a backward glance but, sighting French, strolled slowly towards him, his lean face as grave and smug as a parish priest's.

"Well," he said in an inexpressive tone, "I suppose we might as well be strolling back."

"I suppose so," said French, and then, getting a bit red, he took out his wallet and gave Spike a ten-shilling note. "I owe you that," he added.

"You're quite satisfied about that?" asked Spike gravely, looking first at the note and then at French as if he didn't know whether or not his conscience would allow him to accept it.

"Oh, quite," said French in an embarrassed tone, and then the two of them strode back to town in the evening light.

The Babes in the Wood

I.

WHEN Mrs. Early made Terry put on his best trousers and gansey he knew his aunt must be coming. Terry's mother was dead, and Mrs. Early had taken him to live with her. She was a rough, deaf, scolding old woman, doubled up with rheumatics, and she'd give you a clout as soon as she'd look at you, but her son, Billy, was a nice, good-natured chap. And just as the bell was ringing up the valley for Mass and Billy was scraping frantically at his chin, cursing the bloody old razor, Terry's aunt arrived, blowing into the dark little cottage with her hand out and her big rosy face roasted with the sun. She had a knapsack slung over her shoulder.

"Hullo, Billy," she cried in a loud, laughing voice, "late for Mass as usual?"

"Let me alone, Miss Connors," he stuttered, turning his lathered face on her from the mirror. "I think me mother shaves on the sly."

"And how's Mrs. Early?" cried Terry's aunt, kissing the old woman and fumbling with the strap of her knapsack. "Look, I brought you a couple of things—no, these are fags for Billy." ("God bless you, Miss Connors," from Billy.) "Look, this is for you, and these are some things for the dinner."

"And what did you bring me, Aunty?" asked Terry.

"Now, what would you like, Terry?" she cried, going on her hunkers before him and tossing the mane of loose brown hair back from her shoulders. Her legs were bare; she wore a grey tweed skirt and a green pullover.

"A boat!" cried Terry, who had been promised one.

"Well, well, well!" she said earnestly. "Isn't that astonishing? Do you know, Terry, as I was coming home yesterday, there was a little bird on a tree, and what do you think he was singing?—"Don't forget the boat for Terry."

"What sort of a bird?" asked Terry. "A thrush?"

"A big grey fellow."

"That's the old thrush all right," said Terry. "He sings out in our back."

After dinner the two of them went for a walk up the woods together. His aunt had a long, swinging stride, and Terry had a job to keep up with her, but she was grand to go out with because she talked and laughed and made up games all the time. Terry did his best to be grown-up, though it isn't easy when you're only five and fat. All the morning he had been reminding himself: "Terry, remember you're not a baby any longer. You're nine now, you know." Florrie, Terry's girl friend, was nine.

When they reached the top of the hill, his aunt threw herself on her back with her knees in the air and her two hands under her head. She was wearing dark glasses. When Terry looked through them he saw everything black, the wooded hills at the other side of the valley, the buses and the stream of cars crawling along between the rocks at their foot, and farther down still, almost on a level with the river, the railway tracks. She promised to bring him a pair the next time she came, a small pair his size.

"Oh, Jay!" said Terry. "When will you come again, Aunty? Next Sunday?"

"Why?" she asked, turning on her belly, propping her head on her hands, and sucking a straw as she looked at him. "Do you really like me coming, Terry?"

"I do," said Terry, seeing that he hadn't the words to tell her. "Ah, tell us, Aunty, will you come next Sunday?"

"Terry," she said in an eager whisper, "would you like to come and live with me altogether?"

"Oh, Jay, I would," he replied, dropping his voice as he imitated her air of intensity.

"Are you sure now?" she asked doubtfully. "You wouldn't be lonely after Mrs. Early and Florrie?"

"Ah, no, I wouldn't," said Terry vigorously. "When'll you bring us, Aunty? Now?"

"Maybe very soon," she said.

"Up to town?" (He had never been to town.)

"If I tell you where," she whispered, resting on her elbow and bending closer to him, "will you swear a terrible oath not to tell anyone?"

"I will," said Terry earnestly.

"Not even Florrie?" she challenged.

"Not even Florrie."

"That you might be killed stone dead!" she added in a blood-curdling tone.

"That I might be killed stone dead."

"Well, there's a chap from England that wants to marry me and bring me back with him. Of course, I said I couldn't leave you and go to England, so he said he'd bring you too." She laughed happily and clapped her hands. "Wouldn't that be gorgeous, Terry?"

" 'Twould," said Terry, clapping his hands in imitation. "Where's England?"

"Oh, a long way away," she said, pointing up the valley, "at the end of the railway."

"And would we go there on the train?"

"On the train and the boat as well."

"Chrisht!" said Terry, repeating what Billy said when something knocked him flat. He was afraid that like Mrs. Early his aunt might give him a wallop for it, but she only laughed.

"Of course," she said modestly, "I'd be afraid to go all that distance myself without someone to mind me. Would you mind me, Terry?"

"I would," said Terry with great conviction. "What sort of place is it?"

"Oh, a grand place," said his aunt. "The three of us would live in a big house with lights that went off and on, and every morning I'd take you down to school on your bike."

"A bike of my own?" shouted Terry in stupefaction.

"Oh, a bike of your own," she replied confidently. "And in the afternoons we'd go and sit in the park." She saw he didn't understand, and tried to make it plainer. "You know, a place like the garden in the big house with flowers and trees and seats and a pond in the middle."

"And what else?" asked Terry. He felt he could go on listening to this for ever.

"What more do you want? You could be sailing your boat in the pond, and I could be reading my book, and then we'd go back home on the bikes and have tea, and I'd put you to bed, and tell you grand stories before you went to sleep. Oh, Terry," she cried, "wouldn't it be massive?"

"Oh, 'twould," said Terry eagerly. "Tell us, what sort of stories would they be?"

"Oh, grand stories!"

"But tell us one now."

So she took off the black specs, and hugging her knees and looking away up the valley, she told him the story of the Three Bears, and was so carried away by it that she began to act it, growling and wailing and creeping along the grass with her hair hanging over her eyes till he screamed with fright and pleasure. His aunt was grand like that.

2.

Then, next day, Florrie came up to the cottage to call for him. She lived in the village and had to come all the way up through the woods, but she took a sort of delight in minding him, and naturally Mrs. Early encouraged it. "Your young lady," she used to call Florrie, and Florrie blushed with pleasure. She was tall and thin with jet-black hair, a long, thin, ivory face, and a thin, rather hooked nose.

"Terry!" bawled Mrs. Early. "Your young lady is here for you." And Terry came rushing out from the back with his boat.

"Oh," said Florrie, opening her eyes wide at the sight of it, "where did you get that?"

"My aunty brought it to me," said Terry. "Isn't it grand?"

"Ah, I suppose 'tis all right," said Florrie, showing her white teeth in a rather careless smile which indicated that she thought he was an awful baby to go on so much about an old boat. That was one great fault in Florrie. In lots of ways she was a delightful companion, and a terrible one for making up creepy stories, but whenever she had anything, even if it was only an old raggy doll, you'd think no one in the world before ever had such a treasure, but if anyone else had it she didn't even let on to be interested. "Will you come up to the big house for a penn'orth of goosegogs?"

"Ah, we'll go down the river with this first," said Terry, who had a masterful way with him.

"But these are grand ones, Terry," she said eagerly, and again you'd think that no one had ever seen a gooseberry before. "That size! Miss Clancy gave me the penny and all."

"Ah, we'll go down the river," said Terry cantankerously. "Wait till you see how this sails!"

She gave in, as she always did when Terry had made up his mind, but continued to grumble that Jerry would be gone home, and Mr. Scott, the gardener, would only give them a fistful. She was terrible like that, an awful old worrier. When they reached the bank they tied up their clothes and went in. It was deep enough, and under the trees on the bank it ran beautifully clear over a complete pavement of small, brown, smoothly rounded stones. Florrie tired of it sooner than Terry; the current was too swift, and the little sailing-boat was tossed on its side and spun round and round before it reached the bank. She sat on the bank with her hands under her backside, dipped her feet in the water, and looked at the boat with gathering disappointment.

" 'Tisn't much of a thing to lose a penn'orth of goosegogs over," she said sulkily.

"What's wrong with it?" asked Terry indignantly. " 'Tis a fine boat."

"A wonder it wouldn't sail properly so!" she said, looking at him with an accusing, schoolmarmish air.

"How could it when the water is too fast?" shouted Terry.

"That's a good one," she said, showing her teeth again in ladylike amusement. " 'Tis the first time I ever heard of water being too fast for a boat." That was another very aggravating thing about Florrie—her calm assumption that she was the only one who ever knew anything. "Sure, anyone can see 'tis only a cheap old boat."

" 'Tisn't a cheap old boat," cried Terry indignantly. "My aunt gave it to me."

"She never gives anyone anything, only cheap old things," said Florrie with the same coolness that always maddened him. "She gets them at cost price from the shop where she works. Everyone knows that."

"You're jealous, Florrie Clancy," he cried, throwing at her the taunt he had heard the village children throw when she enraged them like that.

"That's a good one too," she said in a quiet voice, while her long, thin face never lost its air of quiet amusement at his childishness. "What would I be jealous of?"

"Because my aunt brings me things, and no one ever brings you anything," he shouted, moving nearer to her.

"A wonder, as she's so mad about you, she wouldn't bring you to live with her altogether!" said Florrie lightly.

"She's going to," said Terry, forgetting his promise in his rage.

"She is, I hear," said Florrie mockingly, looking at him with her head bowed almost to her chest. "Who told you that story?"

" 'Tisn't a story. My aunt said it."

"She lives with her mother, and her mother wouldn't let her," said Florrie severely.

"She's not going to live with her any more," said Terry triumphantly. "She's going to marry a man in England and bring me to live with her there. So now!"

"In England?" repeated Florrie, and Terry could see that in spite of the air she put on, it had knocked the stuffing completely out of her.

"Yes, in England. Now, what have you to say to that?"

"And I suppose you're going?" said Florrie.

"I am going," said Terry. He could see she was mad, crazy with rage and jealousy because she hadn't an aunt of her own, and he cast round in his mind for anything that would increase it. "And she's giving me a bicycle of my own."

"Is that what she told you?" asked Florrie, with an intensity of hatred and contempt that made him wild.

"She's going to, she's going to," he shouted furiously.

"Ah, she's only codding you, little boy," said Florrie, splashing her long white legs in the water while she continued to fix him with the same dark, intense look. "Why did she send you down here at all so?"

"She didn't send me down here," cried Terry, flinging water at her.

"But, sure, I thought everyone knew that," said Florrie,

turning aside to avoid the splashes, but without breaking her idle tone. "She lets on to be your aunt, but we all know she's your mother."

"She isn't," shrieked Terry, dancing with fury. "My mother is dead."

"Ah, that's only what they told you," said Florrie quietly. "You mother isn't dead at all, little boy. She got into trouble with a man, and her mother made her send you down here to get rid of you. The whole village knows that."

"You're a liar," he said, and began to pummel her with his little fat fists. She could have thrown him in the water if she had cared, but instead she rose, flushed and triumphant, pretending to smooth down the front of her dress.

"Don't be deluding yourself that you're going to England at all, little boy," she said with her grown-up air. "Sure, who'd want you? Jesus knows I'm sorry for you," she added with pretended feeling, "and I'd like to do what I could for you, but I thought even a baby like you would know that."

Then she went off along the river-bank, turning once or twice to give him a strange look. He stared after her and shrieked with hysterical rage. He had no idea of what she meant, but he felt that somehow or other she was the stronger. Then he began to run through the woods to the cottage, sobbing. He knew well that God would kill her for the lies she was after telling, but if God didn't, Mrs. Early would. She was pegging up clothes on the line and looked down at him sourly.

"What ails you now didn't ail you before?" she asked.

"Florrie Clancy was telling lies," he shrieked, his fat face black with fury.

"Ah, botheration to you and Florrie Clancy!" she said. "Come here till I wipe your nose for you."

"She said my aunt wasn't my aunt at all," he cried, indignant at the lightness with which she took him.

"She what?" asked Mrs. Early, blinking.

"She said she was my mother—Aunty that gave me the boat," he said through his tears.

"Aha," said Mrs. Early grimly, "let me catch her round here again and I'll toast her backside for her, and that's what she wants. Whatever your mother was, she was a decent woman anyway, but the dear knows who that one is or where she came from."

3.

All the same, it was a bad business for Terry. Florrie didn't come near him. She knew she had done wrong, and she knew old Ma Early was lying in wait for her. Terry wasn't let go to the village by himself, so he had nowhere to go except across the footbridge and the railway line towards the main road. There were hardly any kids there worth playing with, and the only fun was when there was an engine in from up the valley.

It was weeks and weeks before he saw his aunt again, and this time she came when no one was expecting her.

She had a hat and coat on and her face was powdered.

"Hurry, Terry," she called gaily, "we must change your clothes quick. There's a car waiting for us at the station."

"A car?" gasped Terry.

"Yes, only we'll have to hurry. And wait'll you see what I have for you—a bucket and spade!"

"Cripes!" said Terry.

They crossed the river by the little footbridge, and there in the station yard was a long grey car, and a tall man standing beside it that Terry hadn't met before. He was a well-dressed chap with a grey hat and a pleasant offhand manner.

"This is Mr. Walker, Terry," said his aunt. "Shake hands with him now."

"How're ye, mister?" said Terry.

"Eh," said Mr. Walker, letting on to be frightened of him, "this fellow is a blooming boxer! I say, young Samson," he said, "do you box?"

"Naw," said Terry, not wasting any time on him but scrambling into the back and climbing up on the seat. "Will we go through the village?"

"What do you want to go through the village for?" asked Mr. Walker with a laugh.

"He wants to show off," said his aunt with a chuckle. "Don't you, Terry?"

"I do," said Terry.

"Fine little chap," said Mr. Walker, and away they drove and along the village street just as Mass was over, and Terry leaning out of the back window waved and shouted to them all. First they gaped, then they laughed, and finally they waved. Terry kept shouting messages to them, but they were lost in the whirl of speed. "This is me aunt's car. We're going for a spin. I have a bucket and spade"—whatever came into his head. As they passed the post-office he saw Florrie at the door in her best frock with her head bowed and her hands behind her back. He shouted at her, and his aunt leaned out and waved, but though Florrie raised her eyes to watch them, she didn't even let on to know who they were. That was Florrie all out. She was even jealous of the car.

Terry had never seen the sea before and made up his mind at once that it must be England. You could see it wasn't any place else. There were queer little white-washed houses all along the beach. His aunt undressed him and made him put on bright-blue bathing-drawers, but when he felt the cold wind he shivered and sobbed and clasped himself despairingly under the armpits.

"Ah, Terry," said his aunt crossly, "don't be such a baby!"

Then she and Mr. Walker undressed too and took him by the hand to the edge of the water. After a time his terror and misery went away, and he sat in a shallow place, letting the bright waves break on his fat little belly. He decided that he liked England after all. They had tea on the strand, and his aunt put on her black glasses and lay on her back with her hands under her head. There were other children besides himself, making sand-castles, and Terry decided to do the same. After a while Mr. Walker joined him and helped him with great skill but with such infernal enthusiasm that it got on Terry's nerves. Terry failed to see why, with all that sand, he couldn't go and make a castle of his own.

"Now we want a gate," said Mr. Walker firmly.

"All right, all right," said Terry hastily. "You play there now."

"Would you like to have me for a daddy, Terry?" Mr. Walker asked, squatting on his heels in the sand.

"I don't know," said Terry with a cursory glance. "I'll ask Aunty. That's the gate now."

"I'll make you better castles than that if you come and live with me," said Mr. Walker. "I've got much nicer places than this at home."

"Have you?" asked Terry with interest.

"I have. Roundabouts and swings, and all sorts."

"Where?" asked Terry.

"In England," said Mr. Walker. "Over there, see, across the water."

"Are you the man that's going to marry Aunty?" asked Terry, so astonished that he lost his balance and fell.

"That's right, old chap," said Mr. Walker in surprise. "Who told you?"

"Aunty did," said Terry.

"Oh, did she, by Jove?" asked Mr. Walker thoughtfully. "Did she tell you anything else, Terry?"

"Yes," said Terry. "She said you'd buy me a bike. Will you?"

"Absolutely," said Mr. Walker with a laugh. "You come and live with me in England, and I'll buy you a bike. Is that a bargain?"

"That's a bargain," said Terry.

"Shake," said Mr. Walker solemnly.

"Shake," said Terry, taking his hand. He felt he was going to like Mr. Walker. You could see he was a nice sort of chap that would give you things.

They got back late to the station yard. The little lamps were lit on the platform. At the other side of the valley were the high hills masked in dark trees. When they stopped you could hear the noise of the river. Terry didn't want to leave the car and began to whine.

"Hurry, Terry, hurry," said his aunt briskly, lifting him out. "Say good-night to Mr. Walker now."

Terry stood before Mr. Walker and bowed his head.

"What?" exclaimed Mr. Walker in surprise. "I thought you and I had made a bargain, Terry?"

Terry looked up at the reproach in his voice and then threw himself blindly about his knees and buried his face in his trousers. Mr. Walker patted him on the shoulder.

"That's all right, old chap," he said comfortingly. "I know we're pals."

"Come along now, Terry," said his aunt firmly.

"What's the matter, old man?" Mr. Walker asked, bending down to him.

"I want to go back to England with you," said Terry, and then he began to sob.

"You want to come back with me?" repeated Mr.

Walker. "Well, there's no reason why you shouldn't. You ask your aunty nicely now and see what she'll say."

"Oh, come on, Terry," she said in a loud voice, taking him by the hand.

"You did tell him you were bringing him," said Mr. Walker accusingly.

"I didn't think it was going to stick in his mind," she said apologetically.

"Well, you see it has," said Mr. Walker. "Sorry, Terry," he added gently. "Aunty says it's too late to go to England tonight, but we'll be down again some other Sunday."

"No, no, no," shrieked Terry as she tried to separate them, and he stepped from foot to foot. "She only wants to get rid of me."

"Now, now, Terry," Mr. Walker said in a horrified voice. "You mustn't say things like that."

"She does, she does," cried Terry. "Everyone knows it. She's not my aunt at all. She's my mother."

As he said it, he knew he was saying something dreadful. He knew it even more when neither of them said anything. He heard them talking over his head. He didn't know what they were saying, but he felt that Mr. Walker was for him and his aunt against him.

"Terry," she said, "you're to come with me at once, and no more of this nonsense!"

"I won't! I won't!" screamed Terry as she tried to pick him up and carry him off, kicking and shrieking.

"Leave him to me," said Mr. Walker shortly. "You'll

only make him ill." She let Terry go to him, and at once Terry stopped kicking and nosed his way into Mr. Walker's shoulder. He knew Mr. Walker was for him. He was half asleep already. Crossing the little wooden bridge, he looked up and saw the wooded hills and the river like lead in the last light. Then he fell asleep again and only woke up in the little dark bedroom where he and Billy slept. He was sitting on Mr. Walker's knee, and Mr. Walker was taking off his shoes. There wasn't any light, but he knew it was he by the smell of his breath.

"Me bucket," he whined.

"Oh, by gum, lad," said Mr. Walker, dropping into an easy sort of talk like his own, "I'd nearly forgotten thy bucket and spade."

4.

Every Sunday after that, wet or fine, Terry trotted off across the bridge to the main road. There was a pub at the farther side, and the men all sat on the wall there, waiting for a chance to dive in. In case there might be any danger of having to leave them behind he brought his bucket and spade as well, and sat on the bank, a little below the men, who sometimes said a few words to him. He could see the buses and cars coming in both directions. Sometimes he saw a grey car like Mr. Walker's and waddled up the road to meet it, but it was never the one he expected. In the evenings when the first buses were coming back, he returned to the cottage, and Mrs. Early scolded him for moping and whining. He blamed himself a lot for it, as it all began by breaking his word to his aunt.

One Sunday while he was there, Florrie came up the road from the village. She went past him slowly, waiting for him to speak. He wouldn't. It was her fault. Then she stopped and turned to speak to him.

"Is it anyone you're waiting for, Terry?" she asked.

"Never mind," said Terry.

"Because if you're waiting for your aunt," she went on gently, "she's not coming."

"How do you know?" he asked rudely.

"I know," she replied confidently. "Miss Clancy says it. Miss Clancy knows everything. And the man with the motor-car isn't coming either. He's gone back to England."

The tears sprang to Terry's eyes at that. He had had that fear all along, that Mr. Walker wasn't really in earnest.

"Why wouldn't you be said by me?" asked Florrie, drawing closer till she was sitting beside him on the bank with her long hands on her lap. "You know I wouldn't tell you a lie."

"Why did he go back to England?" he asked through his sobs.

"Because your aunt wouldn't go with him."

"She said she would."

"He was married already, and her mother wouldn't let her," said Florrie. "If she went away with him he'd have brought you as well. Protestants have no proper religion like us."

"But why won't she come down like she always did?"

"Because her mother made her marry the other fellow instead, and he wouldn't like her to."

"Why?" asked Terry.

"Ah," said Florrie in a shocked tone, "because it wouldn't be right. The other fellow was a Protestant, and Protestants don't mind, but he's a big nob, and Miss Clancy says 'tis surprising he married her at all, considering the sort she was. Anyway, she'll be having proper children now."

"Aren't we proper children?" asked Terry.

"Ah, no, we're not," said Florrie broodingly. "I thought everyone knew that."

"What's wrong with us?" asked Terry.

"Lots of things," said Florrie, with her fixed wide-eyed look as if she saw deeper into it than anyone else.

"Florrie Clancy!" shouted one of the men who had been watching them, "what are you doing to that kid?"

"I'm not doing anything to him," she cried in a scandalized tone, blinking as if he had just waked her up from a dream. "He shouldn't be over here by himself. He'll get rolled over. Come on home with me now, Terry, boy," she added coaxingly, taking him by the hand.

"She said she'd bring me away and give me a bike of my own," wailed Terry as she led him past the station yard.

"Ah, she was only codding," said Florrie lightly. "She'll forget about you when she has other kids. Miss Clancy says they're all the same. Miss Clancy says my father has pots of money. If you were in with me I might marry you when you're grown up."

She led him up the short cut through the woods. The trees were turning all colours. Then she sat on the grass and sedately smoothed her frock about her knees.

"Ah, what are you crying for?" she asked reproachfully. "It was all your own fault. I was always your girl. Even Mrs. Early said it. I always took your part when the others called you names. I wanted you not to mind that one and her old goings-on, but you cared more for her and her old toys than you did for me. I told you what she was, but you wouldn't be said by me. If you'll swear to be always in with me I'll be your girl again. Will you?"

"I will," said Terry.

When she put her arms round him he fell asleep, but she solemnly remained holding him fast to her. Then she fell asleep too and didn't notice the evening train going up the valley. It was all lit up. The evenings were drawing in.

The Frying-pan

I.

ONE winter evening Father Foley was sitting by the fire, smoking and waiting for his guests to arrive. If ever—God between us and all harm!—you happen to become curate of Kilforna you will know what that means.

Whitton, the teacher, whom he was expecting, was an old college mate. When the time had come for him to take the vow of celibacy he had contracted scruples of conscience and married the principal one. Foley had to admit that she wasn't without justification.

Then came the knock and she was at the door, all in furs, her shoulders about her ears, her big, bony face blue with cold but screwed up into an amiable monkey grin. Her husband, who wore no hat, came in almost as though he didn't want to come in at all, but Tom was a cantankerous bastard. He was fair-haired, blue-eyed with a face that seemed to have foundered on the jawbone, and quiet-spoken in a way that concealed passion. Una and himself disagreed a lot about the way the children should be brought up. He wanted them toughened.

"Come in, let ye, come in, come in," cried Foley hospitably, showing the way into his warm study with its roaring turf fire and the Raphael print above the mantelpiece; a real bachelor's room. "God above," he said, holding Una's hand a moment longer than he needed, "ye're perished! What'll you have to drink, Una?"

"Whi-hi-hi—" stammered Una excitedly, her eyes beginning to pop. "I can't say the bloody word."

"Call it malt, girl," said Foley.

"That's enough! that's enough!" she cried laughingly, snatching the glass from him.

"Whisky, Tom?"

"Whisky, Jerry," said Whitton quietly. If he wanted it he'd drink it; if he didn't no power on earth would make him. He was like that.

Meanwhile Una, unabashably inquisitive, was making a tour of the room to see if there was anything new in it. There usually was, for Foley, like all bachelors, had a mania for adding to his possessions, and his lumber room was piled high with every possible sort of junk from chest-developers to fieldglasses.

"Is this a new picture, father?" she asked, stopping before a rather nice eighteenth-century print.

"Ten bob," said the priest promptly. "Wasn't it a bargain?"

"I couldn't say," said Una. "What is it?"

"The old courthouse."

"Go on!" said Una.

"That place is gone these fifty years and I never saw a picture of it," said Tom with genuine interest. "This is a bargain all right."

"I'd say so," said the curate with quiet pride.

"And what's the sheet for?" asked Una, studying a tablecloth pinned up between the windows.

"That's not a sheet, woman," said Foley. "For God's sake, don't be displaying your ignorance!"

"Oh, I know," she said joyously. "For the pictures! That's grand!"

Then Bella, a coarse, good-looking country girl, announced dinner, and Foley with a self-conscious boyish swagger led them into the dining-room and opened the door of the sideboard.

"What'll ye drink?" he asked over his shoulder. "There's some damn good Burgundy—'pon my soul, 'tis great!"

"How much did it cost, Jerry?" asked Tom with good-humoured insolence. "The only way I have of identifying wines is by the price."

"Eight bob a bottle," replied Foley at once.

"That's a very good price," said Tom. "We'll have some of that." And he pulled at the knees of his trousers and went off into a schoolboy guffaw.

"You can take a couple of bottles home with you,"

said the curate, who in the warmth of his heart was always wanting to give people things. "The last two dozen he had—wasn't I lucky?"

"You have the appetite of a canon on the income of a curate," said Tom with another harsh laugh.

"Ah, well, we won't always be curates, with the help of God," replied Foley in his sunny way.

"Bella looks after you well," said Una when they were nearly through.

"Doesn't she?" said Foley with pleasure. "Isn't she damn good for a country girl?"

"How does she get on with Father Gubbins's housekeeper?" asked Una.

"They don't talk," said Foley with a broad grin. "Stasia says she's an immoral woman."

"And is she?" Una sounded quite hopeful.

"She entertains Paddy Coakley to my whisky and cigars every Saturday night. I told her I wouldn't keep her unless she had a boy. Gubbins said I was encouraging immorality."

"And did you tell him to mind his own business?" asked Tom, who had frequently done the same.

"I did to be sure," said the curate, who hadn't.

"Ignorant, interfering old fool," said Tom quietly, the ferocity of his sentiments belied by the mildness of his manner.

"That's only because you can't bear to have anyone else in the parish as dogmatic as yourself," said Una, who frequently had to act as peacemaker between the intoler-

2.

A week or two later he went to supper to them. Ita and Brendan were in bed but refusing to go to sleep till he came to say good-night. They were sitting bolt upright in their cots, a little fat, fair-haired rowdy boy and a solemn baby girl.

"Father," said Brendan at once, "will I be your altar boy when I grow up?"

"You will to be sure, son," replied Foley, sitting on the edge of the bed.

"Ladies first! ladies first!" said the baby in a frenzy of rage. "Father, will I be your altar boy?"

"Go on!" said Brendan scornfully. "Sure, little girls can't be altar boys, sure, they can't, father?"

"I can," shrieked Ita. "Can't I, father?"

"We might be able to get a dispensation for you," said the curate. "With a pair of trousers on, you'd do fine."

He was in a wistful frame of mind when he came downstairs again. The house was gay and spotless. They had no fine mahogany suite like his, but Una managed to make the couple of coloured odds and ends they had look deliberate. There wasn't as much as a cigarette butt in the ash-trays. Even Tom looked as if someone had got at him with a scrubbing-brush and a comb, and was very self-consciously wearing a new brown tweed tie.

With his fair hair plastered flat he looked schoolboyish, sulky, and resentful, as if he were meditating on how he could restore his authority in a mutinous household. The thought crossed the curate's mind that they had probably quarrelled about the tie.

"You don't mind if I just drop down to a meeting tonight, Jerry?" asked Tom in his quiet, anxious way. "I won't be half an hour."

"Not at all, Tom," said Foley heartily. "I'll drive you."

"No, thanks," said Tom. "It's only down at the school-house. It won't take me five minutes."

It was clear that a lot of trouble had gone to the making of supper. Out of sheer perversity Tom let on not to recognize any of the dishes. When they had drunk their coffee he rose and glanced at his wrist-watch.

"I won't be long," he said with a smile.

"Tom," said Una appealingly, "you're not going to that meeting?"

"I tell you I have to go," he replied with unnecessary emphasis.

"I met Mick Mahoney this afternoon, and he said there was no need for you to go."

"Mick Mahoney knows nothing whatever about it," said Tom rudely.

"I told him to tell the others that you wouldn't be coming," said Una desperately, half rising almost as though she were fighting for the success of her little evening.

"Then you did something you had no business to do,"

Tom retorted angrily, and even Foley saw that she had gone the worst way about it, by trying to interfere with his infernal committee, whatever it was. He began to feel uncomfortable. "If these fellows come to some damn fool decision while my back is turned, it will be my responsibility."

"If you're late, you'd better knock," she sang out gaily, to cover his insolence. "Shall we go into the sitting-room, father?" she asked over-eagerly. "I'll be with you in two minutes. There are fags on the mantelpiece, and you know where to find the whi-hi-hi—blast that word!"

Foley lit a cigarette and threw himself into the big armchair. He was exceedingly uncomfortable. Whitton was an uncouth bastard and always had been. He heard Una upstairs, and next moment someone turned on a tap in the bathroom. "Bloody brute!" he thought indignantly. There had been no need for him to insult the girl before a guest. Why the hell couldn't he finish his quarrelling while they were alone? The tap stopped, and he waited expectantly, but Una didn't come back. He was a warm-hearted man and could not bear the thought of her, up there alone and miserable. He went softly up the stairs and stood on the landing. "Una!" he called softly, afraid of waking the children. There was a light in the bedroom; the door was ajar, and he pushed it in. Una was sitting on the end of the bed, holding the brass rail, and grinned dolefully up at him.

"I'm sorry, father," she said, making a brave attempt to smile.

"What the blazes ails Tom?" he asked, sitting beside her on the bed.

"He-he's jealous," she stammered, and then with a fresh outburst of sobbing she threw herself on his chest. He put his arm about her and patted her clumsily.

"Jealous?" he repeated incredulously. "Who is he jealous of?"

"You," she gasped, shaking her head.

"Me?" cried the curate indignantly, and thought of the film. "But the man must be mad," he said hotly. "I gave him no cause for jealousy."

"I know," she stammered without looking up. "He's completely unreasonable. He always was. And he hates me like p-p-poison," she added quietly.

"But you didn't say anything to him, did you?" asked Foley anxiously.

"About what, Jerry?" she asked in surprise, looking up at him and blinking the tears from her grey eyes.

"About me," mumbled Foley in embarrassment. He wouldn't have even said that much but that her use of his Christian name had flooded him with emotion. It was years since a woman had called him by that.

"Oh, he doesn't know about that," said Una frantically, shaking her head and putting her hands on his shoulders. "Oh, I never mentioned that to him at all!"

Foley realized that in the simplest way in the world he had been brought to admit to a married woman that he was in love with her, and she had replied that she knew and didn't mind a bit. Obviously, these things happened more innocently than he had thought possible.

"But what the devil ails him so?" he asked truculently.

"You don't understand, Jerry," she said in her eager way. "He's not jealous of me. He wouldn't care if I left him in the morning. He's jealous of you because you're a priest and he's not. Surely you saw that?"

"I did not," said Foley flatly. "It never crossed my mind."

"But he's hardly ever out of your house, and he's always borrowing your books, and talking theology to you, and that's why he hates old Father Gubbins. Don't you see, Jerry," she said, putting her face close up to his, "you have all the things that he wants."

"I have?" said the curate in astonishment. "What things?"

"Oh, how do I know?" she said with a shrug. "Respect and freedom from responsibilities, I suppose."

"He can have them," said Foley mournfully. "What's that the advertisements say?—owner having no use for same."

"I know," she said with another shrug, and he saw that from the beginning she had realized how he felt about her and been sorry for him. It made him feel sorrier for himself. Then she laughed. "Aren't you going to kiss me?" she asked archly. Her face as he did so suddenly ceased to be the face of a mature woman and became weak and girlish.

"It's a change to be kissed by someone that cares for you," she said wistfully.

"Ah, now, Una, that's not true," said Foley gravely, the priest in him getting the upper hand of the lover, who had still a lot of leeway to make up. "You only fancy that."

"I don't, Jerry," she replied, biting her lip. "It's always been the same, from the first month of our marriage. I was a fool."

"But even so," said Foley manfully, doing his duty with a sort of schoolboy gravity, "you know he's still fond of you. It's only his way."

"No, it isn't, Jerry," she replied obstinately. "He wanted to be a priest and I stopped him. That's how he looks at it. I was the temptation, and in his heart of hearts he despises me and despises himself for not being able to do without me."

"But why should he despise you?" asked Foley incredulously.

"Because I'm a woman," said Una passionately. "Because I like my home and my kids."

"But it's not natural," said Foley, shaking his head.

"I'm not so sure, Jerry," she said doubtfully. "I used to think that Tom wasn't like anyone else in the world, but now I'm beginning to think there are more spoiled priests than ever went into seminaries. You see the way it is, Jerry," she went on, growing very red, "he thinks he's a terrible blackguard because he wants to c-c-coort me once a month. . . . I can talk to you like this because you're a priest."

"You can to be sure," said Foley, growing red himself.

and feeling that the priest had been replaced by a particularly fastidious adolescent.

"And even when he does c-c-coort me," she went on, too full of the subject even to notice, "he manages to make me feel that I'm doing the coorting."

"But why shouldn't you?" asked the curate, to conceal the way his heart turned over in him.

"Because it's a sin," cried Una tempestuously.

"Who said it's a sin?"

"He makes it a sin. He's like a bear with a sore head for days after. Don't you see, Jerry," she cried, springing to her feet, "it's never anything but adultery with him, and he goes away and prays for strength to resist it."

"Ah, the man must be a bit queer," growled Foley, though at the familiar word "adultery" his own conscience gave a loud knock that startled him worse than would the sound of Tom's key in the door.

"No, it's I'm going queer," said Una. "It's always adultery, adultery, adultery, and I'm always a bad woman, and he always wants to show God that it wasn't him but me, and I'm fed-up to the teeth with it. I want someone to make me feel like a respectable married woman for once in my life. You see, I feel quite respectable with you though I suppose I shouldn't." She looked in the mirror and her face fell. "Oh, Lord," she said, "I'm a sight! . . . I'll be down to you in two minutes now, Jerry," she said eagerly, swinging round on him and bending double with her hands joined high behind her back; a vital, gay, tense slip of a woman.

"You're lovely," he said in a low voice.

As she was going into the bathroom she turned in a sudden access of joyous emotion and threw her arms about him. He kissed her and she pressed herself close to him till his head swam. There was a mawkish, girlish smile on her face. "Darling!" she said in an agony of passion, and it was as if they themselves weren't there at all; nothing but their unspeakable loneliness mingling. It was the first time a woman had called him "Darling," and in a state of idiotic happiness he went downstairs to wait. He heard Tom's key grate in the lock and looked at himself anxiously in the mirror. He was very red. "Sin," he thought, trying to get used to the idea. "Adultery," he added, and once more in the silence he heard the loud double knock of the old postman, Conscience, at the door.

The Miracle

BOBBY HEALY was the old doctor in our town. He had always got on excellently with the people until Father Ring came. Then Bobby's practice had begun to go down. Father Ring, it seemed, had had a disagreement with an uncle of his many years before; or perhaps it was an uncle of Father Ring's who had had the disagreement with Bobby—in these family rows an outsider is always at sea. Whenever Father Ring was called in to a dying man he took care to ask: "Who have you?" If they said: "Bobby Healy," he nodded and looked grave, and everyone understood that Bobby had killed the unfortunate patient as usual. Whenever the two of them met they were always friendly; and no one could have told from the doctor's tired old face whether or not he knew what was going on. But there was very little Bobby didn't know. There is a certain sort of guile that goes as deep as any cleric's: the peasant's guile. Doctor Healy had that.

Then one day his chance came. He got a call from Bill Enright. Bill was an extraordinary local character, nominally a farmer and breeder of greyhounds, but actually the last of a family of bandits who had terrorized the countryside for generations. To Bobby, Bill was bound by the strongest tie that could bind an Enright, for Bobby had once cured a greyhound for him, the mother of King Kong. He was notoriously living in sin with his housekeeper and hadn't gone to Mass since a little disagreement he had had with Father Ring about a cousin of the same who was up for a job—or perhaps it was a cousin of Bill's. An outsider can never get at the facts.

Bill lived in a fine Georgian house on the edge of the town. It had once belonged to the Rowes, but Bill had got them out of it by the simple expedient of making their lives a hell. The avenue was overgrown, and the house with its fine Ionic portico looked dirty and dilapidated. Two dogs got up and barked at the doctor in a neighbourly way.

"Hullo," said Bobby, pulling their ears, "is he bad again?"

"Rotten," said both the dogs with loud yaps.

"Isn't he a holy terror?" murmured Bobby sympathetically. "'Tis the booze, I suppose?"

"What else?" asked the dogs.

"I'll make him all right for ye, never fear," said Bobby amiably, and the two dogs were so relieved that they nearly knocked him down. They knew Bobby had the knack of putting the boss on his feet again.

Nellie, the housekeeper, opened the door. She was a small, fat country girl with a rosy complexion and a mass of jet-black hair that shone almost as brilliantly as her eyes. The doctor, who was sometimes seized by these fits of amiable idiocy, took her by the waist and she gave a shriek of laughter that broke off suddenly.

"Wisha, Doctor Healy," she said complainingly, "oughtn't you to be ashamed, and the state we're in!"

"How's that, Nellie?" he asked anxiously. "Isn't it the usual thing?"

"The usual thing?" she shrieked. She had a trick of snatching up and repeating the final words of someone else's remark in a brilliant tone a full octave higher, like a fiddle repeating a phrase from the double-bass. Then with dramatic abruptness she let her voice drop to a whisper and dabbed her eyes with her apron. "He's dying, doctor," she said.

"Ah, for God's sake!" whispered the doctor aghast. Life had rubbed his principles down considerably, and the fact that Bill was suspected of a share in at least one murder didn't prejudice him in the least.

"Oh, Christ, God damn the word of a lie there is in it, doctor," she repeated despairingly, shaking her head. "Get out, ye bastards ye!" she shouted, kicking out at the dogs as they tried to slink past her. "Bad luck to ye! Where do ye think ye're going? . . . Oh, he's dying without a doubt in the world," she added in a tone of great complacency.

"But what happened him at all, Nellie?" whispered

the doctor with his withered old face screwed up in bewilderment. "Sure, I saw him in town on Monday and he never looked better."

"Never looked better?" echoed the fiddles, while the beautiful black eyes filled with a tragic emotion not far removed from joy. "And then didn't he go out on the Tuesday morning on me, in the pouring rain, with three men and two dogs, and not come back till Friday night, with the result" (this was a boss phrase of Nellie's always followed by a dramatic pause and a change of key) "that he caught a chill up through him and never left the bed since?"

"With the result, with the result," screeched a man's voice from upstairs. It was nearly as high-pitched as Nellie's, but with a wild nervous tremolo in it.

"What ails you now?" she screamed back, her head over her shoulder.

"What are you saying to Bobby Healy?" asked the voice.

"What am I saying to Bobby Healy?" she echoed mechanically. "I'm saying nothing at all to him."

"If you're telling him I'm dying, you can bloody well tell him now I have no intention," shrieked the voice.

"No intention?" echoed Nellie incredulously. "You won't be asked," she replied, and, exhausted by this brilliant feat of repartee, fell back on simple cheek. "You can tell him yourself."

"How can I tell him anything with you keeping him

down there?" asked the voice indignantly. "Bobby! Bobby Healy!"

"There's nothing wrong with his lungs anyway," the doctor said professionally. "Coming, Bill, coming," he added soothingly as he slowly mounted the stairs. It was bare and damp. It was a lifelong grievance of Bill's against the Rowes that they had been mean enough to take the furniture to England with them.

In a bare but fine-looking room with a decorated ceiling and long windows that overlooked the distant town, Bill was sitting up in an iron bed, propped with pillows. The grey afternoon light and white pillows threw up his brilliant colouring. He was a tall, gaunt man with fair hair and a tiny, gold moustache; perfectly rosy skin like a baby's, and a pair of bright-blue eyes that seemed to expand in a wide, unwinking, almost animal glare. The cheekbones were high and almost seemed to cut the skin. They gave his eyes an Oriental slant, and with the low, sharply sloping forehead, his whole face seemed to point outward to the sharp tip of his nose and then retreat again in a pair of high teeth, very sharp and very white, a drooping lower lip, and a small, weak, feminine chin.

"What was she telling you?" he asked abruptly in his high-pitched voice.

"What was I telling him?" Nellie echoed boldly. "I was telling him that you went out with three men and two dogs and never came back to me till Friday night."

"Ah, Bill," said the doctor reproachfully, "how often did I tell you to stick to women and cats? What ails you now?"

"I'm bloody bad, doctor," said Bill.

"You look it," said Bobby candidly, sitting on the edge of the bed and screwing up his kindly grey eyes. "That's all right, Nellie," he added by way of dismissal. "I'll call you if I want you."

"And make a lot of noise downstairs," said Bill with a snort, "the way we'll know where you are."

"And where else would I be?" she asked wonderingly.

Bobby gave Bill a thorough going-over, back, chest, and sides. So far as he could see there was nothing the matter with him except a chill, but he realized from the way Bill's eyes followed him that the man was in a panic. He wondered whether, as he sometimes did, he shouldn't give him a worse one. It was unprofessional, but it was the only treatment that ever seemed to work. And then the inspiration came to him like heaven opening to sinners, and he sat for several moments looking away and scratching his jaw.

"Well, Bobby?" asked Bill at the end of his patience.

"How long is it since you were at confession, Bill?" asked Bobby gravely.

Bill's rosy face turned the colour of wax, and the doctor felt ashamed of himself for a moment.

"Is that the way it is, Bobby?" he asked in a shrill, expressionless voice.

"Ah, I don't mean it like that, Bill," said Bobby, already wishing he could get out of it. "Perhaps I'd better have a second opinion."

"Ah, your opinion is good enough for me, Bobby," said Bill wildly, sitting up in bed and pulling the clothes about him. "Take a fag and light one for me. What the hell difference does it make anyway? I lived my life and bred the best greyhound bitches in Europe."

"But you wouldn't mind if I went for Father Ring as I'm here?" asked the doctor.

"I wouldn't let that fellow inside my door, Bobby," said Bill with a glare. "He's never done interfering. Do you know that he went to Nellie's brothers and tried to make them bring her home?"

"Is that so, Bill?" exclaimed the doctor in surprise. "Of course," he added, with the comfortable feeling that for once he was getting a bit of his own back, "the poor man hasn't the experience."

"No, but they had," snorted Bill.

"I could easy bring you someone else," suggested the doctor.

"Ah, what the hell do I want with any of them?" cried Bill. "Aren't they all the same—out for nothing but what they can get from you?"

"Ah, I wouldn't say that, Bill," said the doctor thoughtfully as he paced up and down the room, his hands in his trousers pockets, and his wrinkled old face as grey as his homespun suit. "I hope you won't think me interfering?" he added anxiously. "You know I wouldn't talk like this to anyone else."

"I know you mean it well, Bobby," said Bill.

"But you see, Bill," said the doctor, screwing up his left cheekbone as if it hurt him, "the feeling I have is that you want a different sort of priest altogether. Of course, I'm not saying a word against Father Ring, but after all he's only a secular. You never had a chat with a Jesuit, I suppose?"

"Never," said Bill curtly.

"They're a very cultured order," said the doctor.

"What the hell do I want with a Jesuit?" cried Bobby in protest. "A drop of drink and a bit of skirt—what harm is there in that?"

"But that's what I mean, man," said the doctor cunningly. "Tisn't as if you were ever a bad-living man."

"I wasn't," said Bill with a sudden touch of self-pity. "I was a good friend to anyone I liked."

"And you know the way Ring would go on if anything happened you—I'm speaking as a friend."

"You are, Bobby," said Bill, his voice hardening under the injustice of it. "You're speaking like a Christian, which is more than he is. Oh, God, yes," he added with mournful delectation, turning his mad blue eyes on Bobby. "Bill Bloody-well Enright, the fellow that never went to Mass; dead in his sins, and devils coming up through the floor to take him away."

"But you see what I mean, Bill?" said the doctor, cocking his head.

"I do, Bobby," replied Bill with a wicked glint in his eyes. "It's a sort of moral duty to thwart a fellow like that. I could even leave the other chap a couple of quid for Masses. That's the thing that would really break Ring's heart, Bobby," he added with growing enthusiasm.

"Ah, I didn't mean it like that," Bobby said with a trace of alarm. Bill was altogether too apt a pupil for his taste.

"No," said Bill with conviction, kicking his heels in the bed, "but that's what it comes to. He'd be tossing the clothes off himself. All right, Bobby, have it your own way. Bring whoever you like and I'll let him talk."

"I'll run over in the car myself," said Bobby, who was taking no chances of the reception that a Jesuit might get. "I'll spend the rest of the evening with you anyway, just to see you're comfortable."

"Thanks, Bobby," said the dying man. "You're a good pal."

"I'm just running over to Asragh for a priest, Nellie," whispered the doctor as he reached the foot of the stairs. "You might get things ready while I'm away."

"A priest?" cried Nellie in astonishment. "Sure, that devil won't see a priest for you!"

Bobby didn't waste time explaining things further to her, but drove off to Asragh, where there was a little Jesuit with whom he had become rather friendly. He was a stocky, middle-aged man with a tight mouth and little clumps of white hair in his ears. It is not to be supposed that Bobby told him all that was in his mind or that the Jesuit supposed he did, but it is remarkable with just how few direct admissions two intelligent men can come to a complete understanding. As they were driving up the avenue Nellie rushed out to meet them.

"What is it, Nellie?" the doctor asked anxiously.

"He's gone mad, doctor," she replied reproachfully, as though she hadn't thought a professional man would have played a trick like that on her.

"When did he go mad?" Bobby asked doubtfully.

"When he seen me putting up the altar for the priest. Now he's after barricading himself in the room, and he says he'll shoot the first one that tries to get in to him."

"That's quite all right, my dear young lady," said the Jesuit soothingly. "Sick people often behave like that."

"Has he a gun, Nellie?" asked Bobby cautiously.

"Did you ever know him without one?" retorted Nellie. "You may be sure he have a gun."

Bobby, who was of a rather timid disposition, admired the coolness of the Jesuit as he mounted the stairs. While Bobby knocked softly on the door, he stood against the wall with his hands behind his back and his head bowed as if in meditation.

"Who's there?" cried the patient shrilly.

" 'Tis only me, Bill," said the doctor soothingly. "Can I come in?"

"I'm too sick," shouted Bill. "I'm not seeing visitors."

"Just one moment, doctor," said the Jesuit calmly, putting his shoulder to the door and heaving it in as well as the armchair behind it. One glance was enough to show Bobby that Bill had had time to get panic-stricken. He hadn't a gun, but that was the only thing that was lacking to remind Bobby of Two-Gun Joe's last stand. He was sitting well up, supported on his elbows, his head craned forward, his bright-blue eyes flashing unseeingly from the priest to Bobby and from Bobby to the altar that Nellie had improvised in the corner. The Jesuit went up to him confidently with his hand outstretched.

"I'm Father Finnegan, Mr. Enright," he said firmly.

"I didn't send for you," snapped Bill.

"I appreciate that, Mr. Enright," said Father Finnegan, "but any friend of Doctor Healy's is a friend of mine. Won't you shake hands?"

"I don't mind," said Bill, letting him partake slightly of a limp paw while he kept his eyes fixed on Bobby. "But I warn you I'm not a religious sort of bloke. I never went in for that at all. Anyone that thinks I'm not a hard nut to crack has a surprise coming to him."

"If I went in for cracking nuts I'd say the same," said Father Finnegan, holding staunchly to his hand. "You look well able to protect yourself."

Bill gave a harsh snort by way of indicating how much could be said on that score if the occasion were more propitious; his eyes continued to wander unseeingly like a mirror in a child's hand; but Bobby felt the priest had struck the right note. He closed the door softly behind him and went downstairs. The six windows of the long drawing-room opened on three landscapes filling with mist. The lowing of distant cows struck pleas-

urably on his ear. After a time the silence of the house
struck it even more. Nothing disturbed it but the voices
upstairs. Then he swore and threw open the door on
to the hall. Nellie was sitting comfortably on the stairs,
her hands joined in her lap and her head cocked in the
direction of the bedroom. He beckoned her down impatiently.

"What is it, doctor?" she asked in surprise.

"Get us a light," he said wearily. "And don't forget
the priest can't go all the way back to town without a
bit of supper."

"Wisha, you don't think I was listening?" she asked
indignantly.

"No," said Bobby dryly. "You looked as if you were
joining in the devotions."

"Joining in the devotions?" she cried. "I'm up since
six o'clock, waiting hand and foot on him, with the result
that I dropped down in a dead weakness on the stairs.
Would you believe that now?"

"I would not," said Bobby.

"You would not?" she repeated incredulously. "Jesus!"
she added after a moment. "I'll bring you in the lamp,"
she said in a defeated tone.

"Is it sausages and bacon ye'll have?" she asked later,
leaning against the mantelpiece with her fat legs crossed,
a buxom figure of a woman.

"Sausages and bacon will do fine," said Bobby.

"Wisha, Doctor Bobby," she asked, "I wonder would
he ever get round Mr. Enright to go to confession?"

"I don't know," said the doctor cautiously. "Why?"

"Why?" echoed Nellie with a shriek of laughter. "And what would Mr. Enright tell him about me, I'd like to know?"

"I couldn't say," said the doctor innocently. "What would he have to tell him?"

"What would he have to tell him?" repeated Nellie derisively, and for the first time her rudimentary method of communication struck the doctor as being perfectly adequate.

He looked at his watch. He was beginning to feel hungry. Nearly an hour passed before there was a sound upstairs. Then Father Finnegan came down, rubbing his hands briskly and complaining of the cold. Bobby found the lamp lit in the bedroom, and the patient lying with one arm under his head.

"How are you feeling now, Bill?" he asked with rough good nature.

"Fine, Bobby," said Bill with a toss of his head. "I'm feeling fine. You were right about the priest, Bobby. No wonder I couldn't get on with Ring. Parish priests aren't educated at all, Bobby, not compared with that chap."

"I thought ye'd get on well," said Bobby watchfully.

"Oh, he knows his job all right," said Bill critically. "I thought I knew something, but it was only like 'I roved out' to him. There's nothing like the bit of education, Bobby. The only thing I'm sorry for is that I didn't meet him sooner." The wild blue eyes came to rest on the doctor's worn face. "I feel the better of it already, Bobby. What sign would that be?"

"Ah, I dare say 'tis the excitement," said Bobby, giving nothing away. "I'll have another look at you before I go."

"What's that she frying, Bobby?" asked the dying man, sniffing. "Sausages and bacon?"

"So I believe."

"There's nothing I'm so fond of," said Bill poignantly. "Do you think would it make me worse, Bobby? My stomach is raw."

"Ah, I don't suppose it would," said Bobby doubtfully. "But tea is all you can have for the present."

"For the present," echoed Bill bitterly. "It's all I'll ever get if I live to be as old as Methusalem. But I'm not complaining, Bobby. I'm a man of my word. Oh, God, yes."

"Go on!" said the doctor with interest. "You don't mean you're after taking the pledge?"

"Christ, Bobby," said the patient, giving a wild heave in the bed, "that's not a quarter of what I'm after taking. . . . God forgive me for swearing," he added piously. "He made me promise to marry the Screech, Bobby," he said with a look that challenged the doctor to laugh if he dared.

"Ah, well, you might do worse than that, Bill," said the doctor, to whom this was not altogether news.

"How sure he is I'll have him!" bawled Nellie cheerfully, showing her moony face at the door.

"You see, Bobby," said Bill without rancour. "That's what I have to put up with!"

"What you have to put up with!" she repeated wonderingly. "And what about all I have to put up with? Maybe for all you know I might have another fellow."

"Excuse me, Nellie," said the doctor, "I want to have a look at Bill. . . . You had a trying day of it," he added as Nellie went out. "I'd like to make sure it didn't take too much out of you." He sat on the bed and caught Bill's wrist. Then he flashed his torch into his eyes and down his throat while Bill stared at him in a hypnotized way.

"Begor, Bill," he said in a low voice, "I wouldn't say but you're right."

"How's that, doctor?" asked Bill jumping up excitedly in the bed.

"I'd almost say you were a shade better," said the doctor with a frown.

"But that's what I'm telling you, man," cried Bill, beginning to do physical exercises for him. "Look at that, Bobby! I couldn't do that before. It's a bloody miracle."

"Ah," said the doctor with a sniff, "when you've seen as much as I have you won't be so sure about miracles. Take a couple of these tablets anyway, and I'll have another look at you in the morning."

Himself and the Jesuit both came up to take their leave of Bill. He was sitting up in bed reading a tract called *A Saint in the Home*. Bobby had decided in

Asragh that the one on *Keeping Company* was a bit
on the elementary side. There was an empty plate and
a cup and saucer by his bed. "Thanks, father, thanks,"
he said heartily, sitting bolt upright and wringing the
Jesuit's hand. "You made a new man of me. . . .
Thanks, Bobby," he added. "I'll pay that bill of yours
the next time I go to town." Bobby knew that another
item had been placed to his credit beside the mother of
King Kong. His conscience was quite easy on the subject.
A little religion wouldn't do Bill the least bit of harm.

"Well, on the whole, Doctor Healy," said the priest
as they drove off, "I think that was a very satisfactory
evening."

"It was," said Bobby guardedly. He wouldn't have
liked the Jesuit to know exactly how satisfactory it was
from his point of view. He knew the Jesuits, and knew
they could be trusted to take advantage of a break, even
without a miracle. With a miracle, every old woman
for miles around should soon be sending for them. At
a modest reckoning it would bring them in a hundred
a year, which ultimately would have to come out of
Father Ring's pocket. Bobby knew that, for the future,
that officious little man would give him a very wide
berth.

A Thing of Nothing

I.

NED LYNCH was a decent poor slob of a man with a fat purple face, a big black moustache like the villain in a melodrama, and a paunch. He had a brassy voice that took an effort of his whole being to reduce it by a puff, sleepy bloodshot eyes, and a big head. Katty, who was a well-mannered, convent-educated girl, thought him very old-fashioned. He said the country was going to the dogs and the land being starved to put young fellows into professions, "educating them out of their knowl-edge," he said. "What do they want professions for?" he asked. "Haven't they the hills and the fields—God's great, wonderful book of Nature?" He courted her in the same stiff sentimental way, full of poetic nonsense about "your holy delicate white hands" and "the weaker sex."

The weaker sex indeed! You should see him if he had a headache. She havered for years about marrying him at all. Her family thought he was a very good catch, but Katty would have preferred a professional man. At last she suggested that they should separate for a year to see whether they couldn't do better for themselves. He put on a sour puss at that, but Katty went off to business in Dublin just the same. Except for one drunken medical who borrowed money from her, she didn't meet any professional men, and after lending the medico more money than she could afford, she was glad enough to come back and marry Ned. She didn't look twenty-five, but she was thirty-nine. The day of the marriage he handed her three anonymous letters about herself and the medico.

Katty thought a lot about the anonymous letters. She thought she knew the quarter they had come from. Ned had a brother called Jerry who was a different class of man entirely. He was tall and dark and lean as a rake, with a high colour and a pair of bright-blue eyes. Twenty years before, himself and Ned had had some disagreement about politics and he had opened Ned with a poker. They hadn't spoken since, but as Jerry had two sons and only one farm, Katty saw just why it mightn't suit him that Ned and herself would marry.

She was a good wife and a good manager; a great woman to send to an auction. She was pretty and well behaved; she dressed younger than her years in short coloured frocks and wide hats that she had to hold the brim of on a windy morning. She managed to double the business inside two years. But before the first year was well out she began to see rocks ahead. First there was Ned's health. He looked a giant of a man, but his sister had died of blood pressure, and he had a childish craze for meat and pastries. You could see him outside the baker's, looking in with mournful, bloodshot eyes. He would saunter in and stroll out with a little bag of cakes behind his back, hide them under the counter, and eat them when she wasn't looking. Sometimes she came into the shop and found him with his whole face red and one cheek stuffed. She never said anything then; she was much too much a lady, but afterwards she might reproach him gently with it.

And then to crown her troubles one day Father Ring called and Ned and himself went connyshuring in the parlour. A few days later—oh, dear, she thought bitterly, the subtlety of them!—two country boys walked in. One was Con Lynch, Jerry's second son. He was tall and gawkish, with a big, pale, bony face; he walked with a pronounced stoop as if his sole amusement was watching his feet, his hands behind his back, his soft hat down the back of his neck, and the ragged ends of his trousers trailing round the big boots.

He looked at Katty and then looked away; then looked at her again and said: "Good morra." Katty put her hands on the counter and said with a smile: "How d'ye do?" "Oh, all right," said Con, as if he thought she was presuming. Ned didn't say anything. He was behind the counter of the bar in his shirt-sleeves.

"Two bottles of stout, i' ye plaze," said Con with a

take-it-or-leave-it air, planking down the two-shilling piece he had squeezed in the palm of one hand. Ned looked at the money and then at Con. Finally he turned to the shelves and poured out three stiff glasses of Irish.

"Porter is a cold drink between relations," he said in his kind, lazy way.

"Begor, 'tis true for you," said Con, resting his two elbows on the counter while his whole face lit up with a roguish smile. " 'Tis a thin, cold, unneighbourly Protestant sort of drink."

After that Con and his brother Tom dropped in regularly. Tom was secretary of some political organiza-tion and, though very uncouth, able to hold his own by sheer dint of brass, but Con was uncouth without any qualification. He sat with one knee in the air and his hands locked about it as if he had sprained his ankle, or crouched forward with his hands joined between his legs in a manner that Katty would have been too ladylike to describe, and he jumped from one position to another as if a flea had bitten him. When she gave him salad for tea he handed it back to her. "Take that away and gi' me a bit o' mate, i' ye plaze," he said with no shyness at all. And the funny thing was that Ned, who in his old-fashioned way knew so much better, only smiled. When he was going, Ned always slipped a packet of cigarettes into his pocket, but Con always pulled them out again. "What are thim? Faga? Chrisht! Ah, the blessings of God on you!" And then he smiled his rogue's smile, rubbed his hands vigorously, lowered his head as if he were going to butt the first man he met, and plunged out into the street.

It was easy to see how the plot was developing. She was a year married and no child!

2.

One day a few weeks later Katty heard a scuffle. She looked out the shop window and saw Jerry with the two boys holding him by the arms while he let on to be trying to break free of them.

"Come on, come on, and don't be making a show of us!" said Tom angrily.

"I don't give a Christ in hell," cried his father in a shrill tremolo, his wild blue eyes sweeping the sunlit street in every direction except the shop. "I'll go where I'm asked."

"You'll go where you're told," said Con with great glee—clearly he thought his father was a great card. "Come on, you ould whore you, come on!"

Ned heard the scuffle and leaned over the counter to see what it was. He gave no sign of being moved by it. There was a sort of monumental dignity about Ned, about the slowness of his thoughts, the depth of his sentiment, and the sheer volume of his voice, which enabled him to time a scene with the certainty of an old stage hand. He lifted the flap of the counter and moved slowly out into the centre of the shop and then stopped and held out his hand. That, by the way, did it. Jerry gave a

whinny like a young colt and sprang to take the prof-
fered hand. They stood like that for a full minute,
moryah they were too overcome to speak! Katty watched
them with a bitter little smile.

"You know the fair lady of my choice," said Ned at
last.

"I'm very glad to meet you, ma'am," said Jerry, turning his knife-blue eyes on her, his dropped chin and his
high, small perfect teeth making it sound like the greet-
ing of a well-bred weasel to a rabbit. They all retired
to the back parlour, where Katty brought the drinks.
The atmosphere was maudlin. After arranging for Katty
and himself to spend the next Sunday at the farm, Ned
escorted them down the street. When he came back
there were tears in his eyes—a foolish man!

"Well," he said, standing in the middle of the shop
with his hands behind his back and his bowler hat well
down over his eyes, " 'twas nice being all under the one
roof again."

"It must have been grand," said Katty, affecting to
be very busy. "I suppose 'twas Father Ring did it," she
added over her shoulder with subtle mockery.

"Ah," said Ned, looking stolidly out at the sunlit street
with swimming eyes, "we're getting older and wiser.
What fools people are to embitter their lives about
nothing! There won't be much politics where we're
going."

"I wonder if 'tis that," said Katty, as if she were talking

to herself while inwardly she fumed at the stupidity of the man.

"Ah, what else could it be?" asked Ned, wrapped up in whatever sentimental fantasies he was weaving.

"I suppose 'twould never be policy?" she asked archly, looking up from under her brows with a knowing smile.

"How could it be policy, woman?" asked Ned, his voice harsh with indignation. "What has he to gain by policy?"

"Ah, how would I know?" she said, reaching towards a high shelf. "He might be thinking of the shop for Con."

"He'd be thinking a very long way ahead," said Ned after a pause, but she saw it had gone home.

"Maybe he's hoping 'twouldn't be so long," she said smoothly.

"How's that?" said Ned.

"Julia, God rest her, went very suddenly," said Katty.

"He'd be a very foolish man to count on me doing the same," boomed Ned, but his face grew purple from shame and anger—shame that he had no children of his own, anger that she had pricked the sentimental bubble he had blown about Jerry and the boys.

It was a warning to Katty. Twice in the next year she satisfied herself that she was having a baby, and each time put the whole house into confusion. She lay upstairs on the sofa with a handbell at her side, made baby clothes, ordered the cradle, even got an option on a pram. To secure herself against accidents she slept in the spare room. And then it passed off and with a look like murder she returned to the big bedroom. Ned stared at her over the bedclothes with an incredulous, long-suffering air and then heaved a heavy sigh and turned in.

She knew he blamed her. After being taken in like that it would be weeks before he started again. Weaker sex, indeed! One would think it was he that was trying to start the baby. But Katty blamed herself as well. It was the final year in Dublin and the goings-on with the drunken medico that had finished her. For days on end she sat over the range in the kitchen with a little shawl over her shoulders, shivering and tight-lipped, taking little tots of brandy when Ned's back was turned and complaining of him to the servant girl. To make it worse, the daughter of another shopkeeper came home on holidays from England; a nurse with fast, flighty ways that appealed to Ned. He was always in and out there, full of old-fashioned gallantries. He kissed her hand and even called her "a rose." It reached Katty's ears and she clamped her lips. She was far too well bred to make vulgar scenes. Instead, with her feet on the fender, hands joined in her lap, she asked in the most casual friendly way:

"Ned, do you think that was a proper remark to make to the Dunne girl?"

"What remark?" asked Ned, growing crimson—it showed his guilty conscience.

"Well, Ned, you can hardly pretend you don't know, considering that the whole town is talking about it."

"Are you mad, woman?" he shouted, his voice brassy with rage.

"I only asked a simple question, Ned," she said with resignation, fixing him with her clear blue eyes. "Of course, if you prefer not to answer there's no more to be said."

"You have me driven distracted!" cried Ned. "I can't be polite to a neighbour's daughter but you sulk for days on me."

"Polite!" said Katty to the range. "However," she added, "I suppose I have no cause to complain. The man that would do worse to me wouldn't be put out by a little thing like that."

"Do worse to you?" shouted Ned, going purple as if he was in danger of congestion. "What did I ever do to you?"

"Aren't you planning to leave me in my old age without a roof over my head?" she asked suddenly, turning on him.

"I'm not planning to leave anything to anyone yet," roared Ned. "With the help of the Almighty God, when I do 'twill be to a child of my own."

"Indeed, I hope so," said Katty, "but after all, if the worst came to the worst—"

"If the worst came to the worst," he interrupted solemnly, "we don't know which of us the Lord—glory and praise to His holy name—might take first."

"Amen, O Lord," breathed Katty piously, and then went on in her original tone. "I'm not saying you'll be the first to go, and the way I am, Ned," she added bitterly, "I wouldn't wish it. But 'tis only common prudence to be prepared for the worst. You know yourself how Julia went."

"My God," he said mournfully, addressing his remarks out the empty hall, "the foolishness of it! We have only a few short years on the earth; we come and go like the leaves of the trees, and instead of enjoying ourselves, we wear our hearts out with planning and contriving."

"Ah, Ned," she said, goaded to fury, as she always was by his philosophizing and poetry talk, " 'tis easy it comes to you. I only wish the money would come as easy. I didn't work myself to the bone in the shop to be left a beggar in my old age."

"A beggar?" he cried. "Do you think I wouldn't provide for you?"

"Provide for me?" she gibed. "Con Lynch in the shop and me in the back room! Fine provisions I'd get!"

"I never said I'd leave it to Con Lynch," said Ned chokingly.

"Then what is he coming here for?" she shrieked, suddenly bounding into the middle of the kitchen and spreading out her arms. "What is he doing in my home? Can't you do what any other man would do and let them know you're leaving the shop to me?"

"I can't," he shouted back, "and you know I can't."

"Why not?" she said, stamping.

"Because 'tis an old custom. The property goes with the name."

"Not with the people I was brought up with," she said proudly.

"Well, 'twas with those I was brought up with," said Ned. "Women as good as you were satisfied. Ay, and better than you! Better than you," he added with a backward glance as he went out.

She dropped back beaten into her chair. She was afraid to cross him further. He looked like a man that might drop dead at any moment. She was only a stranger, a foreigner, with no link at all between herself and him. Con Lynch was more to him now than she was. It was only then she realized it was time to stop looking after the shop and look after herself instead.

In the autumn she said she was going to Dublin to see a specialist. Ned didn't say anything to dissuade her, but it was clear he had no faith in it. She didn't see a specialist. Instead she saw a nurse she had known in Dublin, another old flame of the medico's. Nurse O'Mara kept a maternity home on the canal. She was a tall, handsome woman with a fine figure and a long face that was growing just the least shade hard. She listened to Katty with screwed-up eyes and a good-natured smile. She was tickled by the situation. After all, if she hadn't got much out of the medico, Katty hadn't got much more.

"And you don't think that 'tis any use?" asked Katty doubtfully.

"I wouldn't say so," said the nurse.

"And I suppose there's nothing else I can do?" asked Katty in a low voice and an almost playful tone, never taking her blue eyes from the nurse's face.

"Unless you'd borrow one," said the nurse mockingly.

"That's what I mean," said Katty slyly.

"You're not serious?" said the nurse, her smile withering.

"Haven't I reason?" asked Katty, her smile growing broader.

"You'd never get away with it."

"Why not, girl?" asked Katty almost inaudibly. "Who's to know? If there was someone that was willing?"

"Oh, hundreds of them," said the nurse, with the bitterness of the childless woman.

"You'd know where to find one I could ask," murmured Katty, still with her eyes steadily fixed.

"I suppose so," said the nurse doubtfully. "There's nothing illegal about it. I'm not supposed to know what you're up to."

"And to have my letters addressed to your place," continued Katty.

"Why not?" asked Nurse O'Mara with a shrug. "For that matter, you can come and stay any time you like."

"That's all I want," said Katty with blazing eyes. "I have a hundred or so put on one side. I'll give it to you, and you can make whatever arrangements you like."

She returned to town triumphant with two new hats, wider and more girlish than those she usually wore. Then she set about a reorganization of the house, running up and down stairs and chattering with the maid.

"Well?" said Ned lazily, interpreting her behaviour with a touch of anxiety. "He gave you some hope?"

"I don't know if you'd call it hope," said Katty, furrowing her brow. "He thought I mightn't come out of it. Of course, I'll have to go back to him if anything happens."

"But he thought it might?" asked Ned.

"Wisha," said Katty, "like the rest of them he wouldn't like to give an opinion."

That, she saw, impressed Ned more than any more favourable verdict could have done. Almost from that on, he looked at her every morning with a solicitous, questioning air. Katty kept her mouth shut and went on with the housework. One night she said with her nunlike air: "I think I'll sleep in the spare room for the present." Even then she could see he only half believed her, but as the weeks passed, he started coming up to her in the evenings, settling the fire, and retailing whatever gobbets of gossip he had picked up in the bar. He started to tell her about his own boyhood, a thing he had never done before.

Jerry called once with Con and was brought upstairs with appropriate solemnity. She knew he had only come to see for himself, and she watched while the electric-blue eyes roved distractedly about the room till they alighted like a bluebottle on her stomach. That settled it so far as Jerry was concerned. He was crafty but not long-sighted. When the game looked like going against him he threw in his hand. He didn't come back, nor did Tom, though Con dropped in once or twice out of pure good nature. To Katty's surprise, Ned noticed and resented it.

"Ah," she said charitably, "I wouldn't mind that. They're probably busy on the farm this weather."

"They weren't so busy they couldn't go to Hartnett's," said Ned, who made it his business to know all they did.

"Ah, well, Hartnett's is near enough to them," said Katty, protesting against his unreasonableness.

"This place was near enough to them too when they thought they had a chance of the money," said Ned resentfully.

She looked at him archly from under her brows. She felt the time was ripe to say what she had to say.

"They didn't send you any more anonymous letters?" she asked lightly.

"They can say what they like now," said Ned, growing red.

Her smile faded as she watched him go out of the room. She knew now she had made herself secure against any suspicions the Lynches might have of her, but the ·change in Ned himself was something she hadn't allowed for and it upset her.

It even frightened her the day she was setting out for Dublin. She saw him in the bedroom packing a little case.

"What do you want that for?" she asked, going cold.

"You don't think I'm going to let you go to Dublin alone?" he replied.

"But I may be there for weeks," she said despairingly.

"Ah, well," he said as he continued to pack, "I'm due a little holiday. I have it fixed up with Bridie."

Katty sat on the bed and bit her lip. Somehow or other the Lynches had succeeded in instilling their suspicions into him and he was coming to see for himself. What could she do? Nothing. She knew O'Mara wouldn't be a party to any deception; it would be too much of a risk. "Mother of God, direct me!" she prayed, joining her hands in her lap.

"You're not afraid I'll run off with a soldier?" she asked lightly.

"That's the very thing I am afraid of," said Ned, turning round on her. Suddenly his eyes clouded with emotion. "It won't be wishing to anyone that tries to get you," he added, with a feeble attempt to keep up the joke.

"Wisha, Ned," she cried, rushing across the room to him, her heart suddenly lightened of a load, "'tisn't the way you think anything will happen to me?"

"No, little girl," he said, putting his arm about her. "Nor I wouldn't wish it for a thousand pounds."

"Ah, is it a fine strong woman like me?" she cried skittishly, almost insane with relief. "What fear there is of me! Maybe I'll let you come up when the next one is arriving."

3.

From Kingsbridge she took a taxi to the maternity home and got rid of some of her padding on the way. O'Mara opened the door for her herself. Katty sat on the edge of a sofa by the window, her hands joined in her lap, and looked expectantly up at the nurse.

"Well," she asked in a low voice, "any luck?"

"You'd better not try this game on too often," said O'Mara with amusement. "You'd never get past me with that complexion."

"I'm not likely to try, am I?" asked Katty complacently. "That girl you wrote about," she added in the same conspiratorial tone, "is she still here?"

"She is. You can see her now."

"I suppose you don't know anything about her?" Katty asked wistfully.

"She's a school-teacher," replied the nurse cautiously.

"Oh, Law!" said Katty in surprise. She hadn't expected anyone of her own class; it sounded too good to be true; and as plain as if it were written there, her pinched little face registered the doubt whether there wasn't a catch in it somewhere. "I don't know her by any chance, do I?" she added innocently.

"I hope not," replied the nurse smoothly. "What you don't know won't harm you."

"Oh, I'm not asking for information," protested Katty a shade too eagerly. "But you think she'll agree?" she said, dropping her voice again.

"She'll be a fool if she doesn't."

"Of course, I'll pay her well," said Katty. "I wouldn't ask anyone to do a thing like that for nothing."

"I wouldn't mention that, if I was you," said O'Mara dryly. "She's not trying to make a profit on it."

"Oh," said Katty, suddenly beginning to shiver all over, "I'd give all I ever had in the world to be out of it."

"But why?" asked O'Mara in surprise. "You're over the worst of it now."

"It's Ned," said Katty with a haggard look. "He'd murder me."

"Ah, well," said O'Mara with gruff kindness, "it's a bit late in the day to be thinking of that," and she led Katty up the stairs past a big Venetian window that lit the well and overlooked the canal bank. The lights were already lit outside. Through the trees she saw brown-red houses with flights of steps leading to hall doors, and a hump-backed limestone bridge.

There was a girl in bed in the room they entered; a young woman of twenty-eight or thirty with a plump pale face and a helmet of limp brown hair. Her face at any rate was innocent enough.

"This is the lady I was speaking about, Monica," said the nurse with a crooked smile. (Obviously she took a certain malicious pleasure in the whole business.) "I'll leave ye to discuss it for a while."

She went out, switching on the electric light as she did. Katty shook hands with the girl and then glanced shyly at the cot.

"Oh, isn't he lovely?" she cried with genuine admiration.

"He's sweet," said the girl called Monica, in a curiously common voice, and then reached out for a cigarette.

"I never smoke, thanks," said Katty, and then hastily drew a chair over to the bed, resting her hands on her lap and smiling under her big hat in a guilty, schoolgirl way that was curiously attractive.

"I suppose," she said, throwing back her head, "you must think I'm simply terrible?"

It wasn't intended to be a good opening but it turned out that way. The girl smiled, and her broad face crinkled.

"And what about me?" she asked, putting them both at once on a common level. "Will you get away with it though?"

"Oh, I'll have to get away with it, girl," said Katty flatly. "My livelihood depends on it. Did nurse tell you?"

"She did, but I still don't understand what you did to your husband to make him do that to you."

"Oh, that's an old custom," said Katty eagerly, seeing at once the doubt in the girl's mind. "Now, I know what you're thinking," she added with a smile, raising her finger in warning, "but 'tisn't that at all. Ned isn't a bit like that. I won't wrong him. He is a country boy, and he hasn't the education, but apart from that he's the best poor slob that ever lived." She was surprised herself at the warmth that crept into her voice when she spoke of him. "So you see," she added, dropping her voice and smiling discreetly, "you needn't be a bit afraid of us. We'd both be mad about him."

"Strange as it may seem," said Monica, her voice growing sullen and resentful, "I'm a bit mad about him myself."

"Oh, you are, to be sure," said Katty warmly. "What other way would you be?" At the same time she was bitterly disappointed. She began to realize that it wasn't going to be so easy after all. Worse than that, she had taken a real fancy to the baby. The mother, whatever her faults, was beautiful; she was an educated woman; you could see she wasn't common. "Of course," she added, shaking her head, "the idea would never have crossed my mind only that nurse thought you might be willing. And then, I felt it was like God's doing. . . . You are one of us, I suppose?" she asked, raising her brows discreetly.

"God alone knows what I am," said the girl, taking a deep pull of the cigarette. "A bloody atheist or something."

"Oh, how could you?" asked Katty in a shocked tone. "You're convent-educated, aren't you?"

"Mm."

"I'd know a convent girl anywhere," said Katty, shaking her head with an admiring smile. "You can always tell. I went to the Ursulines myself. But you see what I mean? There was I looking for a child to adopt, and you looking for a home for yours, and Nurse O'Mara bringing us together. It seemed like God's doing."

"I don't know what you want bringing God into it for," said Monica impatiently. "The devil would do as well."

"Ah," said Katty with a knowing smile, "that's only because you're feeling weak. . . . But tell me," she

added, still wondering whether there wasn't a catch in
it, "I'm not being curious or anything—but isn't it a
wonder the priest wouldn't make him marry you?"

"Who told you he wouldn't marry me?" asked Monica
quietly.

"Oh, Law!" cried Katty, feeling that this was probably
the catch. "Was it the way he was beneath you?" she
asked with the least shade of disappointment.

"Not that I know of," said Monica brassily. Then she
turned her eyes to the ceiling and blew out another
cloud of smoke. "He asked me was I sure he was the
father," she added lightly, almost as if it amused her.

"Fancy that!" said Katty in bewilderment. "But what
made him say that, I wonder."

"It seems," said Monica in the same tone, "he thought
I was going with another fellow at the same time."

"And you weren't?" said Katty knowingly.

"Not exactly," said Monica dryly, giving Katty a queer
look that she didn't quite understand.

"And you wouldn't marry him?" said Katty, knowing
perfectly well that the girl was only trying to take advantage of her simplicity. Katty wasn't as big a fool as
that though. "Hadn't you great courage?" she added.

"Oh, great," said Monica in the same ironic tone.

"The dear knows," said Katty regretfully, thinking
of her own troubles with the medico, "they're a handful,
the best of them! But are you sure you're not being
hasty?" she added with girlish coyness, cocking her little
head. "Don't you think when you meet him again and

he sees the baby, ye might make it up?"

"If I thought that," said the girl deliberately, "I'd walk out of this into the canal, and the kid along with me."

"Oh, Law!" said Katty, feeling rather out of her depth and the least bit frightened. At the same time she now wanted the baby with something like passion. It was the same sort of thing she sometimes felt at auctions for little gewgaws from women's dressing-tables or bits of old china; as if she couldn't live without it. No other child would ever satisfy her. She'd bid up to the last farthing for it—if only she knew what to bid.

Then Nurse O'Mara came back and leaned on the end of the bed, her knees bent and her hands clasped.

"Well," she asked, looking from one to the other with a mocking smile, "how did ye get on?"

"Oh, grand, nurse," said Katty with sudden gaiety. "We were only waiting for yourself to advise us."

"Why?" asked the nurse. "What is there between ye?"

"Only that I don't want to part with him," said Monica steadily.

"Aren't you tired of him yet?" asked the nurse ironically.

"Jesus, woman, be a bit human!" said Monica with exasperation. "He's all I have and I had trouble enough having him."

"That's nothing to the trouble you'll have keeping him," said the nurse.

"I know that well enough," said Monica in a more

reasonable tone, "but I want to be able to see him. I want to know that he's well and happy."

"Oh, if that's all that's troubling you," said Katty eagerly, "you can see him as much as you like at our place."

"She could not," said the nurse angrily. "The less the pair of you see of one another, the better for both. . . . Listen, Mon," she said pleadingly, "I don't care what you do. I'm only speaking for your good."

"I know that, Peggy," said Monica.

"I know you think you're going to do marvels for that kid, but you're not. I know the sort of places they're brought up in and the sort that bring them up—the ones that live. I tell you, after the first time, you wouldn't be so keen on seeing him again."

Monica was staring at the window, which had faded in the pale glare of the electric light. There was silence for a few moments. Katty heard the night wind whistling across the roof-tops from the bay. The trees along the canal heard it too and sighed. Something about it impressed her; the wind, and the women's voices, and the sleeping baby, and the heart contracted inside her as she thought of Ned, waiting at home. She pulled herself together with fictitious brightness.

"Now, nurse," she said firmly, "it isn't fair to push the young lady too hard. We'll give her till tomorrow night, and I'll say a prayer to Our Lady of Good Counsel to direct her."

"I'll give her all the good counsel she wants," said the

nurse coarsely. "If you're thinking of yourself, Monica, you might as well say no now. We won't have to look far for someone else. If you're thinking of the kid and want to give him a fair chance in life after bringing him into it, you'd better say yes while you have the chance."

Monica suddenly turned her face away, her eyes filling with tears.

"She can have him," she said in a dull voice.

"Oh, thank you, thank you," said Katty eagerly. "And I give you my word you'll never have cause to regret it."

"But for Christ's sake don't leave him in the room with me tonight," cried the girl, leaping up in bed and turning her wild eyes on Nurse O'Mara. "I'm warning ye now, don't leave him where I can lay my hands on him. I tell ye I won't be responsible."

Katty bit her lip and her face went white.

"There's supper waiting for you downstairs," said the nurse, beckoning her to go.

"You're sure I couldn't be of any assistance?" whispered Katty.

"Certain," said the nurse dryly.

As Katty turned to look back, the girl threw herself down again, holding her head in her hands. The nurse from the end of the bed looked at her with a half-mocking, half-pitying smile, the smile of a childless woman. The baby was still asleep.

The Stepmother

BOB DESMOND was my great pal. He was a good-looking, well-mannered lad with a plump, good-natured face and big brown eyes—very candid and pleasant when he smiled, but rather gloomy when he didn't. Between us we read every sort of boys' story-book that we could lay hands on, and as we were the only fellows in the district who did, we had the public-school code all to ourselves. We didn't split, we didn't tell lies, anyone that hit Bob hit me as well; and as the monks (our teachers) had never heard of the public-school code and expected us to tell lies, they mistook it for insubordination and beat blazes out of us. Generally we came out of that ordeal well. The great thing was not to shriek and try to get away from the monk, not to stick your damaged hand under your armpit and go back snivelling, but smile serenely as if you forgave them for it and then stroll quietly back to your desk. It made the monks very sick.

Bob's father was married a second time. That came as

a great shock to the neighborhood, for he and Bob's mother were a very united couple. She was a quiet, hard-working woman, while Mr. Desmond was big and jolly and emotional. He was wrapped up in the children; if one of them had a pain in his toe, the doctor was called. I envied Bob because he could always get the books and toys he wanted. Her death made a terrible change in the house. Bob would come in from school and find his father, a big powerful man, lying on the bed with one of her old frocks, kissing it and weeping into it. Bob would sit on the bed and try to comfort him, telling him not to mind, that Mummy was in heaven, and so on and so forth. That was bad enough, but Mr. Desmond did it in public too, and that distressed Bob more than anything. He was a proud kid and rather tongue-tied. Everyone was very sorry for his father. Then inside a couple of months he was going to the pictures with another woman, and finally married her. My mother never forgave him for that. I think she felt he had deceived the neighbours as well as his dead wife.

The second Mrs. Desmond was a tidy little piece, as my father called her, good-looking, rough in the tongue, lively, and very good-natured. She was particularly good to Bob and didn't treat him as a kid so much as a grown-up she could flirt with. In some ways I fancy he was as grown-up as she was. She was mad on amusement, and every evening herself and Mr. Desmond went off arm-in-arm to card-parties and shows. That was Bob's trouble. He had a sister called Sheela who was a real heart-scald,

and as they had no maid, one or the other of them had
to stay and mind the house.

"Which of ye is going to stay in tonight?" Mrs. Desmond would call as she scampered down the stairs and
went to admire herself in the mirror. "Sheela, you mind
the house tonight."

"Why would I?" Sheela would bawl at once. "Can't
Bob do it? I did it the last night."

"You did not do it the last night," Bob would say in
his slow way. It always took time for Bob's anger to get
under way, for he was never quick enough off the mark
with people like Sheela who told lies by second nature.
It gave her a decided advantage.

"But I have to go up to Susie Cross's to get the answers
to my eckera," Sheela would cry, her voice going up to
the top note in her register.

"Ah, you're always the same," Mrs. Desmond would
cry in disgust, shaking herself down inside her frock and
giving the little hat a tug as she smiled into the mirror.
"You have as much old guff about it!"

"Christmas, I have no blooming life in this house,"
Sheela would cry, bursting into floods of tears, and go
upstairs to throw herself face downward on the bed. That
sometimes worked if her father happened to drop in.
He was an emotional man and a bit of despair never
came amiss with him. He would come down with a grave
face and take Bob aside, and sixpence would settle
Sheela's troubles for the evening. But when he didn't
there was sometimes hell to pay with Sheela. They were

no sooner outside the door than she was at it with her long legs crossed and a wild look in her eye. I could hear her myself from our house, bawling across the avenue to the Ryan girl, and it made me wish that someone would smother her. "I can't go out," the long, accusing, half-savage cry would ring out. "I have to mind the ould house." Then the Ryan girl would cross the avenue to her, and Sheela would sprawl across the little gate with her arms folded and her head in her hands. They gabbled away thirteen to the dozen while the dusk came on, the gas-lamp was lit, and the kids in their white pinnies gathered round it. That drove Sheela distracted. By the time I called for Bob she was desperate. She came in with a worried air, plucking at her black pigtails.

"Bob," she would plead unctuously in the tone of a young mother, begging you to look after the baby while she ran upstairs for the bottle, "would you ever mind the house just for five minutes? I only want to run up to Susie Cross's for the answers."

"I'll do nothing of the sort," Bob would growl in alarm. "Why can't she come down to you?"

"Because she have to mind the house too, Bob. As true as God, I'll be killed in school tomorrow. Look, Bob, that the Almighty God might strike me stone cold this minute, I won't be five minutes."

"Yes," growled Bob, who knew her little ways, "and then stop out for two hours!"

"I wouldn't, Bob, I wouldn't, I wouldn't," she would say, joining her hands and waggling her pigtails piously.

"Oh, that's as true as if I was to die tonight."

"Ah, go on!" Bob would say angrily (he hated having to refuse her), "you have no word."

"All right so," she would spit, hands on hips, the very incarnation of a virago of twelve. "You needn't, you dirty, rotten, good-for-nothing, ignorant pig!"

Then she would go to the front door again with an air of great gloom and grandeur, drift towards the gate with folded arms as if she was going to tell the others she wouldn't be out, and then—the voices round the gas-lamp or the twinkling of the first star waking some wild instinct in her blood—one glance back, one hasty, im-modest tug at her garter, and she was off like the wind. You could hear her shrill cries from far away. God, how I hated that girl!

Of course, Bob could have ignored it and come off with me to the barrack, where we had friends among the Tommies, but when his parents came back it would have meant a walloping for Sheela. That, according to Bob, wouldn't have been cricket. It seemed to me a nice point whether cricket applied to people like Sheela, whom I classed among the hill tribes, but Bob took the line that it did, and she was his sister. So, like the captain of the sinking ship, Bob told me to go to the barrack by myself, and I, playing up to the part of the devoted friend, said that of course it didn't matter, and instead of prowling round the barrack in the dusk, picking up cigarette pic-tures and strange characters, we sat down in the front room to a rotten game of checkers. My only consolation was that Bob prophesied gloomily that Sheela would come to a bad end. From my point of view the sooner that happened, the better.

Actually it happened quite soon. One day she stayed at home from school, pretending to be sick, and was left in charge of the house and the dinner by her stepmother. When Mrs. Desmond came back from town just before Bob was due in from school, the door was wide open, the fire out, and the dinner ruined. Of course there was no sign of Sheela. Bob came in and gave her a hand, but she was in a flaming temper, and everything went against her. At last Sheela herself, driven by hunger, came back.

"Where were you?" shouted her stepmother indignantly.

"I was out," said Sheela, fear making her brazen. "Oh, Jay!" she cried, letting on to be astonished at the sight that awaited her. "Did the fire go out on you? And I not gone five minutes!"

"Go and light that fire," shouted Mrs. Desmond.

"Who are you talking to?" asked Sheela impudently.

"What's that you said?" cried Mrs. Desmond, taking a step or two towards her.

"I'm not going to be turned into a skivvy by you or anyone else," said Sheela, beginning to cry.

"Light that fire at once, I say," said her stepmother, taking her by the arm and giving her a good shaking.

"Take your hands off me, you dirty thing, or I'll open you!" cried Sheela through her sobs.

Then it seemed Mrs. Desmond, out of patience, gave

her a good cuff; Sheela went for the pot-stick, and Bob, sick at heart, tried to intervene.

"I wish you'd let Sheela alone," he said in a complaining voice.

"Come on, now," cried Sheela, seeing Bob between her and her stepmother and brandishing the pot-stick for all she was worth, "come on and I'll give you enough of it!"

Now, Mrs. Desmond wasn't a malicious woman by any manner of means, but she had a temper, and a saint in heaven wouldn't have stood the spectacle of this skinny little thing in pigtails waving the pot-stick and inviting her to come on. She came on in one fell swoop, snatched the pot-stick from Sheela, and gave her three or four good hard wallops across the backside with it. "Jesus! Jesus!" shrieked Sheela at the top of her voice. "Me hip is broken!" Then Bob lost his head. He forced his way between them grimly, and when Mrs. Desmond pushed him off he kicked her. She suddenly dropped the pot-stick, doubled up, and collapsed into a chair, nursing her shin. Her face was contracted with agony.

"You vicious little cur!" she cried between tears and rage.

"Well," said Bob in a low voice, "you shouldn't hit my sister."

"All right," she said bitterly, "I'm done with ye now. I'll let your father deal with you."

Bob came and called for me, looking very white. My mother saw that something was wrong. She had a soft spot for Bob, seeing him like that with no mother, and a

father who had so deeply disillusioned her. She felt sure
he was neglected.

"Isn't it early you're out, Bob?" she exclaimed. "Had
you your dinner already?"

Bob smilingly made some excuse about the fire being
out, and she insisted on his having a cup of tea with me.
It was only as we were going down the glen, where most
of our afternoons were spent, that he told me what had
happened. I was shocked, and I think he was a bit
shocked himself—kicking wasn't cricket and kicking a
woman was worse—for he put on a cynical, grown-up
air.

"And what'll your old fellow do?" I asked.

"Oh, I don't care," he said moodily. "Anyway, I can
always go in the Navy."

I had no theoretical objection to the Navy, but we
were both Army men, and it seemed a drastic course to
take for someone like Sheela, who was only half human.
Protecting women and children was all very well, but
the people who had thought of it hadn't met Sheela.

"Anyway," he growled, "she's my sister, and she hasn't
anyone else to take her part."

The glen was great fun that day, for not only was there
firing practice but bugle practice as well, and a young
corporal gave us a lesson on the side. We were late coming home, and by that time we had both forgotten the
very existence of the Navy. Bob had a paper for me, so
I went with him to his house. As we reached the avenue
he suddenly fell silent and said in a low voice: "Wait

here and I'll bring it out to you." I didn't see why I should wait, so after a moment I followed him up to the door. Then I heard his father's voice and remembered what had happened. To my relief, his father didn't sound angry, only a little upset.

"What's this I hear about you, Bob?" he asked. "Is it true that you kicked Mother today?"

"Yes, Daddy," said Bob. He waited a moment and said: "I'm sorry."

"I'm surprised at you, Bob," his father went on. "I wouldn't mind Sheela so much, but I expected better of you. What made you do such a thing?"

"Mother hit Sheela, Daddy," replied Bob in a troubled voice.

"And Sheela was impudent," Mrs. Desmond said scoldingly, "and you know perfectly well she deserved it."

"Is that right, Bob?" asked his father.

"Oh, it's quite right," said Bob candidly. "She's always doing it and I know she needs a licking."

"Then why did you interfere?" asked his father testily.

"Because it's not Mother's place to hit her," replied Bob in a sullen tone.

In spite of my doubts of Sheela's status I nearly said "Hear, hear!" I didn't feel as if I were eavesdropping so much as giving Bob moral support from the door. That was the way I should have liked to talk back to the monks; not defiantly, but just showing them where they were wrong.

"Oh, is that so, Bob?" his stepmother asked mockingly on a rising note. "Thanks for telling me. I'll know better next time."

"What way is that to speak in front of Mother, Bob?" asked his father, and this time he really was angry.

"But it's true, Daddy," Bob said pleadingly. "I know Sheela did wrong, and I know she deserves to be punished, but Mother should tell you instead of punishing her herself."

"You see," said Mrs. Desmond with bitter irony, and in a loud voice, "I simply have no business in this house."

"What do you mean?" Mr. Desmond asked furiously. "Why shouldn't she punish her?"

"Because she's not our mother," Bob replied steadfastly. I had never felt so proud of him as then, but just at that moment I heard a sound that made my heart turn over: just a clout and a cry of pain from Bob. It must have been a real staggerer, for we made a point of not yowling. I nearly went mad, and I am still surprised that I didn't go in then and there and remonstrate with Mr. Desmond. If it had been at school I would, but it was different in another chap's own house. I walked away and shut my eyes. At that age you feel so damnably helpless.

"Isn't she?" asked Mr. Desmond with a vicious intonation I had never heard before.

"She isn't, she isn't," cried Bob, and again he cried out with pain and I could almost see him crouching with his hands over his head from the rain of blows. I had been trying to get away, but this time I went back, in-

tending to knock and ask for Bob. I was halted in this
by Mrs. Desmond's voice.

"Ah, for God's sake, don't hit the child like that,
Charlie," she cried in surprise and concern. "It doesn't
matter. Let him alone!"

"I'll show him who's going to be master in this house,"
snarled her husband.

"Stop it, I say!" she cried sharply, and I knew she was
getting between them. "If you want to punish someone,
punish Sheela. She's the cause of it all."

"I'll knock the lights out of this little puppy first," said
her husband thickly, and then there was the sound of a
scuffle, and I knew she was dragging him off Bob. By
this time the thing had become public property. The
woman next door came out as if she was wondering
when her husband was going to come.

"Stop it this instant," Mrs. Desmond cried shrilly.
"You're worse than the child."

"Let me alone!" he shouted. "I'm going to teach him."

"Fitter for you to teach yourself," she cried. "Leave
the child to me, can't you? . . . And indeed, Bob," she
added bitterly, "you're the last I thought would behave
like that to me."

"I'll show him how to behave," said his father frantically.

"God Almighty," she shouted, "the child has more
sense than you. What way is that for a grown man to
carry on? Do you want to put him into convulsions on
me? . . . Come here to me, Bob," she added gently, and

then the sounds in the kitchen died away, all but Bob's stifled sobbing. I may as well admit that I was sobbing too. "Now look at the state you're in!" she said complainingly. "Here, let me dry your eyes, and look up at me. Are we going to be friends again?"

"Yes, Mother."

"And no more kicking?"

"No, Mother."

"I don't mind you getting into a wax with me, but that's a different thing. You know you wouldn't kick a dog the way you kicked me. That's true, isn't it? . . . Go away, Charlie," she cried in exasperation. "Go out somewhere and let us alone. . . . What did you say, Bob?"

Bob said something that I didn't catch, and neither, it seemed, did she.

"You what?" she cried.

"I promised Mummy not to let you hit Sheela," he said.

"You promised your mummy?" she cried. "But sure, you couldn't do that, Bob!"

"I had to," he said, sniffling. "She asked me to."

"Ah, but listen, Bob," she said with just the least trace of amusement, "sure, I never knew your mummy, son, and your mummy never knew me. She couldn't ask you to do a thing like that. You must have been dreaming."

"I wasn't dreaming," he said indignantly.

"But when was this?" she asked.

"The day before she died."

"The day before she died?" she echoed incredulously.

"Yes, after Father Cronin went. Mrs. O'Regan said she wanted to see Sheela and me, and then Mummy asked me to stay."

"You're not serious, Bob?" she said.

"I am," said Bob. "And then she said when she was gone away Daddy would bring another woman in, and that you wouldn't like us and beat us. So she made me promise whenever you hit Sheela or me that I'd hit you back."

Even I, who had only the very slightest notion of what Bob was saying, felt that he'd said something wrong. There was a pause you could cut with a knife.

"I see, Bob," she said bitterly. "And of course, ever since I came into this house I've hated you and tried to injure you."

"You didn't," he cried passionately. "Now, I never said that. Really, Mother, I didn't."

"God forgive your mummy anyway, Bob," she said in a low voice.

Then I heard Mr. Desmond's step in the hall and was suddenly overwhelmed by an appalling sense of my own guilt. I knew I had been listening to something I should never have heard. I thought I must have made some stir and that he was coming out to see who was the spy, so I took to my heels and bolted up the avenue like mad. At the top I glanced back and stopped. He was going off in the other direction, towards the open country. He hadn't even seen me. Probably he hadn't seen much else either, poor devil!

Friends of the Family

1.

KATE HUMPHREYS worried a good deal about the way Sonny Dorgan treated Gretta. Gretta was a friend of the family and had been since childhood. John Joe, Kate's brother, refused to take it seriously, not because he particularly liked Sonny Dorgan but because he knew Kate and Gretta exaggerated a good deal. John Joe was a nice fellow, quiet and well-spoken, but rather disillusioned.

"Ah, what has she to complain about?" he asked in a disgusted drawl.

"Would you strike a girl, John Joe?" Kate asked with quiet intensity, folding her arms and looking at him. Kate was still beautiful in a quiet way.

"What would her weight be?" her brother asked cynically, smiling only with his eyes. At the same time the question stuck. No man, no matter how cynical, likes to hear of a girl he has been friendly with since childhood being knocked about.

Then Ned Campion appeared on the scene. He was a Dublin man, blue-eyed, fair-haired, and hot-tempered, and he became very friendly with John Joe's sisters. John Joe didn't think much of him. He was far too much at ease in other people's homes and with other people's sisters, and irony seemed to be lost on him. It put John Joe at a disadvantage.

"My goodness," exclaimed his brother, Peter, who seemed to live in a permanent state of wonderment at life, "did you ever see a woman fall for a man as Kate has for Campion?"

"Why?" John Joe asked innocently. "You don't think they're doing a line, do you?"

"Doing a line?" cried Peter indignantly. "My God, where are your eyes, man? They're as good as married already."

But it wasn't till they had the house at the seaside that summer that John Joe really began to wonder where his eyes had been. Of course, he might have known. Kate was still beautiful and still got offers, but they were either from good-living young men who had seen her at the altar on Sunday or middle-aged widowers who thought she would make a good stepmother. They all proposed in writing and told her they preferred the old-fashioned sort of girl. Gretta and her daughter shared the house with them, and Campion came to stay, and John Joe, smiling benignly at the pair of them, wondered at his own stupidity.

"Tell me, Kate," he said one evening when he came in

and found Alice in bed and Kate sitting alone outside the house, "where's Gretta?"

"Gone for a walk with Ned," she replied cheerfully.

"You don't think there's anything between them, do you?" he asked keenly.

"Why, John Joe?" she asked, letting on to be very interested. "You don't mean they were doing anything they shouldn't be doing?"

He realized from her tone that she was stalling, and his tone grew graver.

"I hope you have nothing to do with it," he said.

"Ah, what do you take me for?" she cried impatiently. "Of course, I know Ned is fond of her, if that's what you mean."

"Nothing more than that?" he drawled ironically.

"What do you mean, nothing more?" she retorted quietly, her hands on her lap, her long, pale Madonna face with the limp gilt hair twined about it, raised in the half-light. She looked very beautiful just then.

"Gretta doesn't care for him at all, I suppose?" he added mockingly.

"I never said she didn't care for him," she said placidly. "It would be very surprising if she didn't, considering the sort of husband she has."

"I wasn't considering that at all, Kate," said John Joe with crushing irony. "To tell you the truth, I was under the impression that ye'd forgotten about Sonny entirely."

"Well, if you want to know, John Joe," replied Kate, her face transfigured with a sort of inner light, "I think as little of Sonny as he does about me—and that's not much, God knows!" she added lightly.

"Oh, now, that's all very well, Kate," drawled John Joe with a toss of his head, "but Sonny isn't exactly a cipher. Peter and myself will probably have a lot to say to him from time to time, and I'd like to know where I stand with the man."

"Well, as you asked, you may as well know," said Kate gravely, leaning towards him with her hands clasped in her lap. "Gretta is thinking of leaving him."

"Of leaving Sonny?" John Joe repeated incredulously.

"You sound very surprised, John Joe," she said with quiet mockery. "Doesn't it strike you as surprising that she didn't do it before?"

"I presume," said John Joe, paying her back in her own coin, "that there wasn't anyone to catch her when she jumped. You're not going to pretend she's not doing it on Campion's account?"

"I don't know, John Joe," she said, and for the first time there was a trace of doubt in her voice. "I fancy Gretta is thinking of going to live in Dublin when he goes back."

"Going to live in Dublin?" he repeated in the same incredulous tone, and then grew red with anger at Kate's pious half-truths. "You mean she's going to live with him?"

"But what else can the child do, John Joe?" Kate asked unhappily, leaning still further towards him.

"I don't know," replied John Joe caustically. "What do

people in your church usually do?" (John Joe's disillusionment also extended to religion.)

"Oh," she cried miserably, "I know it's awful, and it's wrong, but what can the girl do? Can't you be a bit human? Her future happiness depends on it. I told her she was crazy ever to marry that man."

"Are you sure," John Joe asked cruelly, "that she's waiting till she gets to Dublin?"

"Oh, how can you ask that?" Kate replied in a hurt tone. "You know her as well as I do."

"So I thought," he said ironically. "Wasn't she supposed to be making Novenas for my conversion or something?"

"Well, indeed," said Kate with a wan smile, "if you'll excuse my saying so, they seem to be having some effect."

2.

At the same time it was disturbing in a girl like that, a friend of the family. He blamed Kate a lot for encouraging Gretta in what, after all, was mere foolishness. He knew what would happen if she did as she proposed. She would have the hell of a time for a fortnight, and then go off to confess it to the priest, and the priest would refuse her absolution and tell her she must go back to her husband. And, of course, her husband wouldn't have her back.

It was like John Joe's luck to run into Sonny the day

he returned from holidays. Sonny's fat, good-natured face lit up at once. He was a born charmer; nuns in particular were dotty about him. John Joe didn't really like him though he was amused by him. Sonny, he felt, believed in far too many things to be wholesome. And he knew Sonny didn't like him, though he wouldn't show it.

"Oh, hullo, John Joe," he said with a smile. "You're looking very brown. Were you on holidays?"

"Will you have a drink?" said John Joe, to cut short the languorous waltz of gab he knew would follow.

"Begor, I never refused one yet," said Sonny, getting brighter each moment. "Sonny by name, sunny by nature," as he described himself. "Sure, I forgot," he added, with a plausible imitation of a man with a short memory. "You were in Bunroo with the family. Gretta was telling me. Ye had a great time, I believe?"

"Ah, not bad," said John Joe without enthusiasm, and he ordered the drinks in his quiet, colourless way.

"Cripes," said Sonny, screwing himself on to a stool and loosening the top button of his trousers, "this beer has a terrible effect on the masculine waist-line. I don't know what Gretta and yourself see in that blooming place. It's too quiet for my taste. Ye had Ned Campion there as well?"

"We had," said John Joe quietly, passing across the drink.

"He was up at the house a couple of times with Gretta, but I never had much chat with him," said Sonny casually. "He seems to be a very smart chap, by all accounts."

"So I believe," replied John Joe cautiously. It was a most embarrassing position. In an inquisitive community it was too much to suppose that Sonny didn't know all about it and didn't assume that himself and Peter were parties to it. At the same time John Joe had no skill in the fencing and probing and shilly-shally that Sonny enjoyed so much. "Of course," he added, "I never had much to say to him, but himself and Kate are very thick."

"And Gretta the same," said Sonny slyly. "Begor, John Joe," he added with a deliberately common drawl, "he seems to be the hell of a lady's man, what? Yourself and myself wouldn't have much chance with a fellow like that around."

"Ah, to tell you the truth, Sonny," said John Joe, seeing the way he was being pumped, "I think he's a decent chap."

"Oh, man alive," said Sonny eagerly, "I'm not saying a word against him. 'Tisn't because he goes round with Gretta. That wouldn't worry me at all." And then the same rogue's laugh as he closed one eye. "And anyone that knocked round with Kate would have to be all right," he added with a conspiratorial air. "That's the girl that would soon stiffen him if he wasn't. Gor, John Joe," he added laughingly, "hasn't she a terrible eye? 'Tis a mercy to God she's not a man or she'd be in the Redemptorists."

Oh, a most embarrassing man to talk to! But John Joe had a stubborn Puritanical streak in him, which only grew more pronounced whenever he was with people like Sonny. He put his hands in his trousers pockets, jangled the coins, and looked at Sonny.

"The trouble with Gretta is that she hasn't friends enough," he said quietly.

"That's the truest word you ever spoke, John Joe," said Sonny approvingly. "It's the very thing I'm always telling her myself. She hasn't friends enough. You should tell her that. Of course, you know she worships the ground you walk on," he added winningly.

"I do not," said John Joe dryly, resenting Sonny's blatant flattery. "Anyway, that's not what I mean," he added with deepening gravity. "I know Gretta since we were kids, and I think I understand her. She's the biggest-hearted girl in the world, but she likes to be made a lot of. . . . Mind you," he added deprecatingly, "I'm not interfering between ye."

"You're not, of course," said Sonny, all the light gone from his face.

"I never discussed you with Gretta, good, bad, or indifferent," added John Joe, "but I can't help noticing when things aren't going right."

"Oh, you put your finger on it, John Joe," said Sonny in a low voice, taking a swig to steady him up. "They're not going right, I know it well. And they're not going right this many a long day."

"And I'm telling you the reason," said John Joe solemnly. "I know it's not your fault," he added hastily, to take the harm out of it, "but a lot of women are like that. They feel you're slighting them if you're not dancing attendance on them night, noon, and morning."

"They do," agreed Sonny disconsolately. "Gretta is the same. And of course I'm not much in the domesticated line. I might meet a couple of the lads, just as I met you, and we might be here the rest of the night. There's not a bit of harm in it, you know," he added eagerly, "but when I go home, I'm the worst in the world."

"Ah, I'm in the same boat," said John Joe, though he wasn't, and he knew Sonny knew he wasn't; it was just that the man had his pride. "But the sort Campion is, he has only to be in a room with a woman for her to start telling him all her troubles as if she knew him all her life. There's no harm in that either," he added charitably, "but you know what it leads to."

"I do, I do," said Sonny, biting his lip. "And I'm very grateful to you for warning me, John Joe. Because the fact is, for all my little vagaries, I'm genuinely devoted to Gretta. Would you believe that, John Joe?"

"I would," said John Joe, and he meant it. He could see that in the odd moments that Sonny devoted to worry, he had worried; men like Sonny always do when they find the woman they have lived with for years hates the living sight of them.

"As true as God I am," said Sonny, shaking his head. "Genuinely and sincerely devoted to her. I'd hate to hurt that girl's feelings."

3.

At least John Joe's conscience was clear. Whatever happened, he had done his best, and for a couple of weeks he was quite satisfied that things were going better with the Dorgans. He knew that because Gretta didn't come to the house so much, and Kate was rather subdued. Then he came home late one night and found Gretta and Kate with their feet over the fender. Gretta looked up at him and giggled.

"Hullo, Gretta," he said, with as much surprise as he ever permitted himself to show. "Isn't it late you're out?"

"Why, John Joe?" she asked with a start, letting on to be upset. "Don't you want to see me home?"

"Oh, well," he said in what he intended to be the same bantering tone, "that depends on who's at home."

"Only Aunty, John Joe," she replied eagerly. "And she's deafer than ever."

"Oh," said John Joe with a bland but watchful smile, taking a pipe from the mantelpiece and looking into the bowl, "is that the way with you?"

"I know," she said between laughing and smiling. "I'm a bad girl."

"It's rather hard lines on Sonny, isn't it?" said John Joe noncommittally, tapping out his pipe on the grate.

"It's awful," she said gravely, "but today I knew I couldn't stand it another week without going mad."

"I wonder you stuck it so long," said Kate, with a touch of complacency that annoyed John Joe. He detached the bowl from the stem and blew through it. Then he sat back in his chair and fumbled for his tobacco.

"Who was it was telling me that Sonny was supposed to be quite a reformed character?" he asked innocently.

"Is he?" asked Gretta with interest, as though that hadn't struck her before. "I suppose in a way he is." Then her grey eyes twinkled wickedly. "Unfortunately," she added demurely, "his ideas of reform are rather limited."

So Gretta and her daughter came back to live with old Miss Curtin, and except that Campion was always knocking round, it would have been quite like old times with Gretta and Kate going shopping together and singing Gilbert and Sullivan in the evenings. As Gretta didn't want her aunt to know anything about Campion, he called for her at the Humphreys', and John Joe purposely stayed out late to avoid meeting him at supper when he came home. He could hardly have trusted himself to be polite. It was bad enough Campion's making himself at home with other fellows' sisters, but when it came to wives, John Joe drew the line. It was very disturbing, and it wasn't only himself. What could you make of a quiet, religious girl like Kate lending herself to such a business?

It didn't last long. Kate grew thoughtful again, and Campion was a bundle of nerves. He snapped and snarled at everybody, and everything he did seemed to

John Joe too demonstrative altogether. One night as John Joe was coming home late, Campion went past him hastily with his head down, hands behind his back, his throat wrapped in a muffler. It wasn't that he didn't see John Joe, for John Joe, startled, called after him in his usual amiable way: "Oh, good night, Ned," and Campion muttered: "Good night," without looking back. By God, as John Joe said to himself, one would think it was Campion's house.

"What's wrong with that fellow?" he asked dryly as he entered the kitchen.

"Who?" asked Kate, looking up from her stool before the fire. "Oh, poor Ned!"

"Poor Ned?" echoed John Joe resentfully. "What's poor about him?"

"He's very worried," said Kate, tossing the hair from her forehead.

"Go on!" said John Joe ironically. "I thought he was supposed to be getting all he wanted in this life."

"He didn't get it yet," said Kate with a sigh.

"But what's the trouble?" John Joe asked in surprise.

"I suppose you might as well hear it now as any other time," said Kate. "Gretta is having a baby."

"Gretta?" he echoed in a dumbfounded voice, and then sank on to a chair beside her.

"You won't mention it to Peter?"

"Why wouldn't I?" he asked suspiciously and then frowned as a fresh doubt struck him. "You don't mean it's Campion's?" he said, aghast.

"Did he look as if it was?" she asked impatiently. "Really, John Joe, I wish you'd have a bit of sense. I only wish to God it was his."

John Joe looked at her in fresh astonishment and then grew very red.

"What's come over you?" he asked angrily. "Or are you losing your senses too?"

"Oh, it's easy for you to lay down the law, John Joe," she cried, as angry as himself. "I don't know how you can sit there, smug and contented, settling other people's lives for them."

"I'm settling other people's lives?" repeated John Joe in bewilderment. "*I'm* settling them. That's pretty good. You bring this bloody man to the house and throw him at Gretta's head; you have the pair of them down at the seaside together, and tell Gretta what a shocking life her husband is leading her; you break up the woman's home, and then you tell me that I settle people's lives for them."

"I didn't, John Joe, I didn't," she said shrilly, her long face pinched with anxiety. "You know that before ever Ned came on the scene, Gretta was sick to death of Sonny; you know that Ned and herself are mad out about one another; and—I suppose it's wrong," she interjected pleadingly, "and I suppose I ought to regret it, but I can't help it, John Joe. Gretta is my oldest friend, and I want her to have some happiness in life. I tell you I'd sooner a thousand, thousand times that it was Ned's child."

She was standing now, looking down at him, slight

and pale, with clenched fists. He looked at her half in pity, half in contempt.

"And what does Gretta herself think?" he asked coldly.

"The poor child doesn't know what to think. It's like the end of everything for her."

"I suppose," asked John Joe ironically, "she feels it's the direct intervention of Providence."

"Ah," said Kate, folding her arms and looking fixedly into the fire, "that's only old doosha-dawsha."

"I'm glad you're prepared to admit that much at least," he said complacently, digging his hands into his trousers pockets as he got a little of his own back for all the prayers that had been said for him. At the same time he saw that he had guessed right. Gretta's conscience had begun to trouble her even sooner than he had expected. "And so Ned is getting the push?"

"I wouldn't say he's getting the push," said Kate unhappily. "It's only that she feels she'd be too much of a burden on him."

"She doesn't know the half of it," said John Joe feelingly. "And what does he think?"

"He thinks just what I think," said Kate firmly, "that it doesn't alter the situation one way or another."

"That's the best thing I've heard about him so far," said John Joe grudgingly, admitting that Campion's attitude was what his own would be in the circumstances. "Still," he said regretfully, "Gretta is right."

"How is she right?" Kate asked.

"Ah, for goodness' sake have sense, girl," drawled John Joe, almost out of patience with her. "At the best of times it would have been hard enough, but with two children of Sonny's and one of them not even born yet! The whole thing is silly."

"Oh," said Kate with quiet intensity, "I don't mind what you say. Anything in the world is better than going back to live with a man you don't care about."

John Joe nearly exploded on her with a denunciation of love and all its absurdities, but when he looked at that pure, spiritual, unhappy face of hers, he held his peace. He even thought for a moment that Peter might have been right and that she was a bit in love with Ned herself. It would be like her to sacrifice the man she loved for the sake of a friend.

And then, lying in bed with a book on his knees, he suddenly saw it all clearly and began to chuckle to himself. He saw that it was entirely Kate's doing that the thing had gone so far, and his that it hadn't gone any farther. "Unfortunately," Gretta had said in her sly way, "Sonny's ideas of reform are rather limited." And Sonny's ideas of reform, however limited they might be, were entirely of John Joe's manufacture. He could hardly help laughing at the comedy of it. Kate, who was a saint, or not far short of one, was deliberately trying to break up Gretta's marriage, while he, who didn't believe in anything, was trying to knock it together as fast as she dismembered it. "Oh, very well," he thought cheerfully. "If that's what Kate wants, we'll see which of us wins."

Next day he rang up Sonny and arranged to meet him for a drink. The moment Sonny arrived, John Joe noticed the change in him. He behaved just the least bit stiffly as became a man whose wife had just left him, meeting one of her friends.

"Well," drawled John Joe with a smile when they were sitting at the table with their drinks, "I believe we'll soon be congratulating you on an increase in the family."

"Oh, is that so, John Joe?" said Sonny without giving anything away.

"So I believe anyway," said John Joe with a grin.

"Oh, of course," said Sonny with a toss of his head, "I'd be the last to know."

"Ah," said John Joe with his innocent smile, "you ought to know by this time what women in that condition are like."

"Well, to tell you the God's truth, John Joe," said Sonny, raising his brows, with affected candour, "I'm easy. As a matter of fact," he added offhandedly, " 'twas only this morning I was seeing Stanton, the auctioneer, about getting a tenant for the house."

"Oh," said John Joe mildly, "that's taking things to the fair, isn't it?" Not because he believed for an instant that Sonny was trying to let the house, but as a warning against any of these dramatic gestures which so often lead to trouble.

"Ah, I don't know, John Joe," said Sonny, wrinkling his brows, "I'm very disappointed in Gretta. Very disappointed!"

"Go on!" said John Joe politely, without being able to conceal a smile. "What disappointed you?"

"Well, John Joe," said Sonny, shaking his head, "you know I'm afraid Gretta is very deceitful."

"You're not serious, Sonny?" purred John Joe. (Really, he thought, there was no limit to the absurdities of married couples, and the men had as little sense as the women.) "When did you begin to notice that?"

"Oh, begor now, John Joe," said Sonny, looking away and raising a plump hand for order, "that's no joking matter at all. And don't tell me you didn't notice it yourself," he added, turning again and pointing an accusing finger at John Joe. "I had occasion to speak to her about it before we were married at all. Gretta is deceitful, John Joe."

"Do you know, Sonny, I wouldn't be a bit surprised," drawled John Joe, feeling the least bit irritated. It was pretty thick of Sonny, who to John Joe's knowledge was a leader of a local Catholic secret society.

"Well," said Sonny reasonably, pulling at the knees of his trousers, "just consider the present situation. As a result of a certain discussion with yourself a couple of weeks ago, I made it up with Gretta—in every sense," he added warningly.

"So it seems," said John Joe with good-natured irony.

"Now," went on Sonny, cocking his head, "I made all the concessions, but that's neither here nor there. I'm not claiming any credit for it. Maybe I was to blame in the beginning. I'm not trying to defend myself, mind you," he said, leaning back and shaking his head earnestly. "I'm not trying to defend myself at all. But then what happens? I come home one night and find Gretta and the kid gone. No disagreement, no explanation, nothing at all. Now, wouldn't you think, if I'd done anything out of the way, that Gretta would come and tell me?"

"That would depend on how you behaved the last time she did it," retorted John Joe dryly, remembering a certain question of Kate's about whether or not he would strike a woman.

"Oh, no, John Joe," said Sonny triumphantly, fumbling for coins in his trousers pocket, "that's want of character. I understand Gretta as well as you, John Joe, and maybe a bit better. Mind you, I had hopes of her. I thought when she was living with me for a few years that I'd be able to draw her out of that moral cowardice and get her to be truthful and straightforward. Up to a point I succeeded, but now—" Sonny made a large despairing gesture—"I'm afraid she's back where she started, John Joe. I can see no hope for her."

"My goodness," said John Joe caustically, as with every moment his dislike for Sonny gathered head, "that's a very serious view to take."

"But what other view can I take?" asked Sonny challengingly. "I hear from you that she's going to have another child. Is that truthful? Is that straightforward? Now, be reasonable, John Joe. If Gretta feels she made a mistake and wants to come back, don't you think it's up to her to come and say so herself?"

John Joe grew very red. It was clear now that Sonny thought he was coming on Gretta's account and, looking on that as a sign of weakness, was doing his best to drive a hard bargain. For the first time John Joe perceived that there might be a lot to be said for Campion.

"That would be a very foolish idea to get into your head, Sonny," he said with murderous quietness.

"Ah, but I'm only assuming, John Joe," said Sonny hastily.

"Oh, no, Sonny," said John Joe, rising, "you're doing nothing of the sort. You imagine that Gretta asked me to come and see you. You never made a bigger mistake in your life."

He turned on his heel, but Sonny made a grab for him.

"You're not going, John Joe?"

"I am," said John Joe firmly. "For the future you can manage your own business."

"You're not, man, you're not," said Sonny with coarse playfulness. "Not till I get a drink for you. . . . I took your advice the last time, didn't I?" he whispered intensely, thrusting his fat face into John Joe's.

"More fool I was to offer it," said John Joe bitterly.

"Now, John Joe," said Sonny warningly, raising a fat finger at him, "you're wronging me. You're wronging me and you know you're wronging me," he added reproachfully, and John Joe was surprised to see tears in his eyes. "Can't you see my position, John Joe?"

"All I can see," drawled John Joe unsympathetically,

"is that you have one last chance of making it up with Gretta, and you haven't sense enough to take it."

"But what chance is there?" asked Sonny emotionally. "It seems she's in love with this fellow Campion."

"I'm hardly surprised," said John Joe.

"Nor I," said Sonny, turning the thrust adroitly. "We all have our little fancies, and there's no harm in them. But what can I do with things as they are?"

"Listen," said John Joe patiently, as though he were explaining a simple problem to a stupid child, "Gretta had her mind made up to leave you for good. We won't go into the wrongs and rights of it. There were probably faults on both sides."

"Oh, there were, there were," said Sonny, nodding eagerly.

"By sheer bad luck, she finds after she has left you that she's having a kid," continued John Joe. "Anyone can see the effect that would have on a woman. Whatever feeling she ever had for you is bound to come on top. At the present moment, if I know anything, her mind is like that," he added, holding his hand edgewise in a presentable imitation of a yacht in a high wind. "The least breath would tilt her."

"That's all I want to know, John Joe," said Sonny with sudden decision, reaching for John Joe's glass. "You needn't say any more. I'm not a man to let pride stand in his way."

"I hope not," growled John Joe in a tone which implied that he doubted it. He was still indignant at the slight

that Sonny had inflicted on him, and if he had happened
to run into Campion during the afternoon, there was
no knowing what he might have done or said. But Sonny
didn't give him a chance. That evening while his elder
sister Rosie, Ned Campion, and himself were sitting in
the kitchen, Kate came in looking tired and distraught.

"You didn't see any sign of Gretta?" asked Rosie,
who was fat and jolly.

"Gretta will probably be late," said Kate noncommittally.

"Go on," said Rosie inquisitively. "What's keeping
her?"

"You'd hardly believe it," replied Kate wearily, sinking into a chair. "Sonny Dorgan."

"Oh!" said Campion, clenching his fists and making
a face as he strode from the fire to the back door.

"And would you believe it," added Kate, half in tears
and half in laughter, "he kissed my hand."

"Oh, you can give her up, Ned," said Rosie in a brassy
voice. "She'll go back to him."

"To tell you the God's truth, Rosie," replied Campion
in a tortured voice, "I wouldn't mind much what she did
so long as it made her happy."

"She will not go back to him, Rosie," cried Kate,
stamping her foot.

"And if she won't," cried Rosie, showing every symp-
tom of hysterics, "why the hell didn't she pitch him out
on his nose? And you're as bad as any of them, you dirty
little turncoat, letting him kiss your hand."

Campion put on his hat and coat and left. John Joe was feeling sorry for him. He had the impression that Campion would probably walk the country roads all night. Then Rosie went off to a meeting in town, and Kate and himself were left alone. There was still no sign of Gretta. Kate rose and walked to the fire and stood with one foot on the fender, her head bowed and her hands clasped before her. In a way John Joe realized that she, almost as much as Campion or Gretta, was a victim of the situation.

"Cheer up, old girl," he said sympathetically. "It's probably the best thing that could happen for everybody's sake."

"I know you think so, John Joe," she said, turning on him with a wan smile, "but I can't feel like that at all. If Gretta were to do a thing like that, I don't think I could ever, ever be the same to her again."

4.

But in spite of that, six months later she went with John Joe to visit Gretta at the nursing home. Gretta was sitting up, looking blooming, and kissed them both affectionately. She was in the highest of spirits. Sonny was a bit tight but he was in high spirits too. But from the moment John Joe saw Kate's eyes fixed on the little figure in the cot, he knew there was something wrong. She grew pale as though she would faint at any moment. To cover up her emotion he stood beside her and rested his hand lightly on her shoulder, and as though she communicated her emotion to him, he found himself seeing what she saw. It was no more than a whisper, a gleam, the faintest hint of resemblance, but it penetrated his knowingness and complacency with a sense of futility.

"I declare to my God," said Sonny gaily, "he's jealous."

"How jealous he is!" said Gretta mockingly. "And all the efforts I made to attract his attention!"

"Ssh!" said Sonny commandingly, and tiptoed to Kate's side. "I think we're rather in the way here just at the moment, Kate," he whispered confidentially, while his tiny eyes, full of mischief, were fixed on John Joe. "I may as well tell you," he added to John Joe, "she thinks the sun shines out of you. . . . Mind you," he said, raising a fat palm conspiratorially, "I'm not asking what there was between ye. I'm only telling you."

Separation and reconciliation seemed to have very little effect on Sonny. "Sonny by name, sunny by nature."

Don Juan's Temptation

" 'Pon my soul," said Gussie with a fat chuckle, "I had one very narrow shave myself."

"What was that, Gussie?" asked somebody. It is extraordinary how we all listen to Gussie. It isn't, God knows, because we like him, or even believe him, but, as I fancy, because deep down in all of us there is a feeling of the insufficiency of our own experience of life. Humanly we understand our wives and sweethearts, but that fat rascal understands them at a level where we never even meet them, like those fairy stories where a girl's soul goes wandering off at dusk and only her body is left behind.

"It was a girl I met at a party in Hannigan's," replied Gussie. "She was quite young, tall and dark and good-looking, but it wasn't so much her looks. It was the naturalness of her among all those wooden dolls in coloured nightdresses. She was only a country-town girl who had never learned to dress up or pose, and however she moved or whatever she said, it always seemed to be natural and right.

"We left together, and she took my arm. It was a lovely night, with the moon nearly at the full. My flat was near the green at the time, and as we were passing I halted and asked her to come in. She gave a slight start. I suppose, having the few drinks in, I didn't notice it at the time.

" 'For what?' she asked.

" 'Oh, for the night, if you like,' said I, and I could nearly have bitten off my tongue when I'd said it. I'm almost ashamed to admit it even now," groaned Gussie, "it was so awkward; just like a schoolboy the first time he goes with a girl. I could feel her go all hard inside.

" 'No, thanks,' she said. 'I have a room of my own to go to.'

" 'Oh, please, Helen, please,' I said, taking her hand and squeezing it in a friend-of-the-family way, 'you're not taking offence at that? It was only a little joke of mine. Now you must come up for a drink just to show there's no ill feeling.'

" 'Some other night,' she said, 'when it's not so late,' and I let it go at that because I knew that anything else I said would frighten her more. She still held on to my arm, but that was only not to make a fuss. Inside she was as hurt as anything. Hurt and surprised. She didn't think I was that sort of fellow at all. Or rather," added Gussie with a good-natured chuckle, "she knew I was that sort of fellow, but she hoped I'd reveal it gradually, so that she wouldn't be expected to notice.

"Anyhow, we reached the canal bridge, and she stopped and leaned over it. I must say it looked very fine in the moonlight, but it wasn't the moonlight she was thinking of. She was getting over her fright, and now it was her pride that was hurt.

" 'Tell us,' she said, letting on to be very light-hearted and interested in it only, as you might say, from a psychological angle, 'do you ask all the girls you meet the same thing?'

" 'But, my goodness,' I said, 'didn't I tell you it was only a joke?'

" 'Now you're not being honest,' she said, resting her head on her arms and looking back at me over her shoulder. I can still see her with the cloche hat shading her face to the chin.

" 'Are you?' said I, smiling at her.

" 'How?' she asked with a start.

" 'Can't you admit that you were warned against me?' said I.

" 'As a matter of fact I was,' she said, 'but I didn't pay much attention. I take people as I find them.'

" 'Now you're talking sensibly,' said I, and I looked at her and thought to myself in a fatherly sort of way: 'Well, the girl is nice. She's a bit shocked now, but she'll have to learn about it sooner or later, and she may as well learn from someone who knows.' Some men are very awkward," sighed Gussie by way of explanation.

"The things their wives tell you about them, 'twould surprise you.

" 'You probably wouldn't believe me,' said I, 'if I told you how few women interest me enough for that.'

" 'But the ones you do ask,' she went on, sticking to her point—oh, quite detached, you know, as if she was only asking out of politeness—'do they come?'

" 'Some of them,' said I, with a smile at her innocence. 'Sometimes you meet a difficult sort of girl who gets offended and won't even take a drink from you after.'

" 'Married women or girls?' she asked in the tone of someone filling up a form, but the quaver in her voice gave her away.

" 'Both,' said I. Mind you, I might have explained that there was only one of the first and not exactly an overflow meeting of the second, but I had the feeling that if she needed to have her mind broadened there was no use shocking her by halves. It's like having a tooth out. 'Why?'

" 'Oh, nothing,' she said lightly, 'but I don't wonder you have such a poor opinion of women if you can pick them up so easily.'

" 'But, my dear young lady,' said I, giving her a cigarette, 'who said I had a poor opinion of women? On the contrary, I have a very high opinion of them, and the more I see of them, the better I like them.'

" 'Have you?' she said, stooping over the match so that I wouldn't see her face. 'It must be a poor opinion of me so.'

" 'I fail to see how wanting to have more of your company proves I have a poor opinion of you,' said I, 'even if I do want to make love to you. As a matter of fact I do.'

" 'You want it rather easy, don't you?' she said with a trace of resentment.

" 'Do you think it should be made difficult?' I asked.

" 'I thought it was the usual thing to ask a girl to go to the pictures with you first,' she said, with a brassy air that wouldn't have taken in a child.

" 'Perhaps so,' I said. 'I didn't think you were the usual sort of girl, that's all.'

" 'But if you get it as easy as that, how do you know whether it's the real thing or not?' she asked.

" 'How do you know whether anything is the real thing?' said I. 'As you said yourself, you take things as you find them.'

" 'It would be rather late in the day to find you were making a mistake about that,' she said.

" 'And what harm?' said I. 'It happens every day of the week. You do it yourself with boys you go walking with. You let them cuddle you for a couple of weeks, and then you find they bore you and you drop them. There isn't any difference. You don't suddenly change your character. People don't say when they pass you in the street: "How different Helen is looking! You can see she spent the night with a man. . . ." Of course, if you attach so much importance to the physical side of it—'

" 'I do,' she said, and by this time she was nearly laughing. I declare to my God, the little minx was laughing! She felt safe now, and when it came to argument she thought she was more than a match for me. 'Isn't it awful?' she said. 'But I'm very queer like that.'

" 'Oh, there's nothing queer about it,' said I, determined not to let her get away with anything. 'That's just ordinary schoolgirl romanticism.'

" 'Is that all?' she said, and though she pretended to take it lightly, I could see she was stung. 'You have an answer for everything, haven't you?'

" 'If you call that everything, dear child,' I said goodnaturedly, patting her on the shoulder. 'I call it growing-pains. I don't know if, with that romantic nature of yours, you've even noticed that there's a nasty wind coming up the canal.'

" 'No,' she said archly, 'I hadn't,' and she rested her elbows on the bridge and looked up at me. 'Anyway, I like it. Go on with what you were saying. Romanticism is thinking you ought to stick to someone you care for, isn't that it?'

" 'No, my dear, it is not,' said I. 'Romanticism is thinking you care very deeply for someone you don't give a damn about, and imagining on that account that you must never care for anyone else. It goes with your age. Come on now or you'll be catching something worse.'

" 'You don't mean you were ever like that?' she said, taking my arm again as we went on down the road.

" 'Oh,' I said, 'we all go through that phase.'

" 'Go on!' she said with a laugh, and her face screwed up with mischief, 'I could have sworn you must have been born like that. How did you get sense so young?'

" 'Quite naturally,' said I. 'I saw I was only making difficulties for myself, just as you're doing now, and as there seemed to be trouble enough in the world, I gave it up.'

" 'And lived happy ever after?' she said mockingly. 'And what about your girls? Aren't they romantic either?'

" 'Not since they were your age,' I said.

" 'Don't rub it in about the age,' she said, giving me a dig with her elbow. 'It's a sore point, and there isn't much I can do about it. Tell us more about your girl friends— the married ones, for instance.'

" 'That's easy,' said I. 'There's only one, at the moment.'

" 'And her husband—does he know?'

" 'It's not a question I ever asked him,' said I, 'but I suppose he finds it more convenient to overlook it.'

" 'Obliging sort of chap!' she said. 'You don't know if he has a younger brother who'd do for me?'

" 'Now,' I said, stopping dead in the path, 'you *are* talking like a schoolgirl.'

" 'Am I?' she asked doubtfully. 'How?'

" 'Why do you speak so contemptuously of someone you've never met?' I asked, and 'pon my soul, I grew quite heated. 'He's a decent, good-natured man. It's not his fault that after sixteen or eighteen years of living together, his wife and himself can't bear the sight of one another. He does what he thinks is the right thing for his family. I suppose you think he should defend her honour at the risk of his life?'

" 'I wasn't thinking of her honour,' she said quietly.

" 'His own, then?' said I. 'At his wife's expense? Is she to be dragged in the mud because some silly schoolgirl thinks his position undignified? His wife would probably have something to say to that. Besides, don't you see that at his age it would be a very serious thing if she was to leave him?'

" 'More serious than letting her go to your flat—how often did you say?'

" 'And now,' said I, 'you're talking like a little cat. But as a matter of fact it would. Where she goes in the evenings is nobody's business. Whether the meals are ready is. They have two daughters at school—one of them nearly one age with yourself.'

" 'Go on,' she said again. 'I wonder does he let them out at night? And the mother, what sort of woman is she?'

" 'She's a great sort,' said I; and mind you, she was; a woman who'd give you her heart out, and the best company in the world.

" 'I wonder what would she say if she heard you asking me in for the night?' said Helen, by way of no harm. Oh, she had a tongue like a whip, that kid!

" 'Ah,' I said a bit feebly, 'I don't suppose Francie has many illusions left,' but the little jade had cornered me, and she knew it. The trouble with Francie was that she still had too many illusions left, even about me.

" 'She can't have,' said Helen. 'But I still have a few.'

" 'Oh, you,' said I. 'You're walking with them.'

" 'They're in the family,' she said. 'Mum and Dad lived together till he died, and Mum thinks he was the one really great man that ever walked the world.'

" 'And I dare say they were often sick of one another,' said I.

" 'I dare say they were,' she agreed. 'They used to fight like mad and not talk to one another for a week, and while they weren't talking Dad went on the booze and Mum said I was breaking her heart and put me across her knee. I'd go up to him with my bottom so sore I could hardly sit down, and there he'd be sprawled in his big chair with his arms hanging down looking into the grate as if 'twas the end of the world, and he'd just beckon me to sit on his knee. We'd stop like that for hours without opening our gobs, just thinking what a bitch of hell Mum was. . . . But the thing is, young man, they stuck it, and when 'tis Mum's turn to go, she won't regret it, because she's certain that the boss will be waiting for her. She goes to Mass every morning, but that's only not to give God any excuse for making distinctions. I wouldn't like to be God if He tries to separate the pair of them. . . . Do you think she will?'

" 'Who will?' said I. I don't know how it was, but whatever way she told the story it gripped me. I knew a couple just like that.

" 'Mum,' she said. 'See the boss I mean?'

" 'Well,' I said, 'there's nothing like optimism.'

" 'I know,' she said quickly. 'That's the lousy part of it. But I suppose she's lucky even to be able to kid herself about it. It doesn't frighten her the way it frightens us. . . . But that's what I mean by love, Mr. D.,' she added light-heartedly.

" 'I hope you get it, Miss C.,' said I in the same tone.

" 'I don't suppose I'm likely to,' she said in a resigned way. 'There doesn't seem to be much of it around. I suppose it's the shortage of optimists.'

"When we reached her flat, she leaned back against the railings with her legs crossed and her hands joined behind her back. She had a lovely figure, that girl, and the beauty of it was, she didn't know it.

" 'Well, good night, Miss Romantic,' said I, kissing her hand.

" 'Good night, Don Juan,' said she. That was what she called me," added Gussie with an almost girlish smile of delight. "Don Juan."

" 'When do I see you again?' said I.

" 'Do you want to?' she asked. 'Old-fashioned and all as I am?'

" 'Oh,' I said, 'I still have hopes of converting you.'

" 'That's marvellous,' she said. 'I love being converted. I was nearly being converted by a parson once. Give us a ring some time.'

" 'I will,' said I, and it wasn't until I reached the canal bridge I realized that what I really meant was 'What

a fool I am!' I felt as if I'd been scratched all over. I suppose the trouble with me was that I was getting things
too easy. I felt like a man with a thousand a year who
finds himself pushed back suddenly into the thirty-bob-a-
week class. I knew what I'd be letting myself in for with
a girl like that: park benches and canal banks with a
sixty-mile-an-hour gale blowing round the corner, and
in the heel of the hunt she'd be detained at the office by a
good-looking chap in uniform.

"Still, I was very attracted by her. I don't know what
possessed me, but instead of crossing the bridge I turned
up along the canal in the moonlight. 'Now this, Gussie,
boy,' said I to myself, 'is what you'll be letting yourself
in for if you're not careful. Moonlight and draughts instead of your nice, warm, comfortable bed.' But in a
curious way she reminded me of a girl I used to know
about fifteen years before. You know," Gussie added
sentimentally, "you mightn't think it, but as a kid I used
to be very lonely. I sometimes think young people are
the loneliest creatures on God's earth. You wake up from
a nice, well-ordered, explainable world and you find
eternity stretching all round you, and no one, priest or
scientist or anyone else, can tell you a damn thing about
it. And there's this queer thing going on inside you that
gives you a longing for companionship and love, and you
don't know how to satisfy it. I used to go out at night,
looking up at the stars, and thinking if only I could meet
a nice understanding sort of girl it would all explain itself
naturally. Then I met this girl called Joan, and I used to

haunt the roads at night, trying to get even a glance at her as she passed. She was a tall, thin, reedy-looking girl, and though I didn't know it she was rotten with t.b. I remember the night before she went away to the sanatorium I met her coming back from town, and as we were coming up the hill she slipped her hand into mine. I held it the whole way home, and we never spoke a word the whole way. In six months' time she was dead.

"And here was I, fifteen years after, feeling the same sort of thing about another girl who reminded me of her, and though I knew well she was talking rubbish, I understood what she wanted all right; something bigger than life, that would last beyond death. And 'pon my soul, I felt a brute, depriving her of her illusions. Maybe people can't do without illusions. I don't know, but I felt, walking there in the moonlight, that I'd give everything I ever had just to be able to feel like that about a woman again. You know the sort of thing. Even a sixty-mile-an-hour gale wouldn't put you off.

"And then as I was coming back the street from the opposite direction, I noticed the way the moonlight was falling on the doctors' houses at the other side. My side was in darkness. I put my key in the lock, and then I nearly jumped out of my skin. There was a figure standing by the door. It was a girl and she was leaning back against the railings with a face as white as chalk as though she was hoping I'd pass in and not see her. And I said to myself: 'It's Joan,' and then I thought: 'She's come back after all the years,' and I thought: 'So it does last beyond the grave,' and I went cold. Then I looked again and saw who it was.

" 'Merciful God, Helen,' said I, 'what are you doing here?'

" 'Well,' she said in a low voice, doing her best to smile, 'you see I was converted after all.' "

There was a long pause, and Gussie's reminiscent chuckle broke the spell. What spell? I don't know. "Poor child!" he added sentimentally.

"I hope you sent her home again," said someone—probably some middle-aged man with a daughter of his own in the Civil Service.

"Why then, indeed," said Gussie with a greasy laugh, "I did nothing of the sort. What do you think I am—a blooming philanthropist?"

A NOTE ON THE TYPE
IN WHICH THIS BOOK IS SET

This book was set on the Linotype in Granjon, a type named in compliment to Robert Granjon, but neither a copy of a classic face nor an entirely original creation. George W. Jones based his designs for this type upon the type used by Claude Garamond (1510–61) in his beautiful French books, and Granjon more closely resembles Garamond's own than do any of the various modern types that bear his name.

Robert Granjon began his career as type-cutter in 1523. The boldest and most original designer of his time, he was one of the first to practise the trade of type-founder apart from that of printer. Between 1557 and 1562 Granjon printed about twenty books in types designed by himself, following, after the fashion of the day, the cursive handwriting of the time. These types, usually known as "caractères de civilité," he himself called "lettres françaises," as especially appropriate to his own country.

The typographic scheme and the binding and jacket are based on designs by Warren Chappell. The book was printed and bound by H. Wolff, New York.